MOODY

Editing: Jessica Royer Ocken
Proofreading and Formatting: Elaine York, Allusion Publishing, www.allusionpublishing.com
Proofreading: Julia Griffis
Cover Model: Philippe Leblond
Cover Photographer: Leda & St. Jacques
Cover Design: Letitia Hasser, RBA Designs

MOODY

PENELOPE WARD

For Shannon

CHAPTER 1

Wren

I get to make people feel better for a living—without having to slice them open or prescribe medication. That's pretty cool, if you ask me. As a traveling massage therapist, I move from site to site, making house calls. That's another thing I love about my day job: I never have to do it in one place. The company I work for, Elite Massage, has an office downtown, where I go once a month to stock up on supplies and check in. When I stopped in this afternoon, my boss, Trina, had an update for me.

"So, I just added something new to your schedule, if you can fit it in tomorrow," she said.

"Where is it?" I asked, stuffing a variety of oils into my backpack.

"Brookline. Actually, you were specifically requested."

I stopped for a moment. "By whom?"

"His name is Dax Moody. Ever hear of him?"

I shook my head. "No. Not at all."

"Well, he came up clean."

Trina always runs a criminal background check on

new clients, which I appreciated since most of the time I was going into their homes and would often be alone with these strangers.

"I also Googled him and got his business page," she continued. "He's the owner of a capital investment company."

Dax Moody. Huh... nothing. "I guess someone must have recommended me to him."

Trina gestured toward her computer. "Check out this property. This is where he lives." She'd pulled up Google Earth and zoomed in on a house. It was a large, brick structure with a black wrought-iron fence around it.

"Wow," I said.

"Yeah. Might want to wear something a little nicer than the usual T-shirt and ripped jeans." She winked. "You know, in case he's single."

"I'm certain if he lives in a house like that in Brookline, he's not. It doesn't matter anyway. Isn't there a rule about mixing business with pleasure?"

She shrugged and zoomed in farther on the house. "You know what they say about rules."

The next day I parked in front of the sprawling estate, unsure where these butterflies in my stomach were coming from. I'd had wealthy clients before. But something about this assignment felt different, though I couldn't put my finger on it.

Brookline was just outside of the city, and a trolley line ran right through the center of town. With its proximity to Boston universities, the neighborhood was a mix of college students and wealthier professionals, depending on the section. This particular street was one of the quieter ones, lined with big, beautiful homes, and not far from where I knew a couple of the New England NFL players lived.

The leaves on the trees surrounding the estate were a multitude of colors, evidence that fall foliage season was in full swing. Looking up at the two-story brick house, I noticed an older-looking Camry that seemed out of place parked in the driveway.

With my supplies hanging in a bag over my shoulder, I carried my portable table as I walked toward the massive black door with a vibrant wreath of autumn leaves hung on it. I rang the bell and anxiously waited.

A woman who appeared to be in her mid-forties, wearing khakis and a pretty cowl-neck sweater, opened the door. *This must be Mrs. Moody.*

She looked down at the table I held and then up at me. "Can I help you?"

I cleared my throat. "Uh, yes. I'm here to see Dax Moody. He scheduled a twelve o'clock massage-therapy appointment with me."

Her eyes narrowed, and she laughed a little.

Is this funny?

"Uh...okay." She waved me inside. "Wait here in the foyer, please."

"Thank you."

I set the heavy table down and walked over to a large, framed photo on the wall. It was a woman in a wedding dress. The background looked like Vegas. I now realized

3

the woman who answered the door wasn't his wife; she must work here. The woman in the photo looked over her shoulder, her long, blond hair cascading down her back. She held a small bouquet of lavender roses. She was beautiful.

The lady returned, interrupting my thoughts. "It seems you have the wrong time. Mr. Moody indicates his appointment isn't until one?"

My stomach sank. "Oh, gosh. Let me see." I rechecked the schedule on my phone. She was right. How could I have messed this up? I shoved my phone in my pocket. "It seems I did screw up the time. I'm really sorry. I'll come back."

Just as I'd turned around and lifted the handle on my table, a deep voice came from behind me. "Wait."

I turned around to find a tall, gorgeous, *shirtless* man wiping sweat off his forehead with a small white towel. He had a six-pack, and his body was insane.

This is Dax? I was expecting someone older. This guy looked like he'd stepped off the cover of *GQ*. He had to be in his early thirties max, was very built, and had light brown hair. He wore black trousers, which was an odd choice to work out in. His tanned skin glistened with sweat.

"We can just do it now," he said.

I gulped. The thought of rubbing my hands over *this* guy suddenly made me very nervous. As someone who touched people for a living, I tried to compartmentalize. But jeez. He was hot as hell. A warning about what he looked like would have been nice.

"Are you sure? I don't mind coming back. It was my fault."

"Yes, I know. But you're here, so we might as well get it over with."

Get it over with? Massage was supposed to be a pleasurable and relaxing experience. "Okay, then. Just let me know where you want me."

Dax stared at me for a few seconds before he said, "My office."

Swallowing, I nodded. "Alrighty, then."

"Let me get that." He reached for my table and headed down the hall.

His housekeeper gave me an amused look. I still wasn't sure what she found so funny about all of this.

As I followed, a waft of his cologne hit me, and I couldn't help admiring the cut of his back. This guy clearly worked out a lot. Which made me wonder...did he expect me to massage him all sweaty like that?

We entered the office and he said, "You can set up in here."

"Your housekeeper seems to think my being here is quite funny."

"Yeah, well, it's not like me to order a massage. And I didn't mention to her that you were coming. She's always telling me I need to try to unwind. So she probably thinks she influenced this."

"I see." I paused. "I'm Wren McCallister, by the way. But you probably already know that since you requested me?"

He ignored my comment, instead saying, "I'm going to jump in the shower while you set up."

"Okay." I smiled.

Grateful to be alone for a bit, and not to have to massage a sweaty person, I blew out a breath and looked around. *Holy crap*. One side of the room had bookshelves built into almost every inch of the wall. His wooden desk was covered in stacks of papers. The large windows let in a lot of sunshine and provided a beautiful view of the colorful leaves outside. A vibrant Persian-looking area rug covered most of the floor. This office was pretty much the size of half of my house.

After unfolding my table and setting it up in the corner, I fished through my selection of oils, contemplating which one would be most suitable for him. Which scent signified darkly intimidating? I settled on vanilla—smoky and mysterious.

About ten minutes later, Dax returned. He didn't say anything, just looked at me. His hair was damp, and he'd changed into a white T-shirt that fit his muscular chest like a glove. He wore the same black trousers he'd had on before, or maybe they were another similar-looking pair of pants.

The sound of a car starting drew my attention to the window. The car that had been parked in the driveway was backing away. Was it the housekeeper leaving? If she was gone, that meant Dax and I were likely alone now. I hadn't heard anyone else in the house. His wife must have been at work, or maybe she was running errands. Did they have kids? I began wondering if I needed to be concerned about this assignment, considering his odd temperament. He didn't seem happy for me to be here.

I forced the words out. "Shall we begin?"

He took a few steps toward me and crossed his impressive arms. "I don't know."

"You don't know?"

"I'm having doubts about this," he said.

I blinked. "About me being here?"

"About the massage, yeah. I think this might've been a mistake."

Any apprehension I had about being alone with him dissipated upon realizing *he* was hesitant.

I'm so confused. "Have you ever had one before?"

"No." He looked out the window and back to me. "I haven't."

I swallowed. "Well, it's pretty simple. You just lie on your stomach, and I take it from there. You don't have to do anything."

"Well, I *do* have to give up control."

"That's the idea, though."

"I'm not good at that." He tilted his head. "What do you do exactly?"

"I...stand beside you and rub my hands into your skin and work to get some of the knots out of your muscles."

He shook his head. "No. I meant, what do you *do*? Is this your full-time gig?"

Is that an insult? "Yes. I went to school for massage after college, and I make a good living. Being a massage therapist is not something you do on the side. It's a great, fulfilling career in and of itself," I said defensively.

"I didn't mean to imply it wasn't." He fidgeted with his watch, which looked like it cost more than my car.

I blew out a breath. "I do have other aspirations, but this pays the bills and allows me to put some money away, too. I'm currently saving for a trip to Europe."

"I see." He stared out the window, almost looking as though he wanted to escape.

What's with this guy? "Look...I can leave if you're not comfortable."

"No." He walked over to a cabinet and took out a bottle of some kind of liquor. "I just need something to take the edge off." He poured himself a glass of amber-colored liquid.

I stared at his big, masculine hands. "Well, this is a first."

"A first what?" he asked.

"The first time a client has ever had to relax before a relaxing massage." When I laughed, I accidentally snorted.

His eyes narrowed. "What the hell was that?"

"Sorry. I didn't mean to snort. That happens sometimes when I'm nervous. It just comes out."

"Why are *you* nervous?"

"Maybe your attitude is rubbing off on me."

He chugged the alcohol and slammed the glass down. "I'm sorry. I don't know *how* to relax. It's my nature. Even when I'm supposed to be freaking relaxing...the thought of relaxing stresses me out."

I nodded. "That's actually a real thing. It's called relaxation-induced anxiety."

He chuckled. "Thanks for the diagnosis."

"I used to be like you. I'd get panic attacks from the quiet when I tried to meditate."

He licked the side of his mouth. "I suppose that defeats the purpose."

"Exactly. And sitting still, like in the hair salon or dentist's chair, used to make me panicky when I was younger."

"Younger? You're pretty young. How long have you been doing this massage thing?" he asked.

"A couple of years."

"What made you get into it?"

"I wanted to make people feel good. And it doesn't bore me. I never have to be in one place."

"Does it pay well? How much of the fee do you get to keep?"

My eyes narrowed. "You ask a lot of questions."

"Well, maybe I need to get comfortable with you before I let you put your hands all over me."

For some reason that comment rubbed me the wrong way. *Let me* put my hands on him? As if it was a privilege? (As if he could read my mind and sense my attraction? *Ugh.*)

I raised my voice. "I thought you told the company someone recommended me. Why are you so apprehensive?"

"Okay." He sighed, scrubbing his hand over his face. "Let's get this over with. What do I do?"

Jesus. He's wound tight. "Take off your shirt and lie down on the table. You can leave your pants on or take them off."

He let out a guttural laugh. "Take my pants off?"

"Yes. That's actually customary. But it's always the client's choice. I can leave the room, if you wish, while you undress. There's a towel to cover yourself. But you can totally leave your pants on, too."

"I *will* be leaving my pants on, thanks."

"Okay. Just make sure you take the stick out of your ass one way or the other."

He glared at me but finally cracked a slight smile. I'd take it.

I laughed. "In all seriousness, just breathe. That's all you need to worry about." I took a deep breath in, willing myself to take my own advice.

Dax slowly pulled his shirt over his head, once again granting me a view of his rippled muscles. There wasn't an inch of anything soft on his body. I turned away suddenly when I caught my eyes lingering a little too long.

He then lay down stomach-first on the table and within seconds, I heard the pitter-patter of paws and the clanking of a metal collar coming from down the hall.

A large English sheepdog pushed through the door and entered the room, barking profusely at the sight of me. Then he jumped up on the table and landed on Dax's back.

"Damn it, Winston!" Dax yelled.

I didn't even know a dog that big could jump so high. The dog shot me the evil eye. *This house is just full of welcoming people.*

"Hello," I said awkwardly.

He growled. It seemed Doggy was just as *extra* as his owner.

"Get off me, you fluffernutter!" Dax groaned.

The dog kept growling at me while I covered my mouth to keep from laughing. "Why is he so angry?" I asked, trying to stifle my amusement.

"He's protective to a fault. He was napping upstairs when you arrived. I hoped he'd stay sleeping. I hadn't planned on him coming down, although I should've."

Dax sat up and somehow got the beast of a dog off him. He hopped down off the table. "I'll be right back," he said, guiding Winston out of the room and down the hall. The sound of the collar disappeared into the distance.

Left alone for a moment, I exhaled and wandered over to a shelf that displayed various things, including a large, white seashell that seemed completely out of place, given the room's otherwise masculine vibe. It was beautiful. Remembering what my mother had told me when I was little, I lifted the shell and placed it against my ear in an attempt to hear "the ocean." Met with the ambient noise that resonated from within, I closed my eyes and smiled.

"Please don't touch that," Dax called from behind me.

Shaken by his abrupt tone, I jerked, and the shell slipped from my fingers and crashed to the ground.

He let out a jarring shriek.

My hands shook. "I'm so sorry... I..." I bent to clean up the pieces, but he bolted to stop me.

"Don't touch anything!" His tone was grating.

"Why? It's my fault," I insisted.

"Please just get up," he commanded in an even harsher tone.

Burning with embarrassment, I stared down at the mess. That's when I realized something had fallen out of the shell. It was a plastic bag filled with...ashes.

I slowly stood up and pointed to the ground. "What is that?"

His eyes lifted to meet mine, and after several seconds he finally answered.

"My wife."

CHAPTER 2

Wren

Trina kept shaking her head. "I don't even know what to say."

"There is nothing to say. There are no words at all. It's been a week, and I still can't seem to figure out how to describe what happened."

I'd just recalled for my boss my odd experience with Dax Moody, starting with his reluctance to let me anywhere near him, and ending on the horror of having dropped the shell containing his wife's ashes. Thankfully, although the shell broke, the ashes had remained safely inside that sealed bag—unlike my guts, which felt like they'd been splattered everywhere. I couldn't imagine how I'd feel if those ashes hadn't been protected, if God forbid, they'd been strewn all over the floor. I might've needed therapy.

"So how did you leave things before you walked out of there?" Trina asked.

"After he picked up the pieces—because he wouldn't let me touch anything—he said his wife had passed away suddenly about a year and a half ago. He didn't offer any details about what happened. We both agreed it was best if I left, so that's what I did—right after I used his bathroom quickly since I'd nearly pissed myself."

Trina frowned. "Gosh. That's so sad."

"Me nearly pissing myself?"

"Well, that, too, but mainly his wife dying. And it explains the dog's territorial behavior."

"Yup. Winston was probably like 'Who the hell is this bitch with my lady's man?'" I shook my head. "When I first walked in there, I thought Dax was just an uptight asshole. But man, by the time I left I could see why he was so guarded. I mean, to lose your wife so young..."

My time at Dax's haunted me. I'd thought about little else since that day last week. There were so many lingering questions—ones I had no particular right to the answers to. *How did she die? Is he lonely?* I wished he'd let me massage him so he could've escaped reality for a while. Although, I was also relieved that I hadn't had the opportunity to botch that up, too.

That evening, I hung out with my dad in the kitchen. We often sat at the table cracking pistachios after dinner and watching *Jeopardy!* on the nights he didn't have to work second shift at his factory job.

I had no shame about still living at home with my dad at age twenty-four. There was plenty of space in our house, and we got along well. It didn't make sense to spend my savings on rent. Dad didn't want to be alone, and I helped him with cooking, cleaning, and bought groceries. So it worked out for both of us. I made enough money to have my own apartment, but this helped me save for an eventual trip overseas. Pretty sure it would be Europe. I hadn't settled on an exact location there, but I knew I wanted to explore a new land at some point before I turned thirty. I had some time to figure it out.

"You might be interested in this." My father handed me a pamphlet. "Came in the mail today."

It was from my alma mater, Boston College of Music, advertising a program designed for alumni to teach music in France. On the front was a photo of a woman holding a trombone, surrounded by kids in what looked like the countryside. It included information on how to access the online application.

"Hmm..." My eyes lit up. "I'll definitely be looking into this."

"I assumed you would." He smiled. "I'll just have to figure out how to deal with worrying about you when you're so far away."

"I wouldn't be that confident about it, if I were you."

He broke open a pistachio. "Think positively."

My phone dinged with a notification from Elite Massage's scheduling app. An assignment had been added to my roster. My heart nearly stopped when I got a look at the update.

"What's wrong?" my father asked.

A rush of heat ran through me. "I...just got a text from work about a new assignment for tomorrow night."

"Is everything okay?"

I shared almost everything with my dad, but I hadn't told him this story and didn't want to rehash it now. So I simply said, "Yeah."

Of course, it wasn't merely the assignment that had shaken me. It was the person who'd booked the appointment.

Dax Moody.

It was already starting to get dark out when I pulled up to Dax's on Wednesday night. I heard Winston barking before the door even opened. To my surprise, it was Dax himself who greeted me, not the housekeeper from before.

Dax nodded. "Hello, Wren." He stepped aside. "Come in. It's cold."

"Where's Winston?" I asked. I'd expected him to come charging toward me.

"I put him in the other room for a bit so he doesn't bother you. I have an area gated off."

"It's fine. I can handle his attitude."

"Let me get that." He reached for my table.

I took a few more steps inside. "I have to say, I wasn't expecting to be called back here again."

Dax's lip twitched. "I felt like I needed to apologize."

"*You* need to apologize? What I did was unforgivable."

He shook his head. "You didn't know. And it was an accident. But I sensed you were upset when you left. So I wanted to apologize for my harsh reaction."

I looked around. "Why make another appointment to apologize to me? You could've sent me a message through the company."

"Well, I'm also still in need of a massage. So I figured I'd kill two birds with one stone." He paused. "Unfortunately, the massage isn't going to be able to happen tonight as I'd originally planned. Something's come up at the last minute, and I didn't have a chance to cancel before you arrived."

"What happened?"

"Shannon, my housekeeper, had to leave early, and Rafe isn't feeling well."

"Rafe?" I tilted my head, pretending like I didn't know who that was. Since the last time I was here, I'd read his wife's obituary, which said she'd left behind a son.

Before Dax could answer, a boy made his way down the staircase. He paused at the bottom and looked at me. He seemed to be about twelve or thirteen.

I lifted my hand in a wave. "Hello."

"Rafe, this is Wren," Dax called.

Rather than acknowledge me, the boy walked through the foyer past us.

Dax cleared his throat. "He's...shy."

"I didn't realize you had a son," I lied.

He lowered his voice. "Rafe is not technically my son."

That caught me off guard and piqued my curiosity all at once.

Dax looked toward where Rafe had disappeared. "My late wife adopted him when he was eight—before she and I got together. When Maren died, he was suddenly left in my care. Day by day, I'm still figuring out how to be a proper guardian to him. We're in a situation neither of us chose. I don't know what I would do without Shannon's help."

"Is Shannon the woman I met the last time I was here?"

"Yes. She's here every weekday until eight. She basically runs this house while I work. Her two sons are grown, so she has the flexibility." He sighed. "Anyway, she wasn't feeling well tonight and left about ten minutes ago. So, like I said, I didn't have time to cancel before you got here. Rafe doesn't normally need a babysitter, but he's under the weather tonight, too—it's his ear. So I can't proceed with the massage. I'm sorry." He looked me up and down. "Would you like a cup of tea or something? You came all this way."

As I pondered the offer, Rafe reappeared briefly before jetting past us back up the stairs. I watched him until he disappeared. My eyes were still glued to the stairs when I said, "I don't want to impose."

With the late cancellation, the appointment was already paid for and non-refundable. While the curious side of me wanted to stay, I felt strange about intruding when Dax seemed to have so much on his plate tonight.

"I'm making some tea anyway," he said. "It's no imposition. I insist."

"Okay, then." I nodded. "Tea would be nice."

A chill ran down my spine as I followed him into the kitchen, which was a cook's dream—huge, rustic center island featuring a countertop made of butcher block. There was a bowl of papayas on it. Behind the top-of-the-line Viking stove was a wall of exposed brick. Off to the side was a brick oven. I imagined happier times in this house where perhaps Dax and his wife had made pizza together while sipping wine. My heart clenched.

I took a seat at the table and watched as Dax opened the cabinet and seemed to fumble with some things, eventually taking out two mugs.

"I have black tea, green tea..." He lifted a tin can and squinted to read it. "And this cinnamon one with orange peel. I think that's Shannon's."

"Cinnamon sounds great. Thank you."

"Do you take it with milk?"

"Just a splash." I smiled.

Things were quiet until the whistle blew on the tea kettle. After Dax prepared two steaming hot teas, he carried them over to the table and placed one in front of me.

"Thank you." I took a sip too fast, burning my tongue. I winced. The cinnamon taste was sweeter than I'd expected.

"Too hot?" he asked.

I blew on it. "It'll be perfect in a minute."

There was a bowl of various candies on the table. He must have noticed me eyeing it because he pushed it toward me. "Feel free to help yourself. Shannon apparently picked up some of the Halloween candy they're starting to put out early in the stores."

I faced my palm toward him. "No, thank you."

He reached into the bowl and took out one of the mini bars of chocolate, placing it in front of me. "I think this one is fitting."

Oh my God. *Butterfinger*. That was a total dig at my breaking the shell. I sighed. "Mr. Moody, was that an attempt at humor? That's really out of character for you."

"A poor attempt, yeah." He chuckled. "Sorry. I couldn't help myself."

"You didn't plant these here just so you could say that, did you?"

"No. It was luck."

After a few moments of awkward silence, I asked a nagging question. "Were you...able to replace the shell?"

He stopped mid-sip and put his mug down. "I ordered another one online. It should be arriving this week."

"Glad to hear." I should've offered again to pay for it, as I did before I left the other day, but I knew he'd never let me. Instead of offering a second time, I stared down into my mug. "I'm so sorry again."

He nodded. "Why did you have the shell up against your ear when I interrupted you that day?"

I laughed nervously. "The ocean."

His eyes narrowed. "The ocean..."

"Yes. You've never heard of that? If you put a seashell to your ear, you can hear the ocean inside?"

"Can't say I have." He continued to stare at me like I was crazy.

"It was something my mother told me when I was younger...before she died. She passed away when I was five."

He frowned. "I'm sorry, Wren. That's terrible."

I nodded and looked around the kitchen. "Can I ask what happened to your wife?"

He hesitated a moment. "Brain aneurysm. No one saw it coming."

"She was so young."

He swallowed. "Forty-two."

"Older than you…"

His brow lifted. "How do you know how old I am?"

I didn't want to admit my Googling. The write-up in *The Boston Globe* about Maren's death hadn't stated how she died. But I did notice that she hadn't taken his last name. She still went by Maren Wade.

"Just an assumption," I finally answered. "You seem younger."

"She was twelve years older than me. I'm thirty-two." He paused. "How old are you?"

"Twenty-four."

He bounced his legs, seeming tense as ever. That massage definitely would've done him good.

Rafe suddenly appeared at the entrance to the kitchen.

"What's up?" Dax asked.

The boy said nothing, just pointed to his ear.

"Shit. Your ear is worse?"

He nodded.

Rafe had thick, light brown unruly hair and big, beautiful hazel eyes that held a hint of sadness.

"Let me see where Shannon put that medicine." He turned to me. "I'll be right back."

Dax stood, leaving a cloud of his masculine scent in his wake, and followed Rafe out of the room. I felt a little guilty for checking out Dax's ass as he left. But his dark jeans hugged it quite well.

I could hear the two of them going up the stairs together.

After sitting alone for a while, the sound of a dog collar registered. The next thing I knew, Winston had entered the kitchen.

"Where did you escape from? You broke down the gate?"

He growled and barked before settling down on the kitchen floor.

I lifted my mug and walked over to where he'd planted himself near the center island. I sat on a stool and put my tea down. "You know, Winston, you're awfully fluffy and cute for someone so mean. I don't normally want to bury my nose in the fur of people who hate me."

He growled again. *"Ruff!"*

"Look. I'm not here to make trouble, okay? I know you've been through a lot. Clearly everyone in this house has."

"Winston is probably the most balanced of anyone under this roof."

Startled at the sound of Dax's voice, I turned so suddenly to face him that my arm hit the mug, causing it to crash to the floor and shatter.

Not again.

I covered my mouth. "Oh no."

Dax held out his hands. "Stay back, Winston." He walked around and led the dog out of the room.

I bent down to pick up the pieces.

A minute later, he returned to find me down on my hands and knees. "Stand up, Wren."

Refusing to listen, I kept at it. "I'm so mortified right now."

He spoke louder. "Stand up. I have the dustpan and brush. I'll take care of it."

I reluctantly stood and watched as Dax knelt in my place to pick up the pieces.

I paced. "This is déjà vu. How could this possibly have happened a second time?"

"It's okay." He glanced up at me. "Nobody died."

His choice of words gave me pause. "Nobody died? Are you trying to be funny again?"

"Actually, I wasn't. But now that you mention it, that could've been a dig at the last time this happened, huh?"

Oh great. So *I'm* the one making jokes about his dead wife's ashes now.

Dax dumped the ceramic pieces in the trash. He went over the area with a small hand vacuum before mopping up the remaining tea. Then he put all of the supplies away in a utility closet off the kitchen.

"All set," he said. He examined my face. "You don't look so good."

I wanted to crawl into a hole. "I'm not. I feel like I have PTSD or something from the first time I broke something here." I let out a shaky breath.

He walked over and placed his hands on my shoulders. "Relax."

Oh. My pulse reacted to the weight of his hands on me. His touch felt damn good, but I had to be crazy for getting a little aroused at a time like this. "You're telling me to relax? Isn't that somewhat ironic coming from you?"

He smiled, removing his hands from my shoulders—much to my dismay. "Come sit. I'll make you another tea."

I was about to tell him that wasn't necessary, but he'd already turned on the kettle, so I let things be.

I sat in silence and watched as he prepared it, my eyes again falling to his derrière. Dax had broad shoulders, and you could make out the muscles of his back through the material of his cream-colored shirt. It was strange to be intimidated by someone who was also waiting on you. It wasn't every day that a handsome man served me like this.

After the kettle went off, he poured my tea and walked over to hand it to me. He then poured the remaining hot water into his mug.

"Thank you." I cleared my throat. "How is Rafe?"

Dax returned to his seat across from me. "He gets these chronic ear infections. I managed to find where Shannon put the ibuprofen she bought today. I'll have to get him to the doctor tomorrow." He let out a long breath. "Rafe is in a...silent stage right now. He prefers not to talk, so it's hard to know the extent of his pain."

"Okay, so he's *choosing* not to talk. I wasn't sure."

Dax nodded. "Doctor says it's a form of mutism."

"I thought maybe he had a developmental delay."

"No. He spoke perfectly fine before his mother passed. All of this came on after."

Oh man. "How old is he?"

"Thirteen."

"That's a tough age. I can't imagine how difficult losing her must have been for him."

"Yeah. He was eleven at the time. And now he's stuck with a guy he never liked to begin with, and who certainly wasn't cut out to be a parent."

"I'm sure you're doing the best you can."

"How do you know that?" he asked, almost defensively.

"Well, I was raised by my dad. As I mentioned, my mother, Eileen, died in a car accident when I was five. My dad and I are very close. But I understand how hard it is, because I know how much my dad struggled with being a single father. Still, he did a damn good job."

"So, you assume I must be like him? Worthy of the responsibility of a child? I'm not. I didn't choose to adopt Rafe. That was all Maren long before I came along. When she and I got married, I made it clear that I wasn't ready to be a father to her son. And she said that didn't matter because Rafe was hers. She said I could choose the role I wanted to have in his life. The problem is, we never figured that out, nor did we discuss what the hell would happen if she wasn't around anymore." His voice was strained. "I can run my company and provide investment expertise until kingdom come. But when it comes to that boy? I basically know shit. And he won't talk to me on top of everything. So that makes it harder." He let out a long breath.

The stress resonated off of him. I could feel it. I didn't know what to say. What came out was: "He probably just needs time."

"It's been a year and a half." Dax laughed angrily.

"*More* time?" I shrugged and offered a sympathetic look.

He stared at me for several seconds, then changed the subject. "Wren is an interesting name."

"It means little bird. My mother picked it out."

"Little bird." He nodded. "It fits you."

My cheeks burned. His eyes lingered on mine, causing me to fidget with the buttons on my sweater. I felt like I was on an eternal job interview with him. At the same time, he was so attractive it was almost painful. I wasn't used to feeling like this—so obviously flustered that I was certain it must have showed on my face. I never wanted to stop looking at him, and at the same time, I wanted to run. It was a strange contradiction. And it seemed so wrong to be lusting after some poor dead woman's husband.

"So..." he said. "The first time you were here, you said you're saving for a trip to Europe?"

"Yes. That's the plan."

"Good for you. I wish I had traveled more for leisure before I got tied down."

When he looked away, I examined his profile. He had the perfect nose and just the right amount of chin scruff. But like Rafe, his eyes held a sadness that made me yearn to wipe it away. "Are you okay, Dax?"

He turned to me suddenly, his eyes narrowing. "Why are you asking?"

"Does no one ever ask you that question?"

He sighed, running his finger along the rim of his mug. "I don't have anything to complain about. I'm alive. I'm wealthy. I have the means to hire help. There are plenty of people who've lost their spouses and don't have that privilege."

"That's true, but money can't buy happiness. It can't bring your wife back." I paused. "It helps to talk sometimes. I get the impression that you don't open up about all of this very often. You just go through the motions."

His mouth curved into a slight smile. "You get that impression...because I'm wound so tight?"

"Frankly?" I arched my brow. "Yes. You have to learn to let go somehow, find some joy in each day for no one other than yourself. It doesn't matter how successful you are if there's no joy in your life. Otherwise, what's the point? You could have all the money in the world, but it doesn't matter if you're miserable."

"What's the point..." he muttered. "I've definitely asked myself that question from time to time lately." He stared down into his cup a moment. "What do you do for joy, Wren?"

"It doesn't have to be anything elaborate. Sometimes it's just breathing the air outside on a fall day and being alone with your thoughts. Or enjoying a cup of tea with a virtual stranger whom you find intriguing and a little frightening at the same time."

His eyes widened. "I frighten you?"

"I should clarify. I'm more frightened by the way I seem to keep making an ass of myself around you." I cleared my throat. "Anyway, as far as bringing joy into your life, it doesn't matter what you're doing as long as you're being mindful in the process—not letting your mind go to that place where it bombards you with toxic things that take you out of the present."

"You have a good outlook. Can you bottle some of it for me in a pretty little jar?"

"I would, but I might break it." I winked.

He bent his head back. "Ah, yes. That's very true."

Our eyes locked, and I felt my knees quiver. *Yeah. That's your cue to leave.* I stood up and placed my mug on the counter—gently. "Well, this tea was very good. But I'd better let you get back to your evening."

He got up from his chair. "You don't have to go."

"I really should."

Dax nodded and followed me to the foyer. Sensing him behind me, the hairs on the back of my neck stiffened. I lifted my portable table and placed my bag of supplies over my shoulder before heading to the door. I'd just turned the doorknob when he called my name.

"Wren..."

I turned. "Yes?"

"Thank you for your question—when you asked if I was okay. Thank you for caring enough to ask. Most people don't. And thank you, too, for your insight. I'm sorry the massage didn't work out—again."

"Yeah." I shrugged. "I guess it's not meant to be."

"I may try again sometime," he said.

"Maybe third time will be the charm?" I grinned. "Who knows what else I might break."

He chuckled. "I'll have to bubblewrap the glassware before you come."

The prospect of seeing him again gave me goose bumps. I hoped to God he scheduled something, because I'd never have the balls to reach out to him if he didn't. And then I might never see him again. Even though I barely knew him, the thought of that didn't sit right with me.

Before I walked outside, I looked up at the top of the stairs to find Rafe looking down. I waved, but once again, he didn't reciprocate.

CHAPTER 3

Dax

Adriana rolled out of her bed and rushed to put her clothes back on. We were both late for work. After Rafe left for school on Monday morning, rather than go straight into the office, I decided to give myself a little "joy." At least, I tried. It wasn't quite *joyful* with Adriana, though—just a meaningless escape of a quickie with a woman who had been an occasional friend with benefits for a few months now. If there were feelings, it would've defeated the point, which was *not* to feel anything.

Adriana was the ex-wife of a business adversary. She'd messaged me out of the blue one day to tell me about her divorce. Then she'd asked if I wanted to grab drinks.

Most unsettling was that in the middle of sex with Adriana this morning, I'd been thinking about...Wren. How incredibly messed up was that? Her pretty face. Her short copper hair and delicate neck. Her gigantic blue eyes. The way her breath seemed to quicken when I'd touched her after she dropped that mug of tea. Given the circumstances of my life—not to mention the fact that she was eight years younger—my dick's reaction to that was completely fucked up. I'd thought about Wren a lot in the five days since she'd come over, and that needed to stop.

But our conversation the other night had also had some kind of effect on me, making me realize I hadn't been truly living. Why were these thoughts of her so pervasive? That's why I'd called Adriana and done the one thing I could think of to wash Wren out of my brain. Unfortunately, it seemed to have backfired.

"I was surprised you called," Adriana said as she buttoned her blouse. "Usually I'm the one calling you. We should do this again soon. It'd been a while. I thought you'd forgotten about me."

I slipped my pants on and buckled my belt. "I've just been busy. Lots of stress at work."

She fluffed her long, brown hair. "Well, I'm happy to take your mind off things anytime."

"I know. And thank you. It was...fun."

"Busy day ahead?" she asked.

I knotted my tie. "Yeah. The day is fully booked after ten."

"Well, good luck."

"Thanks." I gave her a chaste kiss on the cheek before heading for the door. Our encounters always reminded me of a business transaction.

As soon as the air hit my face outside her apartment building, relief came over me. I always felt guilty when we fucked. I hadn't slept with anyone since Maren died before my first encounter with Adriana a few months ago. And I'd only allowed myself to be with her because she'd made it clear she was fresh off her divorce and didn't want anything serious. That was perfect because I had absolute-ly nothing to offer her besides my dick. We barely even kissed. It was just pure sex. No intimacy. The only way it could be.

Once I got to work, I led a couple of back-to-back meetings before returning to my office. Almost as soon as my ass hit the chair, my assistant rang in with a call.

"I have Serena Kravitz from Phillipson Academy on the line."

Rafe's school. Shit. "Thank you," I said before picking up the call. "This is Dax Moody."

"Mr. Moody. Everything is fine with Rafe, so please don't worry. But do you have a moment to discuss some things with me?"

My pulse slowed a bit. "Yes, of course."

"As you know, Rafe has been refusing to talk for some time. We've done the best we can to accommodate him. But we have an upcoming declamation program he's not going to be able to participate in. I'm afraid his grades are going to fall behind if we can't find a way to get him to speak."

"Do you have a magic wand, Ms. Kravitz? Because I'm honestly at my wits' end."

"I know his mother's death was traumatic."

"*Traumatic* isn't a strong enough word. He'd only had a few years with her, but she was his everything—the only person in his life who'd ever given a damn about him." I hadn't meant to shout that, but I was so damn frustrated.

"I understand that."

"His therapist can't get him to talk, and neither can the woman who takes care of him most of the day. I'm going to be the last person able to get him to speak. He and I were working on our relationship before his mother passed, but everything stopped after. The world stopped. So we've made zero progress." I scratched my head. "I don't think he trusts me."

"Perhaps we should plan a meeting soon—with the school psychologist and his therapist. Form a team to help." She paused. "Have you considered medication?"

"I'm not fucking putting him on medication when I'm not sure what's causing his issue." I stopped to get a grip and lowered my voice. "Excuse my language. But I'm not going to blindly treat him when he can't even tell me what's going on in his head. Is it depression? Is it anxiety? A mix of both?" I pulled on my hair. "Anyway, a meeting would be fine. I'll do whatever you need me to do."

"Mr. Moody, I really am sorry for your predicament."

If I had a penny for every time someone said they felt sorry for me, I'd be richer than I already was.

"Thank you," I said.

After I hung up, I decided to clock out early.

The only thing that brought me out of the ever-present funk my life had become was going to the gym. I had a workout room in the basement of our house, but I also kept a membership at the luxury gym on the top floor of my office building in downtown Boston.

As I pumped iron, my energy went through the roof. I knew it was anger manifesting itself as strength. As I dropped the seventy-pound weight, I wished I could rid myself of the weight on my shoulders—the one I couldn't put down.

That night, Rafe and I sat across from each other at the dinner table. Shannon always prepared supper on weeknights. She had the weekends off, and I usually picked up takeout on those days. But tonight she'd made a nice chicken and broccoli pasta dish.

I fiddled with the penne. "Your ear feeling better?"

Rafe shrugged as he looked down at his plate.

"What does that mean? Yes or no?"

He tugged on his ear and shook his head.

"Shit," I muttered.

I'd put off taking him to the doctor for one day—or having Shannon take him—because everything seemed to upset him lately. I'd thought maybe his ear infection would magically go away. But a doctor visit would be unavoidable now.

"We'll get you to the doctor tomorrow. You probably need antibiotics again."

I hated that he'd taken more than his share of antibiotics this year. That couldn't be good for his system.

When he continued to look down, I said, "Look up at me, please."

He did as I said. The phone call from his school earlier today had made me realize I'd let this situation go on long enough.

"Rafe, at some point you're gonna have to talk again. You can't live like this. It's not like being silent is going to bring her back, you know? You need to let stuff out, and you're doing just the opposite. This is starting to become a big problem at school." I exhaled. "They called me today."

His ears turned red as he looked up from his plate.

"They want to set up a team to try to help you. But, Rafe, we won't be able to help you if you don't let us. I know you're not completely comfortable with me, but your mom expected me to look out for you. And that's what I'm trying to do. You and I, we're both in the same boat. We both miss her. We both wish things were different. So we need to work together to try to be happy. She would want that, you know? She would hate the way things are right now."

His ears turned redder, and I suspected it wasn't the ear infection. It was anger and frustration. He wanted nothing to do with this one-sided conversation.

"Alright, I'll stop bugging you—for now. But I hope you heard what I said."

After Rafe washed his hands and headed back to his room, Shannon gave me a sympathetic look. She'd been on the other side of the kitchen listening in. She now had her purse over her arm and was readying to leave.

Slapping my cloth napkin on the table, I let out a long breath. "I wasn't cut out for this."

She walked toward me. "And yet somehow you were chosen for the task. Someone up there must disagree."

"Someone up there has a sick sense of humor if they think I can handle parenting a teenager who hates my guts."

She took a seat across from me and leaned her elbows on the table. "Look, it's not you. You're not the reason he's silent. I know you think if he were in someone else's care, this wouldn't be happening."

I rubbed my eyes. "I know it's not directly about me, but I can't help thinking that if a better man for the job were in my position, things *would* be different. If I had worked harder to connect with him before Maren died, maybe we wouldn't be here."

"You know dwelling on the past is a waste of energy, right? Dwelling on the past is regret. Dwelling on the future is anxiety. The only place of peace is in the middle, the present moment."

That reminded me of what Wren had said the other night about mindfulness.

"When did you become so zen, Shannon?"

"I've got fifteen years on you. Wisdom comes with age." Shannon smirked. "Speaking of zen, how did your massage go the other day?"

Here we go. I'd been waiting for her to ask me about that. I'd noticed the expression on her face when she got a look at Wren, and she'd probably wondered if there was something more to the appointment. But I'd had no clue the girl was going to be so goddamn attractive. With the way Shannon left the house soon after Wren arrived, I got the sense she was trying to give me privacy in case I'd ordered *more* than a massage. She had it all wrong.

"It didn't work out," I said.

"What do you mean?"

"The massage. It never happened. It's a long story."

"You sent her home?"

"I changed my mind."

I didn't have the energy to tell her the story about the shell or deal with her reaction. And she didn't even know about Wren's second visit. But I was too damn spent tonight.

"It surprised me that you'd even arranged for a massage," she said. "I thought it was a great idea, though. I was proud of you for finally recognizing the importance of self-care. You work too hard, in my opinion. Like I always say, you should take more time for yourself. You can't be there for Rafe if you're burned out."

I rubbed my temples. "Noted."

I didn't know what I'd do without Shannon. Rafe's previous nanny had moved away shortly after Maren died. I went through a nanny agency and got really lucky the day Shannon showed up on my doorstep. She'd offered to handle most of the household stuff as well, so we really got a package deal. I paid her well, but I still counted my blessings to have found her.

She got up from her seat and fished through her purse for her keys.

"Hey, Shannon?"

"Yeah?"

"Don't ever leave us, okay?"

She smiled. "You guys are stuck with me."

"Thank God." I smiled back.

"Well, until I retire to New Orleans."

She was obsessed with all things New Orleans and had vowed to settle there eventually. Last year for Christmas, I'd paid for her and her husband, Bob, to take a trip there in the spring. They'd renewed their wedding vows under a tree. The week she was away had been the longest of my life. But she'd deserved the respite.

"I'd better start looking at real estate in New Orleans for Rafe and me, if you're planning on moving. You don't think you can get rid of us, do you?" I teased.

"NOLA, here we come!" She laughed.

After Shannon left for the night, I stayed at the table for a while, contemplating. Rafe was lucky to have Shannon, too, but he needed so much more to fill the gap left by Maren's death. He needed an actual father, not an imposter like me, raising him. He needed a sense of family. Most of all he needed his mother back, and that was the one thing I couldn't give him.

In bed later that night, I Googled Wren McCallister. What popped up first was the last thing I expected—a link to an online audition posted by the City Symphony.

It's her. Wren was seated, and after a brief introduction, she began playing a cello, which was almost bigger than she was. She hugged the instrument as her fingers moved over the neck, the bow in her other hand gliding across the strings. The music was somber, her expression even more so. She was...really good. *Wow.* I listened for a while as I stared at her beautiful face. Wren's short hair suited her. She certainly had the bone structure to pull it off. In the clip, she had her hair tucked behind one of her ears and wore a crisp, collared white shirt, buttoned all the way up. That was a more formal look than the ripped jeans and T-shirt she'd worn to my house the last time I saw her. Even more prominent than her beauty, though, was her talent. It blew me away.

I couldn't tell you how many times I watched the video, each time drowning myself in the hypnotic sadness of her music, an expression of the trapped emotions inside of me.

When I finally shut it off, I went to the Elite Massage website and scheduled another appointment for Friday.

CHAPTER 4

Wren

My skin tingled as I waited for someone to answer the door. Dax Moody had booked a third massage. Well, technically it would be his first massage, if it actually happened. This time it was early on a Friday evening. Having zero clue what to expect, I was both nervous and excited to see him.

When the door opened, Dax stood behind it.

"Hello, Wren. Good to see you." He gestured for me to come in.

A waft of his cologne hit me. "You, too, Moody." I wiped my feet before entering, since it had been raining a bit.

"Is that my new name?"

"It's not only your last name, but you were a bit moody when I first met you, so I think it fits you perfectly." I smiled. "I wasn't sure if I'd hear from you again."

"Well, you said third time would be the charm, right?"

"Yes, I did."

"Here, let me take that from you." He grabbed my table and settled it in the corner of the foyer.

"Thank you." I dropped my bag in the same location and looked up toward the stairwell. "Is Rafe here?"

"No, actually. He's with Maren's mother for the weekend. She lives in Palm Beach, but she's in town staying at the Ritz. She's always traveling around the world, and she wanted to spend time with him while she was here. She insisted he stay with her."

"Ah. Well, that's sweet."

"I warned her that she shouldn't expect much in the way of conversation."

I nodded sympathetically, but my pulse raced at the realization that we were likely alone. Except for maybe the dog.

"And Winston?" I asked. "Where's my buddy?"

"He's confined to the back room for now. I didn't want him bothering you."

"He really is no bother." I rubbed my hands together and looked around. "Is Rafe doing better?"

"You mean, is he still not talking at all?"

"I was more referring to the ear infection. But yeah, also that."

"His ear is better. Thanks for asking. But unfortunately, he's still not talking."

"Okay." I frowned. "Well, glad to hear about his ear."

As I followed him into the kitchen, he asked, "Can I get you something to drink? A glass of wine?"

"I can't have wine. I'm on the job."

"Well, I'm gonna open a bottle for myself. You know, the whole need-to-relax-before-the-relaxing-massage thing. If you want a glass, I won't tell."

God, did I need to relax right now. If there were ever a time to break the rules... "Maybe just one," I blurted before I could change my mind.

"White or red?"

"Either is fine."

"Red it is, then."

I watched as he uncorked the wine. He had such beautiful hands, big and rough-looking. I imagined how his callused fingers might feel against my bare skin, and then shook the thought away. *You're here to work, Wren, not to ogle him.*

He walked a glass of cabernet over and handed it to me. "If you have somewhere else to be later, let me know. I won't take up too much of your time. We can get right to the massage. I imagine you must have plans on a Friday night."

"Not tonight, actually. So it's no rush." Taking a sip of my wine, I let my eyes wander around the kitchen. I immediately noticed something on the table. It was a black book with a hard cover and a gold fleur-de-lis on the front. "Is that a journal?"

"Yes." He reached over and grabbed it. "Shannon actually designs them."

"What's the significance of the fleur-de-lis?"

"She's obsessed with all things New Orleans. She has an online shop of New Orleans memorabilia and trinkets that she makes. She left that journal here for me. She thinks I need to express myself more and suggested I start writing my feelings down in it." He rolled his eyes.

"The nerve of her," I taunted.

"Not my thing."

I shrugged. "Still, she's right. Journaling is the best. It's the only way I ever fully express myself. It's very therapeutic."

He took a sip of his wine. "It sounds like more work to me—something I don't have time for."

"It shouldn't be work. It should just be like a purge of your thoughts, frustrations...anything, really. It doesn't have to be articulate."

"Mine would be filled with expletives, then."

"That would be better than nothing. Probably even more therapeutic, actually. I highly recommend it."

"Well, since *you* highly recommend journaling, I must try it."

I squinted. "Are you mocking me?"

"No." He laughed behind his glass. "I swear. I'm not."

It was nice to see him more jovial tonight.

"I have to confess something, Wren."

"Okay. What is it?"

He set his glass down. "I Googled you."

I took a long sip of my wine. "Find anything interesting?"

"How long have you played the cello?"

My eyelid twitched, as it often did when I was nervous. I wasn't sure why knowing he'd watched me play made me jittery.

"I started lessons when I was eight."

"You're amazing. The song you played during your audition for City Symphony was hauntingly beautiful. That was the video I watched. I'd heard that song many times before, but somehow it never sounded like that."

"*Bach Cello Suite Number One.* I can't tell you how many times I've played that. It feels like the alphabet to me."

"Listening to it made me sad in a sense, but not in a bad way... In a way that brought out some things that maybe needed to come out."

"The cello is good for that. It has a reputation as one of the saddest of instruments."

"I'd have to agree with that." He leaned back in his chair. "Whatever became of that audition? Why are you massaging people when you should be traveling in some kind of orchestra? You're certainly talented enough."

"That audition was two years ago, and it was for a substitute cellist role, someone who can play at the last minute if one of the regular symphony cellists calls out." I picked some lint off my pants. "I didn't get the job, though."

"That's a shame. You're very good."

"I might seem good to you, but I'm not quite good enough for the symphony."

"I wanted to hear more than just that song. But I couldn't find anything else."

"You clearly didn't do enough online research." I winked.

He gave me a look. "What am I missing?"

"I have my own channel."

His eyes went wide. "Really..."

"It's one of the only ways to get myself out there, to continue practicing and playing so I don't throw away everything I've learned. It keeps me active and professional, and I make a little money on the side, depending on the number of views." I grabbed my phone and pulled up my channel on the streaming site. "It's not under my name, which is why it didn't come up," I explained as I showed him.

"RenCello. Spelled with no W." He smiled. "Ten-thousand followers. Very cool. I'll check it out. I admire your perseverance. I would imagine this channel is not something that's easy to keep going when you're working another job."

"Well, with music, it's first and foremost about the passion. You have to make the time. I mean, my dad was the one who chose to enroll me in lessons years back, but ultimately, I made the decision to continue because I love it."

He stared at me a moment. "I'm curious about you. Do you mind if I ask some questions?"

"What made you ask for permission all of a sudden?" I teased, trying to keep it light. "Your massage appointments are definitely not the norm."

"You think it's strange that I want to know more about you?"

"No. I just have a hard time understanding you, in general. You were so aloof when I first met you. And you're still guarded when it comes to yourself, yet you have this curiosity at the same time." I chuckled. "You know what you remind me of?"

"What?"

"A deer."

Dax massaged his chin scruff. "Well, that's a first. I've been called many things, but a deer is not one of them. Care to explain?"

"My dad's mother lives in New Hampshire. Growing up, I'd play in the woods by her house. This beautiful deer would appear from time to time and give me this curious stare. But whenever I'd approach, it would run away. It wanted to stare at me, but as soon as I returned the attention, it would run."

"Ah." He nodded. "I suppose you're right. I don't want to share myself or give up control, but I do like learning about other people."

"Well, you're in luck, because I have nothing to hide. What do you want to know?" I straightened in my chair.

He took a drink of his wine and set it down. "You said your dad raised you alone. Obviously, I have a vested interest in learning more about that scenario because of my own situation. What was that like for you, not having a mother around from a young age?"

I twirled the stem of my glass between my fingers. "I hit the jackpot with my parents. Even though I only had my mom until I was five, I have fond memories of her. And my dad helps to ensure that I never forget her. There were always photos of her around, and not a day goes by that he's not sharing some story about her. He also worked really hard to make sure I never felt different because I didn't have a mother around. Of course, I felt the loss, but my father really filled both roles as best he could. Dad has always been my rock. We're lucky to have each other. I couldn't imagine life without him."

"Your parents didn't have any other kids?"

"No. My mother was unable to have children, and my father never remarried. Like Rafe, I was adopted. Except I was a baby when my parents got me."

He scratched his chin. "I see."

"My birth mother was apparently very young and made the choice many in her situation have to make. She chose not to have contact with me, but I never felt unwanted because my parents gave me all the love in the world. After my mother died, my father taught me that you can find reasons to smile even in the darkest moments. He's definitely my hero."

"He sounds like an amazing guy."

"He is." I smiled.

"I suppose if you were immersed in music from the age of eight, you were the type of teenager who didn't get into too much trouble?"

"Ha." I chuckled. "Don't be so sure about that. I gave my father many sleepless nights—getting into cars with boys, sneaking out of the house, et cetera."

He flashed me a mischievous look. "I'm curious about the et cetera."

I shook my head. "Why do I feel like I'm being interviewed for the *privilege* of massaging you?"

"That's not what this is about. I'm just interested."

I tilted my head. "Then it's only fair if I turn the tables a bit, Bambi."

He crossed his arms. "Depends on what you want to know."

I came out with it. "I want to know about your wife."

You could've heard a pin drop.

Dax swallowed. "Okay…"

"I know she was older than you. I'm curious about how you met her, I guess."

"That's all you're curious about?"

"No. I'm curious about a lot when it comes to you, but I haven't had the balls to ask about most of it. But since *you're* being so intrusive…"

He looked down a moment. "When I met Maren, she was my boss, actually. I was successful in my own right at the time, but she was a little further up the chain. She didn't pursue me until I left the company for another job." He poured himself some more wine and lifted the bottle toward me, but I held my hand up. I wasn't going to have any more.

"I had a great deal of respect and admiration for her from the moment I met her. It wasn't love at first sight for me, but it was a very strong *like*. She made no secret of the fact that she was interested in me once it was appropriate for her to express that, and I was flattered to be the object of her affection. In time, our relationship grew romantic. But I always viewed us as more of a partnership of mutual respect than your typical fairytale love story. We had our issues. A lot of them—mostly having to do with the fact that I wasn't completely ready for marriage when we eloped one crazy weekend. But I was determined not to fail and convinced myself that the connection we had was strong enough to make a marriage. I have an issue with failure, so I vowed to make it work. We were still a work in progress when she died." He exhaled. "She was an amazing woman, and her death was a tremendous loss to this world. She truly cared about people, myself included. I didn't deserve her. And she certainly didn't deserve to die." He shut his eyes and muttered, "That's the very short version of the story."

As brief as he might have been, it was a lot to take in. "I'm sorry," I whispered.

His voice was barely audible. "Thank you."

"The fact that she adopted Rafe proves what a wonderful person she was. You said he was eight when she got him, right?"

He nodded. "When she set out to adopt, she insisted on an older kid, someone who might otherwise not have been adopted so easily. She really loved him. And he loved her. I think that's why his relationship with me got off to such a rocky start. When I moved in, he saw me as a threat. That certainly wasn't my intention, but he was very protective of her."

"That's sweet, though."

Dax stared down into his glass. "This is the most I've opened up about it, sadly." He looked up at me. "I don't know what it is about you that makes me want to do that. Maybe it was the cello—some kind of weird musical hypnotism." He shook his head. "You seem too good to be true, Wren."

"What do you mean?"

"You're very balanced for someone who lost her mother so young. That makes me hopeful for Rafe, I suppose. The musical talent. Good girl who loves her dad. You appear to have a decent head on your shoulders. What am I missing here?"

I laughed. "I don't have any dead bodies hidden or anything, but *good girl* is not exactly a fitting description."

His eyes filled with mirth. "I'm intrigued."

"Yeah, well, you're not getting my whole life story over one glass of wine, Moody."

"You can tell me more during the massage, then?"

"Nope. I don't talk to clients during the massage. That would impair your ability to shut out the world and relax."

"What if I want to talk because I don't like silence?"

46

"Then you're out of luck." Feeling suddenly anxious to get started, I checked my phone. "I should probably set up. Where do you want me?"

A look of disappointment crossed his face. I think he wanted to keep talking.

"We can do it in my office, like the first attempt. You're not allowed to touch anything but me, though," he teased.

My nipples stiffened, his comment reminding me that I was about to touch him for the first time. Feeling flustered, I cleared my throat. "Very funny. And don't worry. I'm never touching a damn thing in your office again."

"Okay." He got up from his seat, taking my empty glass to the counter. Dax then fetched my table and bag from the foyer, and I followed him into the other room.

"I forget what I'm supposed to do," he said. "You'll have to direct me."

"Well, it's your choice whether you want to take your pants off or not."

"Jesus," he muttered. "You seriously massage men who are naked under a towel?"

"Yes. Sometimes. Other times, they leave their underwear on. And don't even think about that other question in your head, because the answer is fuck no, I've never given a happy ending, and I never would."

His eyes widened. "I wasn't thinking that at all."

"You may not have thought I did it, but you thought about it. Because everyone seems to wrongly associate massages, even legitimate ones, with happy endings. We get a bad rap."

"Maybe in the back of my mind I thought about it for a fleeting second, but only in the sense that many men are pigs, and I would imagine you must have come across a few bad apples who might have tried something. It can't be safe going into strange homes."

"I've been pretty lucky—only one or two bad apples. Our clients are all background checked and vetted. So sketchy people are very rare. And if someone gives me a weird vibe, I just stop the massage. I carry mace as a precaution, too."

"Ah. So, I've been under the threat of getting maced this entire time. I shouldn't have pried so much."

"You're one intrusive question away from getting hit with it." I winked. "Nah. You're safe."

He pretended to wipe sweat from his forehead.

I chuckled. "You know what I think?"

"What?"

"You're stalling again because you're still not comfortable with the idea of this massage, for some reason."

"You're right."

"I know I'm right."

He folded his hands together. "Okay. Let's get this show on the road, then. How do I make this easier for you?"

"You signed up for a full-body massage. It's easier if you take your pants off since I'll be working on your legs. You can leave your underwear on. I put a towel over your backside anyway."

He swallowed. "Okay."

"But seriously, whatever you're comfortable with."

"I'm comfortable with not making your job more difficult," he said.

"I'll step outside so you can get...comfortable."

"Comfortable. We've used that word a lot, haven't we? So it's ironic how *uncomfortable* I am right now." Dax laughed.

"You won't be for much longer," I said matter-of-factly. If there was one thing I knew, it's that I was good at my job, and he'd be feeling good and relaxed in no time.

I stepped out of the room. Despite putting on a front of calmness, I *was* nervous to touch him. I refused to show it, though. If he called me out, I'd have to admit that *he* made me nervous. I did this for a living. It was supposed to be a piece of cake. And I was only flustered because I was attracted to him. I definitely wouldn't be admitting that.

After a few minutes, I knocked. "All set?"

"Yes. Come in," he answered.

Dax lay on his stomach with his head turned toward me. He'd placed the white towel over his backside, although it did nothing to hide the sculpted contours of his derrière. The band of his gray boxer briefs peeked out from the top of the towel.

His body looked amazing, beautifully bronzed and hard as a rock. I took a deep breath in and willed myself to get a grip. Once I got going, I would feel more at ease.

I'd thought maybe he would still seem anxious, but it seemed lying down had already relaxed him somewhat.

"I'm just gonna rub some oil onto your back. It's warmed, so it will feel good."

"Okay," he whispered.

To my dismay, when I squeezed the bottle, it made a funny fart sound.

Dax added fuel to the fire. "Excuse yourself, Ms. McCallister." His back shook in silent laughter.

"The only one in danger of passing gas here is you," I retorted.

Dax's body froze. "Don't tell me that happens a lot."

"That's pretty much the most common thing I see."

"That will *not* be happening with me."

"Sometimes when people reach a certain level of relaxation, they don't have full control of their functions."

"Just when I was starting to relax into this, you're telling me I'm in danger of unwillingly ripping one?"

"Not necessarily. Just letting you know it's okay if it happens."

He turned around to face me. "Look, I may not know the first thing about massage. But what I *do* know? It's *not* fucking okay if that happens."

"Okay." I chuckled. "No more talking."

"Yes, ma'am." He repositioned his head into the face hole at the edge of the table.

I took a deep breath in and began rubbing the oil into his back. His skin was warm, his muscles tight—so knotted and tense. I stood off to the side, using the weight of my body to press both of my palms down, moving them slowly in a straight line from the bottom of his back to the top. He expelled a long, guttural breath that made my body buzz. While unwanted desire flowed through me, I could feel some of the tension lifting from him. So at least one of us was having an appropriate response.

After a couple of minutes, I applied even more of my body weight as I switched to moving my forearms along the length of his back, this time landing lower, closer to the top of his ass. His breathing became a bit more labored, and even though I was conscious of the shift, my own nerves had calmed. I was now comfortable, despite maybe enjoying this a little too much. But honestly, I'd have to have been dead not to enjoy this. He didn't need to know I'd be going home later and replaying it all in my head.

When I began to use my elbows to dig into his back, he let out a groan and muttered, "Fuck, that's good."

Those words felt like they vibrated through my entire body and landed on my clit. Still, I vowed to focus my attention on the job of making him feel good and not on the fact that he was making *me* feel good, too.

I moved to the front of the table so I could better work the top of his back and lower neck. My abdomen brushed along his hair. It wasn't intentional; there was simply no way to reach over him without that contact. It normally didn't even faze me, but with Dax, even the slightest things affected me. He surprised me at one point when he lifted his head to look up at me. His eyes locked with mine, and I nearly froze, because I didn't want him to see the look on my face. I worried I couldn't hide how aroused touching him had made me. I thought maybe he'd say something, but he just stared a moment before he returned to his spot.

I eventually moved down to his legs, rubbing both of my hands in a firm line up his left calf and the back of his thigh.

"Is this level of pressure good?" I asked. "Or do you want it deeper?"

"The way you're doing it is perfect."

His feet were as large as I might have expected, given his height, and I noticed his toes curling. He was definitely enjoying this. It gave me pleasure to know I could help such a tightly wound man decompress.

As I moved over to the other leg, he seemed so relaxed that I thought he might have fallen asleep. It wasn't until he let out another slight groan of pleasure that I realized he was awake.

After finishing the back of his body, I lightly tugged on his towel and said, "You can turn over now."

He tensed and didn't move. Finally, he said, "No. I'm sorry. I can't."

CHAPTER 5

Dax

A rush of adrenaline shot through me the second she asked me to turn over. I don't know what I was thinking, but I absolutely did *not* realize this massage involved the *front* of my body, too. What the fuck did I think *full body* meant? This wasn't good. I'd had a plan. I was going to wrap the damn towel around me and leave the room before I let on that she'd given me a hard-on. But now what?

Now I had no choice but to end this immediately or turn over and salute her—or maybe offer her the opportunity to hang her coat on my cock.

I turned my head to look at her. "I...can't turn around right now."

"Why not?" she asked.

I glared at her.

She got the drift pretty quickly. "Oh."

"Earlier when you said people in this situation could lose control of their bodily functions, it didn't occur to me that I could get a..."

"You know that happens all the time, too, right?"

"Well, that's fucked up."

"It's involuntary. High levels of oxytocin are released during a massage and can cause it to happen."

"You make it sound so scientific."

"You don't have to turn over. I'll just go over your upper back again to make up the time. It's not a big deal. You were really relaxed. It was great. So try to go back to that."

Thankful for the opportunity to stay facing down, I did my best to close my eyes again and forget about the fucking awkwardness. I would've loved to feel her hands on my chest, too, if I could do it without my dick pointing at her face. But it wasn't going to happen. The level of control I'd apparently given up had far exceeded what I'd imagined. It was probably a good thing I couldn't look at her from this angle. That would've undoubtedly made my predicament far worse.

Her hands were like silk, and the strength in her movements was impressive. It felt like she'd worked years' worth of knots and tension out of my back. She deserved triple what I'd paid for this session; actually, you couldn't even put a price on it. But I knew it wasn't just about her physical touch. It was *her*. She'd made me feel like it was okay to let go long before she ever laid a hand on me.

What killed me, and what probably led to my dick's awakening, were the little breaths she'd sometimes let out when she was applying pressure. I could feel them on my skin. And that made me want to feel more than just the air that escaped her. This was a problem. But I couldn't let myself feel guilty right now because this massage was too damn good. It was the best thing I'd felt in a very long time. I needed this.

When it finally came to an end, I felt almost drunk off of how relaxed I was. As Wren turned around to clean up, I told her I'd be getting dressed upstairs and would meet her back downstairs in a moment. Wrapping the towel carefully around me, I picked my clothes up off the floor and rushed out.

I was still fully erect, and I needed to take care of that before I said goodbye to her. So I jumped in the shower and in less than a minute rubbed out one of the most intense orgasms I'd had in a while. After my cum shot into the tub, I felt a bit of shame for getting off on her. But never in my life had I experienced something as sensual as being touched by her.

Wren was all packed up and waiting in the foyer when I arrived back downstairs. I'd wanted to ask her to stay for a bit, but all things considered, that wasn't appropriate.

"That was fast. You're leaving?" I asked instead.

"I am."

I stood in front of her. "Wren..."

"If you're going to apologize for you-know-what, please don't, okay?"

I looked down at my feet and chuckled. Her choice of words was better than *the party in your pants*, I supposed.

"I won't," I said.

"How do you feel?" she asked.

"I feel amazing. Truly. Like a new man. I hope you know how good you are at what you do."

"Well, you gave me a standing ovation earlier, so..." Her face was red as a beet.

Jesus. "That's a fucking good one. I have to admit."

"In all seriousness, I'm glad the massage helped." She smiled and turned toward the door.

I was still *this close* to asking her to stay for another drink. I did *not* want her to leave. Maybe I could've gotten away with it if it weren't for pitching a tent earlier. But realistically, she had to go—for many reasons.

"What will you do tonight?" I asked. "The night is still young."

"I don't know. I'll have to see what kind of trouble I can get into." She winked. "You should do the same. Take advantage of Rafe not being home."

"My body is so damn relaxed right now, I feel like I'd have jelly legs if I left the house." I laughed.

"That'll probably lessen in a half hour or so. Then you can go out on the town."

"Going out on the town isn't exactly my thing anymore."

"I would think all you have to do is walk into a room full of people, and they flock to you."

I shrugged. "Usually those aren't the right kind of people."

She nodded. "I hear you."

I much preferred being around people I naturally gravitated toward. And this girl was a magnet.

I stood there saying nothing, clearly stalling. I didn't want to say goodbye to her because I liked the way she made me feel. *Alive.* That was the only way to describe it.

"'Night, Moody," she finally said, ending my awkward procrastination.

"Goodnight, Wren."

She walked away without further ado. I stayed at the doorway and watched as she packed her stuff into her small SUV and took off.

The second the door closed, it felt lonelier than it had in a while in this big, empty house.

An hour later, I'd done nothing productive with my night. The massage had not only relaxed my body but seemed to have brought to the surface so many of the emotions trapped inside me. Now that they were released, I needed to put them somewhere. So I decided to do something I'd never done before.

I took that journal off the kitchen table and brought it up to my bedroom. Lying in bed, I settled into my pillow and opened the blank notebook. The paper was a heavy stock. I grabbed a pen from my side-table drawer and began to write out my thoughts.

Why do I feel guilty for the euphoria I'm experiencing right now? Maybe because I feel so alive, and that's an even bigger reminder that Maren isn't. I feel amazing and terrible at the same time. Who knew you could feel both at once?

You would think Maren's death would be a constant reminder of how life is short, but I've done nothing but bury myself deeper into work since she left us. And I know that's because I don't want to feel anything. I don't want to have to feel the guilt over not having given Maren the love she deserved. I'd all but told her our marriage was a mistake in the weeks before she died. The signs were there, and she knew it. Maren deserved a man who was ready for that commitment. I'd taken a chance when

I married her, and I failed miserably. I hope she knows how sorry I am for that. I wanted so desperately to love her the way she deserved to be loved. I will spend the rest of my life trying to make it up to her in the only way I know how, which is to look after Rafe and to try to be a better person for him.

But as Shannon always says, I can't be anything for Rafe if I'm miserable. I know I need to work on my mental health. So, I guess writing in this journal is the first step in that direction.

I've spent so much time trying to feel nothing, but tonight that was impossible. Tonight I felt EVERYTHING.

I closed the journal and put it inside my drawer.

That was the first night in a year and a half that I truly slept.

In the weeks that passed after the massage, I kept flip-flopping about whether to contact Wren again. While sitting at my desk at work one afternoon, I went so far as to open the massage company's scheduling portal. I finally gave in, only to find that there was no longer an option to request Wren as the massage therapist in the dropdown.

Perplexed, I picked up the phone and dialed their main number.

A woman answered. "Elite Massage. How can I help you?"

Fiddling with my pen, I said, "Yes, I tried to book an appointment online, and it wasn't allowing me to select

Wren McCallister for a massage. Can you help me with that?"

"I'm sorry. Wren is no longer working with us."

What?

My fingers tightened around the pen. It took me a few seconds to respond. "She's not..."

"Correct."

"I know it's none of my business, but can I ask what happened?"

"She decided to part ways with us."

I gripped the pen harder, nearly breaking it in half. "Is she working anywhere else?"

"If she is, I'm not able to disclose that."

"Oh, man," I muttered.

"Is everything okay, sir?" the woman asked.

"Uh, yes." I shook my head. "Thank you for the information."

"I'll be happy to book you an appointment with one of our other qualified massage therapists."

"No, thank you." I hung up before she could say anything else.

Pulling on my hair, I let out a long, frustrated breath.

Maybe this was a sign that contacting her was the wrong decision.

Maybe I'd dodged a bullet.

CHAPTER 6

Wren

I almost never checked the messages I received through my RenCello account. Most of the time, they were special requests for songs I couldn't accommodate or dirty messages from men. But for some reason, I clicked on the inbox one Tuesday night, just to be sure I wasn't missing anything of importance, like a job opportunity. The last thing I expected to see was a message from Dax Moody. It had been sent a couple of weeks ago.

Hi Wren,

It's Dax Moody. I'm sorry if contacting you on here is out of line. I wasn't sure how else to reach you. When I went to book another appointment with you at Elite, I was surprised to learn that you'd left. I guess I'm writing just to make sure everything is okay. You left an impression on me, and I want to wish you well. I hope you got a better opportunity. I also wanted to let you know how much I enjoyed talking to you during our last appointment and to thank you again for the massage. That was the first night in forever that I slept without waking up a dozen times. I consider that magic and have you to thank for it. If you're so inclined, drop me a note to let me know all is well with you.

Sincerely,
Dax Moody

P.S. I've been enjoying perusing the archives of this account. My favorite performance has to be "The Swan," but there are so many good ones. You're very talented.

I sat there in shock. I never thought I'd hear from him again. Leaving Elite had been unexpected. The day after I last saw Dax, I'd been contacted by another company in need of a massage therapist after one of their staffers left unexpectedly. One of my previous clients turned out to be the owner of this new company, and I had been unknowingly vetted for the position. The new company took a smaller cut of my earnings, so it was a no-brainer to take the job. As much as I liked Trina, I knew she wouldn't budge on the financial arrangement from previous experience with others who had left Elite. So, I gave her my notice and took the other gig. Unfortunately, my second day on the job, things went sour. The new company sent me to the house of a man who harassed me. Apparently, he was a top client, and when I complained, the message I received was basically to "suck it up." I quit that same day. I soon learned Trina wasn't interested in hiring me back after my "betrayal," so I was currently searching for another job.

I'd thought of Dax often, but I didn't think he would reach out again. He'd seemed embarrassed about getting aroused during the massage, so it surprised me that he'd tried to book another. I didn't really understand our connection. But there *was* a connection. We came from two totally different worlds, and yet somehow, at least in my mind, when we talked to each other, time stood still. I'd considered reaching out to let him know I left Elite but had decided not to be presumptuous. Deep down, I knew if he really wanted to get in touch again, he would find a way. And it seemed he had.

I sat in front of my computer for about fifteen minutes before responding.

Hey Moody,

It's good to hear from you. It makes me happy to know the massage had its intended effect and you were able to relax that night. Everything is good with me, although I'm currently not working. Long story short, I left to take a position with another massage company. But they turned out to be terrible. So I'm currently looking for another job. My attitude is that everything happens for a reason, so I'm trying to use this time as a gift, spending more hours making music and meditating. I'm sure I'll find another position soon. I hope you're well? How is Rafe? My buddy Winston?

Wren

P.S. "The Swan" by Saint-Saens is one of my favorites as well.

I tried to avoid checking the site for a response like a madwoman. So I closed out and vowed not to look again for at least an hour.

At 10 PM, I went back and saw that Dax had responded.

> **God, Wren. I'm really sorry to hear about the job situation. Are you working independently at all? If so, I would love to book another session.**

My heart beat faster. I wouldn't normally be working independently because it was too much work to vet customers myself. In fact, I'd never worked as a freelancer. I much preferred being attached to a company. But since I "knew" Dax, this would be different. It would be some money in my pocket, and who was I kidding? I'd get to see him again. That was the real reason I'd say yes. He could've asked me to come over and clean his floors for free, and I probably would've said yes.

> **I don't typically work independently, but since I know you, I'd be happy to come by. You could just pay me whatever you paid Elite for my services. Let me know what timeframe you have in mind in terms of scheduling.**

His response came within five minutes.

> **That sounds great. I appreciate you making an exception for me. Would you happen to have availability this coming Friday around noon? I took the day off and would prefer to do it before Rafe comes home from**

school. No worries if that doesn't work out. We can fig-ure out another time.

Goose bumps peppered my skin as I responded.

Friday at noon works great. See you then.

I hadn't been able to concentrate on anything else all week. When Friday arrived, I'd already spent way too much time debating what to wear. Deep down, I knew this was much more to me than an appointment. I wondered if it was all in my head or if the vibe I'd gotten from Dax since our last meeting was real. Did he like me, or did he just want another massage?

He was a complex man. And his life was understand-ably too complicated right now to deal with a relationship of any kind, so I wasn't sure why my hopes were up. What did I want from him? All I knew was that any time I was about to see him, an inexplicable excitement filled me.

Once I got to his house in Brookline, butterflies swarmed in my belly as I knocked on his door and waited.

About a minute later, the door opened. Dax looked gorgeous in dark jeans and a slim-fitting, beige ribbed sweater that displayed his muscles beautifully. His hair was damp from the shower. He was more stunning than ever.

"Hey, Wren. Good to see you." He waved me inside. "Come in."

"Good to see you, too." I stepped into the house.

He reached for my table and carried it to a corner of the foyer.

The sound of paws scratching against the floor registered, and then Winston appeared. He immediately started barking.

"Sorry about him," Dax said. "I was going to put him behind the gate, but the groomer is coming to get him."

"Your groomer picks him up?"

"For an extra fee, yeah."

"Wow. That's cool."

"They'll call Shannon to pick him up when he's ready. She's out running some errands."

I turned to the big, fluffy beast. "You know, Winston, I read online that English sheepdogs are known for liking to cuddle. I wish you would let me hug you. But I'm afraid to upset you."

He growled.

"Winston was Maren's dog," he said. "It took a while for him to get used to me, but now we're attached at the hip. He's quite territorial."

"You don't say..."

Dax chuckled. "Anyway, I can see they just pulled up. Excuse me while I bring him out to them." He clipped on the leash. "Come on, you fluffernutter."

Ruff!

"Goodbye to you, too, Winston." I waved.

I looked out the window and watched as Dax spoke to the groomer guy and helped get Winston into the car.

A few minutes later, he returned. "Sorry about that."

"No worries. I'm determined to get him to like me eventually. I'll kill him with kindness. Although I haven't garnered the courage to pet him yet." I laughed.

"Thank you again for agreeing to come today," he said.

"Of course. Thank you for hiring me. It's not like I currently have a job or anything."

"I was just about to make some espresso. Want one?"

"Sure. I could use a pick-me-up." I smiled as I followed Dax into the kitchen.

He served me while I told him the full story of what had gone down with the last massage company.

He drew in his brows. "That guy didn't lay a hand on you, though, right?"

"No."

"I'm sorry that happened."

"It's a risk of the job." I shrugged.

"Which is a damn shame. It shouldn't have to be."

"Actually, like I said, everything happens for a reason. Losing my job lit a fire under my ass to look for other opportunities. I applied for a potential opportunity to travel abroad and teach music. If I get it, I'll be leaving this summer. It's probably the only way I'd be able to afford to go to Europe so soon."

He seemed to ponder my news. "So...you may be leaving, then?"

"If I'm lucky, yeah." I studied his expression, searching for hints of disappointment, but I couldn't read him.

"That's amazing."

"Thank you. Fingers crossed."

"Now's the time for adventures, right? While you're young."

"I suppose," I said. "I mean, if I had a strong reason not to go, I'd stay. But I don't have anything tying me here."

"Yeah." He stared into my eyes.

"You never answered when I asked how Rafe was in my message."

He nodded. "I'm sorry. Thank you for asking about him. He's the same, actually. We have another meeting this week at the school. He sees a therapist regularly, but she hasn't been able to get him to talk. The therapist has been attending these meetings, and we're all brainstorming on next steps."

"I've been doing some reading up on mutism. His is not really selective, right? Because people with selective mutism speak comfortably in certain situations but not others..."

"Correct. Rafe won't speak at all. But he has the ability to speak. He's just choosing not to, or perhaps feels like he can't. His therapist has him illustrate his emotions on paper, but it's typically abstract and not always easy to interpret. He's actually an amazing artist. Before his mother died, he used to draw more often."

"You said the mutism started after Maren died?"

He nodded. "Like clockwork. They definitely link it to the trauma of losing her. But Rafe's exact situation is not something his doctor has ever seen before. It typically doesn't last this long. Although there is apparently a name for it—traumatic mutism."

"I'm sorry you guys are going through this. The mind is very complex, isn't it? I hope that it works itself out somehow."

"Me, too," he whispered.

I looked down at his long fingers wrapped around the small espresso cup. I had a weakness for sexy hands, and Dax had the most beautiful pair.

He snapped me out of my trance when he said, "I've been listening to your music."

I looked up and met his gaze. "That sort of makes me nervous, but I'm flattered."

"You're so good. There's nothing to be nervous about."

I felt my face heat up the way it did when anyone complimented me on my music. "Thank you."

"You're blushing."

"Yeah. I don't handle compliments well."

"Well, then I'll stick to insults. I'm better at those anyway." He winked.

We shared a smile.

"Seriously, though, that just means you're humble," he said.

"Who *are* you, Dax?" I asked.

He drummed his fingers along the table. "What do you mean?"

"I mean, who were you before you became this successful man? What led you to where you are today?"

"It wasn't all pretty." He offered a sad smile. "I grew up in New York state. The Catskills. My mother was a wonderful woman, but my father was verbally abusive. He owns a large cement company, and the expectation was always that my brothers and I would take over the business. I deviated from the pack and decided to do my own thing, built my success from the ground up. That was important to me. I also had no passion for the cement business. My father wasn't happy with that, so he disowned me about seven years ago. Still won't speak to me to this day. My mother and I have a cordial relationship, but it's been on the down low so she can keep the peace with my father.

My two brothers and I are also not on speaking terms because they decided to side with my dad. The whole situation sucks, for lack of a better word."

I almost felt bad for asking about it now. "That must be so hard for you."

He nodded. "So, naturally, I've always put this enormous pressure on myself to succeed. Because I wanted to prove myself to them." He ran his hand through his hair. "But really, what did I attain in the end, if we're still not speaking—if my father sees it all as an abandonment rather than being proud of me? The hardest part has been losing touch with my brothers, though."

That broke my heart. "I've always wondered what it would be like to have siblings. But honestly, who needs siblings like that? Your family should've supported your dreams. No one should be told what to do with their life for someone else's gain. Your brothers are probably bitter because they wish they'd had the balls to do what you did. People don't typically act like that unless they have a problem with themselves. They're jealous of your success."

"As always, you're very insightful, Wren." He sighed. "But it is what it is. Like you said, success isn't the measure of joy, right?"

"You remembered." I smiled.

"I've tried to let it sink in a little. I suppose it's one of the reasons I called you back. The last time I experienced joy...was with you."

Oh God. A shiver ran down my spine. Hearing him say that was both beautiful and heartbreaking. And the feeling was mutual. I had a good life, nothing to complain about, but nothing in recent years had lit a fire inside me, either—

until Dax. I wanted to tell him so much but couldn't find the right words.

He looked down into his cup. "I hope that didn't come across as inappropriate. I just meant that in order to experience joy, you have to let your guard down. And the first time I'd done that in a long while was during that massage with you."

"That makes me very happy." I wanted to reach out and touch his hand, but I stopped myself. "And thank you for sharing a bit of your history. I hope your family comes to their senses someday."

He took a deep breath. "When I met Maren, part of what drew me to her was the way she saw me and the way she made me feel. She looked at my self-made success, my hopes, dreams, and flaws the way I'd hoped my family would. And she filled the void they left...somewhat. We didn't have a perfect marriage. But she was basically the only family I had and my best friend." He shook his head. "Are you sorry you asked now?"

"Not at all," I said, humbled by his openness.

He circled the tip of his index finger along the rim of his cup. "I took your advice and started journaling."

"Really? I'm so glad to hear that."

"It's a work in progress."

"*Life* is a work in progress, a series of ups and downs. What matters is that we pick ourselves up when we're down and keep going. You've had a lot of practice with that as of late."

"Well, that's true. What's that they say? God doesn't give you anything you can't handle? I feel like crying uncle so He knows I'm done." He chuckled. "Anyway, now I suppose it's my turn to ask you something, yes?" He flashed a mischievous smile. "I'm still curious about your bad-girl history—what you alluded to last time. I think it's time you dispel my theory about being so put-together."

I laughed. "There are probably too many stories to fit into this one appointment."

Dax stared through me. "Share only one, then."

I wracked my brain. There were several to choose from. "Well...okay..." I picked a memory at random. "For a brief period of time, I was a scrap-metal thief."

"What now?" His eyes filled with amusement. "I gotta hear this."

I sighed. "About ten years ago, my father became temporarily unemployed. We were in danger of losing our house. He'd been through so much and worked so hard to support us that I felt like I needed to do something— even if it was desperate. This kid from the neighborhood found out about my predicament and showed me all the best places to go to steal scrap metal. I'd sell what I gathered, and then leave the money in an anonymous envelope in our mailbox. My dad didn't know where the cash was coming from."

"Wow." He chuckled. "Where did you steal the metal from?"

"Lots of places. Taverns that left their unsecured kegs out at night, construction sites... I refused to take anything from graveyards or playgrounds, though."

"Did you ever get caught?"

"Yup. It scared the crap out of me. A woman caught me taking a bronze statue from her yard. I was lucky she didn't have me arrested. When I explained why I'd resorted to stealing it, she actually let me have it and agreed not to press charges. But on the condition that I promise not to steal anymore. She also made me tell my father what I'd been doing. She knew him because we lived in the neighborhood. Once my dad found out, he was livid. So he and I did her snow removal that winter."

"But you didn't lose the house?" he asked.

"No. Thank God my dad got a new job before that happened. But I can't say I regret helping him keep a roof over our heads. If I go to hell for that, so be it. I'd never have the balls to do something like that today. And I realize, of course, how wrong it was. So don't worry, your metal is safe."

"I'm glad you clarified that. I was fearing for my wrought-iron fence outside." His smile lingered. "Okay, so even your bad-girl story has an undercurrent of good in it. You make stealing scrap metal seem heroic. I can appreciate why you did it, even if it was wrong. There should be nothing we wouldn't do to protect the ones we love. I admire the bond you have with your dad."

That made me feel sorry for him. Family *should* always have each other's backs. Dax's family clearly didn't have his.

There was a long moment of silence. I'm not sure what compelled me to utter exactly how I was feeling in that moment, but I did.

"I missed you," I said.

Dax had been looking down into his cup, and he suddenly met my eyes. He said nothing.

Ugh. Why did I do that? My mouth opened and closed a few times. "I'm sorry if that sounded awkward, but I thought I'd never see you again." I shook my head and looked down. "You know what? Forget I said that, please."

"No," he finally said. "I love your honesty. And it's good to see you, too. I'd be lying if I said the only thing I wanted today was a massage. I enjoy your company. It's nice to see your face again and talk to you. It feels good."

Speaking of feeling good, wasn't I supposed to be giving this guy a massage? It must have been getting late.

I looked at the time. "We should probably get started since Rafe will be home soon, right?"

He glanced at the clock on the kitchen wall. "Another hour and a half, yeah." He stood and took our cups to the sink.

"I'll go set up." I hopped out of my seat so fast that I tripped. My bag went flying, and so did much of its contents.

Shit! Why am I always such a disaster in this house? "Butterfingers is at it again." I shook my head. "Would it kill me not to drop shit or break something every time I come here?"

Everything seemed to have fallen out—my wallet, coins, receipts, energy bars, and unfortunately, tampons. At least ten of them. Yes, ten.

Dax rushed over to help me pick up the mess. "Always helps to be prepared," he teased, putting a couple of the tampons back in my purse.

Clearing my throat, I explained, "I had a bad experience once where I needed one and didn't have one, so I make sure that can never happen again."

"I think you might be set for the next five years." He lifted my daily planner off the ground. It was held open to today's date with a binder clip.

"You had a pretty busy morning," he said. "Reiki at 9 AM?"

"Yeah. You're not the only one partaking in a little self-care." I smiled.

"What's BDE? That's our timeslot."

Oh no. I nearly pissed myself. BDE was what I'd written to signify this meeting. "You don't know what it means?" I asked, snatching the planner and putting it back in my bag.

"Afraid not."

"Seriously?"

"Seriously."

"Then I'm not telling you."

He arched a brow. "Is it bad?"

"No."

"Tell me, or I'll have to guess." He handed me the last item off the ground. "Boston Dumbass Extraordinaire?"

I chuckled. "Nope."

"Bad Dumb Elephant?"

I shook my head and sighed. He was only going to Google it later, and then I wouldn't be around to explain myself. "It means big dick energy."

"Oh...yeah. I've heard of that. Didn't make the connection with the acronym."

"It has nothing to do with an actual...dick. The term isn't even exclusive to men. Women can have big dick energy, too. It's like when someone exudes confidence, but they're not cocky. That's the vibe you give off. You don't see it about yourself because you're too busy doing your thing—managing your company, looking out for Rafe. You're not *trying* to have BDE. You just do."

"Well, it's a hell of a lot better than small dick energy, I suppose."

"Absolutely. It's totally a good thing."

"I've been called much worse in my life, so I'll take it."

I cleared my throat. "Now that I'm thoroughly mortified, let's get on with the massage, shall we?"

"Sure." He smiled.

Relief washed over me.

Dax brought my equipment into his office, helped me with the table, and left me alone in there for a bit while I set up the rest. I felt more nervous to touch him now than the last time. And I knew why. I'd agreed to come here not only to massage him, but because I *liked* him. At the same time, he intimidated me, and I felt so very out of my league. I worried that a man like Dax Moody would never be truly interested in starting something with me. It was possible he found me attractive and thought I was nice. But at this stage in his life, he was likely looking for someone who had their shit together. After all, he went for older women.

Still, even knowing the harsh truth, and vowing to not mix business with pleasure, I felt jittery going into this massage—as if it were some kind of date. *Am I delusional?* I had to wonder.

"Is everything okay?"

I flinched at the sound of his voice. Thankfully, there was nothing in sight to break this time. I turned around to face him. "Yeah. Why do you ask?"

"You were mumbling to yourself."

"Oh..." I laughed nervously. "I do that sometimes."

Without having to be asked, Dax lifted his shirt over his head. *Okay then.*

He was clearly more confident this time. I swallowed at the sight of his naked chest, which awakened an awareness between my legs. I wanted him like I'd never wanted a man before. But I had to remain professional. I wasn't here to gawk at his body or get off on this relentless and inappropriate attraction. I was here to perform a simple task, and I needed to focus.

Get it together, Wren. You have one job to do. And it's not a blowjob. Get your damn head out of the gutter.

Like last time, he stripped down to his boxers and covered himself with a towel. After he lay down, it was like déjà vu as I poured the oil and began to press my hands into his back. I was eventually able to get over my anxiousness as I lost myself in the process. As expected, he relaxed, too.

When I reached the end of my work on the back side of his body, I asked a burning question. "Do you want to turn over?"

His body tensed, and he didn't say anything, so I knew he was hard again. Maybe he needed some encouragement.

"I think you should turn over. I couldn't care less if you're hard."

His back just kept rising and falling.

I cleared my throat and went out on a limb. "Would it help if I told you I get aroused, too? You just can't see it."

"Fuck," he muttered.

Okay, maybe that was a bit much. But it was true.

To my surprise, Dax slowly turned over, swiftly adjusting the towel over himself. He was indeed erect, based on the prominent bulge I could see. It looked like he might have been hiding a large snake under the towel.

Big dick...energy.

Wow.

Okay.

Focus.

I pressed my palms into his rock-hard chest and slid them down slowly, applying just the right amount of pressure. Now I could see his handsome face, which was a definite distraction. I tried not to look at it, but I kept failing. His eyes were closed as his neck arched a little. His Adam's apple moved, and his chest rose and fell. He ran his tongue along his bottom lip at one point, and it was so sensual I felt like my panties were going to melt right off. The fact that he seemed turned on did not make my situation any easier. It was hot as fuck.

Standing at his side, I once again willed myself to focus on doing my job. Then I continued to slide my hands down the length of his chest to his torso, eventually working my way to his legs. Touching him from this angle was a glorious experience, even if it never went any further than this. I knew one thing: I would never forget this. And even if he never called me again, I would certainly never forget *him*.

A little while later, I moved to his head so I could work on his shoulders and eventually make my way down his chest from this angle. My breasts ended up positioned above his face, and I could feel the heat of his ragged breaths over them. My nipples turned to steel, craving each puff of air from him more than the last. As I rubbed my hands over his skin, I became consumed with an intense desire far greater than before. My imagination came out to play. I thought about what it would be like to lie on top of him, to grind over his rigid cock. My panties were wet from merely touching him. I couldn't imagine what it would feel like to actually *be* with him.

Moreover, I was confused about what *this* actually was. Did he really only want a massage? Because from the moment I walked in today, he'd made me feel like he wanted *me*. I hoped that was true. The feeling was mutual.

His eyes fluttered open, and he looked up at me. They were hazy, and I could see even more clearly that he was just as turned on as I was. In fact, the current look in his eyes seemed like an invitation. That look convinced me to take a leap of faith, and I lowered my mouth—not to kiss him, but in the hopes that he would reach up to kiss *me*.

But he didn't. Instead, he gripped my wrists, the sudden force jarring. "No," he rasped.

Is he talking to me or himself?

The relaxed and aroused expression on his face turned to one of pure torment.

My stomach sank, and all I managed to utter was, "I, um..."

"I can't," he muttered. "I'm so sorry."

I stepped back as he lifted himself to an upright position, holding the towel for dear life over his crotch. "Fuck." His eyes filled with regret. "I'm sorry, Wren," he repeated.

What have I done?

Before I could say anything, I heard a door slam.

Dax hopped off the table and ran to grab his pants. He slipped them on as if we'd been caught in the act of something inappropriate.

Had we?

"Is that your housekeeper?"

"I think so."

There was a knock on the door, but she opened it before he could say anything.

She started talking before she'd fully entered. "They told me tha—" She stopped at the sight of me, and then looked over at him.

His hair was disheveled. His pants were still undone. And given the looks on both of our faces, I was sure she assumed she'd walked in on *something*.

"Oh...I'm...sorry to interrupt."

Winston then stormed into the room, barking like crazy as he circled around Dax.

"I didn't think you'd be back until three," he told Shannon.

"The groomer called and said Winston was ready early, so I figured I'd bring him back here before I picked up Rafe. I had no idea you had...an appointment."

Winston looked beautifully fluffy and clean. His tongue hung out, and he seemed out of breath. I could smell the shampoo from across the room. As much as he hated me, I wouldn't have minded burying my nose in his shiny fur—you know, if I weren't currently in the middle of the most mortifying moment of my life.

She looked over at me. "You're the same massage therapist who was here a while back."

"Yes." I cleared my throat. "We're finished, and I was just leaving."

Dax turned to me. "You don't have to leave, Wren. We should talk first."

No way I was gonna subject myself to that so he could elaborate on why he'd rejected me. Some things were better kept a mystery. Come to think of it, some things were better not spoken or thought of *ever again*.

"Yes, I do have to leave. Talking is not necessary. Truly."

Utterly humiliated, I threw all the oils into my bag as fast as possible and worked to fold up my table. Dax tried to help me, but I held out my hand to stop him. Seems he got the message because he took a step back—unfortunately still looking painfully sexy with the top of his pants unbuttoned.

The housekeeper continued to stand there, watching the whole thing unfold.

I finally packed everything up and headed out the door.

He called after me as I made my way down the hall. "Wren, wait..."

"I really need to go," I said as I proceeded to exit the house.

Dax stood at the doorway shirtless. I realized I'd never gotten my towel back. *Oh well.* I hoped it lived a long and happy life in Dax's possession because I sure as hell wouldn't be coming back for it.

He watched as I loaded my SUV. I slid my table in the back and dumped my bag next to it before slamming the rear door closed. I still sensed his presence in the doorway as I started my car as quickly as I could.

Before I drove off, I took one last fleeting look at the stunningly beautiful man standing at the door, certain I'd never lay eyes on him again.

The worst part? All the way home, my damn nipples were still hard.

CHAPTER 7

Dax

I sat at the dinner table, staring blankly into my wine glass. Rafe had just gone to his room, leaving me alone with my thoughts. My eyes landed on the bowl of candy Shannon had been putting out on the table lately, and the mini Butterfinger bar immediately made me think of Wren—not that I needed a reminder to think about her. I thought about her every damn day.

A month had passed since the afternoon she'd stormed out of my house. Christmas had come and gone, and it was now early January—the start of a fresh, new year in which I vowed to stop fucking up. Deciding not to reach out to Wren again had been part of that resolution. That had been difficult, but I was convinced it was for the best. Any action I took would only make the situation worse.

When she'd lowered her mouth toward mine that day, I'd wanted nothing more than to kiss her. The ball had been in my court. Wren had very firmly placed it there. But instead of taking it and running with it, I'd freaked out. I

knew if I'd let things go in that direction, there would be
no turning back—even if kissing her would have been the
most natural thing I'd done in a long time. I'd been a hair
away from inserting myself in places I didn't belong, both
literally and figuratively. Plain and simple, my attraction
to Wren was selfish. I wasn't the right man for her in any
way, shape, or form. So I made the difficult choice to end
what was happening before it got out of control.

I was sure she'd drawn the wrong conclusion as she
bolted out of my house. I hoped she didn't feel ashamed
for attempting to make the first move, especially when I'd
led her on. *I* should've been ashamed—ashamed for contacting her after she quit her job at Elite when I should've
left well enough alone. Ashamed that I couldn't hide my
damn arousal—both times she massaged me, but especially the last time. Ashamed for the fact that I still watched
her goddamn music uploads every night and that it was
the only way I could sleep. That was the hard part—I *did*
still see her. Every night. Just not in the flesh.

Shannon spoke from somewhere behind me, interrupting my rumination. "You've been preoccupied lately.
Well, more preoccupied than usual."

"I'm glad you clarified that last part because I'm pretty much always preoccupied."

Shannon was my employee, but we'd crossed into the
friendship zone a long time ago. It wasn't unlike her to pry
if she felt something was off.

As if she'd been reading my mind, she said, "Maybe
it's time for you to book another *massage*."

My jaw tensed. This was the first time she'd brought
it up in the month since Wren's awkward exit. I was sur-

prised it had taken her this long to bust my balls about it, but apparently my grace period was over. I cleared my throat. "That won't be happening anymore."

"Why not?"

"Just not my thing."

"That little massage therapist was very attractive."

"What does that have to do with anything?" I snapped.

"I don't know. I just sensed something that day when I came back early. I thought there might have been something more going on."

"Well, you thought wrong."

"It's none of my business, Dax. But you know it would be perfectly acceptable if there *were* something going on, right? It's been almost two years since Maren died. She would want you to move on."

"How do you know what Maren would want?"

"Well, I can only assume she would want you to be happy. There's no shame in allowing yourself the human contact we all need."

I arched my brow. "Who says I don't get human contact? Maybe I do and you just don't know about it."

"I'm aware of that woman who came by here looking for you once. Adriana or something? I didn't get the impression she was anyone important. Not like the impression that massage therapist gave me. You seemed really *affected* when she stormed out of here, like she mattered to you. Again, it's none of my business, but I don't think you should feel guilty about anything that might or might not have happened."

"For Christ's sake, I didn't sleep with her," I barked. I took a deep breath and lowered my voice. "But there was...

something there. An attraction. I'll admit that. That's all it was."

"So, suppose, you know, you did decide to get another massage..."

I arched my brow. "What?"

"We should come up with a code. Like if I see a T-shirt around the doorknob, that means don't enter your office."

I rolled my eyes. "Shannon..."

"What?"

"I know you're just looking out for me. And I appreciate that. But I'd rather not discuss this anymore."

"Okay." She smiled sympathetically. "You're the boss."

The following Saturday, I dragged Rafe out of the house. Getting out wasn't just going to be good for him, but for me as well. Both of us spent too much time on our devices, wasting the weekends away because we didn't quite know how to interact with each other. I needed to do better, and it was going to start today. Even if he still wouldn't talk to me, I would force some bonding time.

I decided we would go downtown for lunch, and I'd picked a ramen restaurant. He slurped down his soup pretty fast, so at least I knew he enjoyed it.

We then headed to a bookstore. Rafe liked Japanese comic books, so I told him to pick out a few. He separated from me to browse, and I kept an eye on him from afar while I perused the fiction aisle.

At one point, I looked up to find someone standing next to him. I squinted to get a better look at her.

It can't be.

It was.

It was her.

My heart felt like it was beating out of my chest.

Wren said something to him. When I walked over, she looked up at me.

Her skin immediately reddened. "Hey, Dax." She set a book back on the shelf. "I...recognized Rafe. I didn't realize he liked manga. I was telling him about the time I went to the anime convention when it was in Boston a few years back."

Rafe smiled.

He fucking smiled.

It was the first genuine smile I'd seen on his face in... well, forever.

"Really?" I swallowed. "That's cool."

"How have you been?" she asked.

"Good. We, uh, just decided to come downtown today."

"We both had the same idea, then. I love this bookstore. I think Rafe was surprised to realize I knew all about *Death Note*." She turned to him. "It was nice seeing you, Rafe. I hope you pick out a good one."

My body came alive at the sight of her. I'd nearly forgotten how beautiful she was in person. Her short hair had grown out a bit. Her delicate knee peeked through the hole of her ripped jeans. Her black-and-white-striped T-shirt slipped off her shoulder and was tied in a knot just above her waist. It might have only been a month, but it seemed like forever.

Rafe held up his hand and waved goodbye to her before returning his attention to the books.

She exhaled. "Well...I'd better get going."

"Don't let her go," a voice inside me said.

"Do you have to be somewhere?" I pointed my thumb back toward the café area. "Can we grab a coffee over there?"

"I actually do have somewhere I need to be." She bit her bottom lip, seeming tense. I got the impression that was just an excuse, but I wasn't going to push it. She had every right to run away from me after the way I'd handled things.

"Okay, well, it was really nice to run into you," I said.

"You, too." She forced one last smile before brushing past me.

Inhaling the remnants of her flowery scent, I watched until she disappeared from view.

For the rest of our time at the bookstore, I couldn't stop thinking about her, occasionally looking over at the door, as if she were going to come back. But what really got to me was the connection she'd seemed to have with Rafe. No one had gotten him to smile like that in nearly two years. I was already second-guessing my decision not to have contacted her all this time. More unsettling was how invigorated I'd felt for those few minutes of being in her presence again.

Rafe and I went back to the house not long after she left. I was in sort of a daze the entire evening. After dinner, Rafe retreated to his room with the three books I'd bought him, leaving me once again alone with my thoughts.

Later that night, I was lying in my bed when I received a text.

My heart sped up when I saw it was from Wren.

I'd forgotten that I'd messaged her my number before the last massage appointment so she would have it if she needed to reach me.

Hi, Dax. It's Wren. I'm sorry if I acted awkwardly during our run-in today. It was good to see you. And Rafe is amazing. I was thinking about how attentive he seemed when I was telling him about the anime convention. It occurred to me that sometimes we try too hard to get people to relate to our version of the world. Find out what he likes, what makes him tick, and use it to connect with him. Anyway, I figured I would pass that along.

My chest tightened. I wanted to hear her voice.

Dax: Can I call you?

The dots moved around as she typed.

Wren: Sure.

I pressed the call button under her name.

She picked up after two rings. "Hey."

"Hi." I exhaled, fisting my sheets. "How are you?"

"Good."

After a moment of silence, I said, "I feel like I scared you away today. The way you rushed out of there..."

"I guess seeing you did trip me up."

I shut my eyes. "I've felt like shit ever since you left my house that day, Wren. I've thought about you a lot."

"Well, you could've called. You have my number. You chose not to."

She was right.

"Not because I haven't wanted to. Please know that."

"That's the thing. I somehow *do* know that you liked talking to me, that you liked spending time with me. And I also suspected that when you called me for a massage that day, it wasn't only about the massage. I guess that's why I'm confused. Did you never...like me in that way? Did I misread things? Because you definitely gave me a vibe that you were interested in me, Dax."

How the hell am I supposed to explain myself? "Wren... I do like you. A lot. But there's nothing I can do about it."

"You don't feel you're ready?"

That was a fair question. "It's not that..."

"What is it, then?"

"I'm not...right for you. And I like you too much to just fuck around. So that means I have to control my actions."

"You think you're too old for me? Because I've been with older."

Well, fuck. "No, it's not that, either."

"You're not attracted to me?"

If only... "I think you know by the way my body reacted that I am very attracted to you. You're absolutely beautiful. In every way. Don't ever doubt that."

"Then what is it?"

My stomach twisted. "It's...complicated."

She paused. "Have you had sex since your wife died?"

I hesitated but told her the truth. "Yes."

"Wow, okay. So it's not a need to stay loyal somehow. I wasn't sure."

"I've only been with one person. And it's meaningless. Just someone I know who doesn't expect anything more from me."

"So it's an ongoing thing?"

I tugged on my hair. "I don't know if it will happen again. I don't typically reach out to her. Like I said, it doesn't mean anything. I'm not in a position for anything serious."

"Hmm..." She paused. "I thought maybe from how... *reactive* you were to me that you hadn't been with anyone in a long time. I wrongly assumed that I was the first woman who'd touched you in a while."

She *was* the first woman who'd made me feel anything. I wanted to tell her that, but I had to be careful with my words. "My resistance had nothing to do with my feelings or lack thereof toward you physically...or otherwise."

The frustration in her tone was apparent. "You don't owe me an explanation. But why did you ask to call me just now? I only texted to get that simple message to you about Rafe because I've been thinking about him all day. You don't want more from me, so maybe it would've been best to leave well enough alone if you seem to think everything is so complicated. This conversation is only messing with my head even more."

She was pissed. And she was *right*. I shouldn't have called her.

We both just breathed into the phone for a while.

"I'm sorry," she finally said. "It's just that...I'd never put myself out there like that before, the way I did that day in your office. And I certainly never did so while on the job. It just didn't feel like work with you. It felt like something entirely different, like we were really connecting. It'd felt like that for a while. I misinterpreted where things were going with us—what you wanted. That's my bad. I've got to get better at reading people so I don't embarrass myself in the future."

I sighed. "You read me just fine. We *do* have a connection. That's undeniable. And I very much *wanted* things to continue that day. I..." My words trailed off as I rubbed my temple. *Watch what you say, Dax.* I wanted to explain more, but I couldn't.

"I'm gonna let you go, Dax. Okay? I hope you have a nice life. I mean that. I'll never forget you or Rafe...or even fluffernutter Winston who hates me. I'll pray that everything works out for you all. Be well."

My pulse raced. "Wren..."

Before I could get any more words out, she hung up.

CHAPTER 8

Wren

I'd finally taken a new job with a massage company based in Wellesley. So far, it was a good move, even though it paid a bit less than Elite. Things were going pretty well overall in my life, in fact. In addition to the new job, I'd started dating a guy I met through a friend.

Sam Benson worked for his family's chain of restaurants and had grown up in the same general area as me, though we'd never crossed paths when we were younger. He lived farther north of the city now, though. Things were casual between us, but I enjoyed spending time with him.

From the outside, it appeared that I'd moved on from my obsession with the mercurial Dax Moody. It had been a month since he and I had last spoken on the phone. So why did I still think about him all the time? That I couldn't tell you. But despite still finding him on my mind almost every day, I was coming to terms with that small chapter in my life—and the unfulfilled desire and confusion that would likely exist in perpetuity.

This time, I'd really assumed I would never see Dax again—especially after the way I'd hung up on him. But you know what they say about assuming things, right? I found that out the hard way one night after work.

I'd just gotten out of the shower when my father knocked on the door to my bedroom.

"Wren, there's a man here to see you. Something you want to tell me?"

A man? "Who is it?"

"His name is Dax Moody. He's waiting downstairs."

My heart nearly jumped out of my chest.

"What? Dax is here?"

"Yes. Who is he?"

I spoke against the door. "He's...a former client."

"He looks rich—drives a really nice car from what I see parked outside. Something going on between you and this guy? I thought you were seeing that Sam."

"Dax and I aren't dating. I haven't even seen him in over a month. I have no idea what he wants."

"You want me to send him away?"

My pulse raced as I frantically searched for my clothes. "No! I just need to finish getting dressed. Tell him I'll be right down."

"Okay...whatever you want."

I threw on jeans and a shirt and ran the blow dryer through my hair before dabbing on some light makeup.

A lump formed in my throat as I descended the stairs. The sight of him made my knees weak. I'd always known Dax was tall—at least six-two—but compared to Dad, who was only five-eight, he looked even taller. He wore a black wool coat with a scarf wrapped around his neck.

"Hi, Wren."

"What are you doing here?"

"I know you're probably shocked to see me right now. I apologize for not calling first. But I was hoping we could talk."

"Oh...kay." I swallowed, glancing over at my father.

Theories as to what he could have to say flooded my brain at warp speed. Did he change his mind about wanting to date me? Had he been thinking about me and felt bad for the weird way things ended between us? I even wondered if he felt sorry for me and came to offer me a job.

He snapped me out of my thoughts. "Can we possibly take a ride? Or if you prefer, we can talk here." Dax fidgeted with his watch. He was definitely nervous in a way I hadn't observed before.

I looked back over at my father, who seemed as confused as I was. It would probably make sense if we went somewhere for more privacy. The house was small, so Dad would overhear the whole thing no matter which room we were in.

"Let me get my jacket," I said. "We can take a ride."

My father followed me to the coat closet at the back of the house.

"Are you sure this guy is safe?" he whispered.

"Yes. He's a good person. I'm not in any danger. You don't need to worry." *Trust me. I could throw myself at him, and nothing would happen.*

"Okay." He sighed. "Text me in a half hour if you're not back."

"I will."

I shivered in the cold February evening air as Dax and I walked to his Porsche, parked in front of my house. There weren't a lot of spots on the hilly street where we lived in Boston's Roslindale section, so I was surprised he'd managed to find a spot at this time of night when everyone was home from work.

He disarmed the car, and I got in. The leather beneath me was cold.

Dax turned on the heat as he settled into the driver's seat. "If you want the seat warmer on, the button is there on your left."

"What's going on, Dax?" I asked, ignoring his suggestion. "How come you didn't call me first?"

"This was an impulsive decision. I didn't want to give myself time to change my mind because this talk is necessary."

"How did you get my address?"

He started the car and took off. "It came right up on Google."

"Where are we going?" I asked as we headed down my street.

"You tell me. We can't go to my house because Rafe is there, and we won't have privacy."

"Let's just park somewhere," I said. "There's a field about half a mile down the road. Go down to the end of the street and turn right."

Five minutes later, Dax pulled into a spot overlooking a baseball field. He kept the engine running and the heat on as he put the car in park.

He stared out at the field for a bit before he turned to me. "Wren, you deserve so much more than the hot-and-cold treatment I've given you in the short time we've known each other. I just hope you can forgive me for all this."

"What is going on, Dax?"

He balled his fists, taking a long breath in. "When I set out to find you, I never imagined that I would connect with you in such a way, to the point where I feel like an entirely different person around you, a better version of myself. That was very unexpected."

My stomach sank as I absorbed his words. "What do you mean...set out to find me?"

"When I first called you to my house for a massage, I had an ulterior motive. It wasn't about the massage. It was about *you*, Wren."

A rush of adrenaline hit. "You need to go faster, Dax. Because you're freaking me out."

"I'm sorry. Please don't be freaked out. It will make sense." He exhaled and repositioned himself to face me. "Okay..." He took a deep breath. "You know I've felt completely lost when it comes to Rafe. I've never felt like he belonged in my care, but I've still vowed to do my best... for Maren's sake." He paused. "He has no one else but me. Maren's mother's too old and is never in one place. It was *my* responsibility, as Maren's husband, to look after her child."

I gulped. "Talk faster, please..."

"A year ago, I came to the conclusion that he needed more than just me. I felt like I owed it to him to find out if there was someone else who could love him like Maren did—in the way he deserved. It didn't seem fair that this woman who'd loved him with all of her heart and soul was ripped away from this Earth, and then he was left with me. Someone who'd never even wanted a kid."

I shook my head slowly and whispered, "I don't understand..."

"I hired a private investigator to find Rafe's blood relatives—not to relieve my responsibility, but in the hopes of finding someone who could bring light into his life, someone who would innately love him. My intention wasn't to pawn him off. I fully intend to take care of him."

My heart thundered against my chest. "What does this have to do with me?"

"The investigator located his birth mother, who divulged that she'd given up a daughter more than a decade before Rafe was born." He looked into my eyes. "Wren, you're his biological sister."

My vision got hazy, and everything began to spin.

Dax continued talking, but it sounded jumbled now. "It's been verified many times over. I'll let you look at everything I have. I would've never brought this to you if I wasn't absolutely sure."

My hands shook, and a tear fell as reality sank in. "I don't understand..." I wiped my eyes. "Why didn't you just tell me from the beginning?"

"That's a very fair question, and I hope you'll let me explain." He swallowed. "There were a number of reasons. At the beginning, I felt like I needed to get to know you. When we first met, it was about vetting you, to see if there was any reason I might not want you around him. Obviously, I quickly realized you were a beautiful human he'd be lucky to have in his life. Still, I didn't know if it was fair to throw this on you, to disrupt your life. I didn't even know if you'd *want* to know. So I constantly debated whether telling you was the right thing. But then I saw the way you interacted with Rafe that day at the bookstore, and my guilt kept growing from there."

I rubbed my temples. "Back up, Dax. So the massage was never about the massage..."

"Correct. I had no other way to connect with you besides ordering a massage. Once I found out where you worked, it seemed to make sense."

I let out a long breath and closed my eyes.

"What I wasn't expecting..." he continued, "was to develop feelings for you in the process. Despite the reasons for finding you, the connection you felt between us was real. It had nothing to do with anything else." Dax paused. "I sought you out for Rafe, but I started wanting you around...for me. Because you made me feel things I hadn't in a long time. And that's not fair. I was playing with fire because nothing can happen between us."

My head whipped toward him. "Why couldn't it happen?"

"Because I was hiding something major from you, and even if I'd told you the truth, I knew I couldn't get involved with Rafe's sister. That's the harsh truth of the matter. It wouldn't be fair to either of you. If things went sour between us, that would affect him. So the two of us being anything more than friends is out of the question, despite my strong personal feelings about you. My feelings can't matter."

I placed my head in my hands. "I'm sorry. I just need a moment."

"Take your time," he whispered. "I understand what a shock this must be."

I thought back to Rafe's sad eyes. I tried to remember all of his features, now that I knew he was my brother. From the moment I'd met him, I felt inexplicably drawn to him. Maybe it *was* an innate sense.

"You met my mother, too?" I asked.

"The investigator did. From what he said, she was a bit messed up. She didn't want any involvement. But she did say the two children she gave up had different fathers."

That was upsetting. But I couldn't focus on my so-called birth mother at the moment, especially if she didn't want to know me. Rafe was what mattered now.

I finally turned to Dax again. "You want me to be part of his life?"

"Not unless that's what you want. There's no obligation. But I needed to tell you the truth because it's been eating away at me. I've debated whether telling you was the right decision—for both you and him—since the moment we met. I've realized you're the type of person who would want to know you have a brother." He looked in my eyes. "I'm sorry to have put you in this position. I really did have the best of intentions."

I shook my head in disbelief. "I just wish you'd told me from the beginning. Then I might not have misconstrued your intentions and gotten wrapped up in my feelings for you."

He closed his eyes and nodded. "In retrospect, I wish I had as well. But I needed time to sort it all out, and in the process, I grew to care for you in a way I didn't expect. It's the biggest conundrum of my life. And I'm so fucking sorry I handled it poorly."

I thought back over everything that had happened, like a movie in reverse. "This explains so much—like why spending time with you sometimes felt like a job interview."

His voice was strained. "Do you hate me?"

I knew in my heart of hearts that he'd never set out to hurt me. And I now believed he *did* have genuine feelings for me. He just wouldn't act on them. "I want to hate you. But I can't. I don't. I get why you did it."

He reached for my hand and let out a long sigh. "Thank you."

We held hands in silence for several seconds. "Where do we go from here?"

He squeezed my hand and let it go. "That's totally up to you. You don't have to do anything with this information, Wren. He will never have to know, if you don't want him to. You have a right to your privacy, which I violated."

"I can't just...ignore this information."

Dax nodded and looked out toward the field. "I think, either way, now is not a good time for him to find out. He's too unstable—still not speaking or opening up to anyone. I don't think he could handle it."

"I think you're right," I agreed.

He looked back toward me. "But if you want to be in his life, we can work something out. You can come to the house under a different pretense, get to know him naturally. Then we can figure out how to tell him when the time is right. But again, you have no obligation here, Wren. I can't emphasize that enough."

"He's my brother!" It came out louder than intended. Saying those words brought tears to my eyes. My voice was shaky. "I can't just unknow this. There's no question what I want."

"Okay," he whispered. Dax reached out to wipe my tears. I closed my eyes, relishing the feel of his warm fingers against my face.

Then I opened my eyes and cracked a smile. "Holy shit...I have a brother."

"Yeah." He grinned.

Sniffling, I wiped the last of my tears. "Can you take me home? I need to talk to my dad."

"Of course."

The ride back to my house was quiet. I was still in shock and assumed I'd be this way for a while. Before I went inside, Dax and I agreed to meet for coffee sometime in the coming week to discuss the next steps.

My life would never be the same again.

CHAPTER 9

Dax

Over coffee, I'd shown Wren the folder where I kept all the information the investigator had provided me about both adoptions. I didn't want her to have any doubts about the situation. We'd also decided she would spend time at our house under the guise of being my friend. It wasn't like Rafe hadn't seen her here before, so that story worked out well. He'd likely already assumed she was a friend of mine. It made sense to continue under that pretense.

She had come over twice in the two weeks since the conversation in my car. Each time she'd attempted to bond with Rafe over anime and manga, bringing him a couple of new comic books I'd confirmed he didn't have. She also showed him photos from the time she'd attended the anime convention in college. I was relieved to see her handling everything so well, and even more relieved that I no longer had to hide such a major thing from her.

While he still refused to talk, Rafe appeared to be in better spirits lately, appearing more engaged and spending more time at the dinner table before rushing off to his room.

I decided to tell Shannon the truth about everything, knowing she'd see Wren at the house and draw the wrong conclusion about us once again. She was shocked, to say the least, but she supported the idea of Wren getting to know Rafe before we announced the news to him.

One Friday evening, Wren joined us for an early dinner, her third visit since learning the truth. Shannon had made chicken and roasted Brussels sprouts. I insisted she sit down and join us, which she occasionally did if she didn't have plans with Bob. I knew she'd take me up on my offer tonight because she'd been very curious about Wren since discovering who she was.

Shannon and Wren led the conversation for most of the dinner, while Rafe and I remained quiet, although I noticed he was paying attention to what they were saying. Shannon spoke about her last trip to New Orleans, and Wren seemed particularly interested in Shannon's stories from the ghost tour she'd gone on.

Then the conversation somehow moved to the topic of unusual physical traits. Shannon noted that she had two different-colored eyes, which I hadn't noticed. It was a subtle difference, but when she pointed it out, I could definitely see it.

"I have you beat, I think," Wren said. "I have twin toes."

"What are twin toes?" I asked.

"It's when two of your toes are stuck together. It used to bother me when I was younger, but I've come to appreciate them now."

"Another term for that is webbed toes, I think," Shannon said.

I smiled. "I have to see this."

"Well, I'd pull my foot out, but that's not really appropriate at the dinner table," Wren said.

"I have twin toes."

I dropped my fork. *Who said that?*

The three of us turned to Rafe at once.

It was as if God himself had spoken.

Wren looked at me, and then back at him. "Really? I've never met anyone else with them."

He nodded.

"That's so cool," she said, looking as frazzled as I felt.

We sat there frozen. I knew that if I acknowledged it, Rafe might withdraw, so I tried to act nonchalant. But inside, I was ecstatic.

"I never knew that about you, Rafe," I said. "I guess I haven't looked closely enough at your feet."

"I was thinking the same thing." Shannon glanced over at me and smiled.

We waited in silence, but he didn't say anything else.

Rafe didn't utter another word during the rest of dinner, even when prompted. But that was okay. Because we'd all heard it. *"I have twin toes."* The four best words ever to be spoken. They'd given us hope.

After dinner ended, Rafe went to his room. Shannon started clearing the table, but I stopped her.

"Go home to Bob. I've got this."

Wren took some dishes to the sink and said, "Yup. We've got this."

"You're sure, Dax?" Shannon asked.

"Yup. Get outta here."

Shannon beamed. "Tonight was a good night, huh?"

"Indeed, it was," I said. "I can't get over it."

"I think Wren is bringing him out of his shell," she said.

Wren shook her head. "I didn't do anything."

Shannon threw her bag over her shoulder. "Well, you clearly gave him something he could relate to enough to want to speak. None of us have been able to do that."

After Shannon left, I told Wren I'd handle the clean-up, but she insisted on helping. She finished clearing the table while I got started on the dishes.

"What are you thinking?" she asked me.

"I'm in shock," I said, placing a tray on the drying rack.

"Me, too, but in a good way," she said.

I shut off the water and wiped my hands. "All this time, and all we had to do was talk about twin toes?"

Wren laughed. "Apparently."

"But it wasn't really about the toes. It was the fact that he feels comfortable around you. And you managed to tap into something that mattered to him, just as you did with the anime stuff. Maybe the problem all along has been that neither Shannon nor I can relate to him on a personal level. I've tried to implement the advice you gave me about finding things he's interested in, but nothing I do seems to resonate. With your vibrant energy around, his anxiety lifted just enough to make him *want* to say something."

Wren's cheeks turned pink. "Whatever the cause, it's wonderful. And a good sign."

When there were no more dishes to be done, Wren and I stood in the kitchen, facing each other. Despite my declaration that her being Rafe's sister made her off-limits, the sexual tension between us had never waned, not even a little. You could cut it with a knife. In quiet moments like this, I really noticed it. I knew Wren was dating someone now, and that made the situation both harder and easier. As long as he made her happy, I was good with it. I didn't have to *love* it. But it was a part of our dynamic I had to accept.

"Are you going out tonight?" I asked.

"Sam has to work, so I was going to head home and watch something on Netflix."

"Sounds exciting," I teased.

"You got any better ideas?"

"I'm kidding. Watching TV may not be exciting, but sometimes that's what you need. It's been a long week for you, I'm sure." I tilted my head. "Everything going okay at work?"

"Yeah. They've kept me really busy, one massage client after another. I end up making more money because of the volume, even though the hourly rate is less."

"Well, I guess that's good, so long as you don't mind more work."

"I don't. I need to keep busy."

Wren looked beautiful tonight. Not that she ever looked less than gorgeous, but on this particular evening she wore a short, floral dress with a cut-off denim jacket. I tried hard not to let my eyes find the tiny bit of cleavage peeking out from her neckline, or the scattered beauty marks there. She'd never shown this much skin before. But what killed me was her nipples poking against the thin fabric. They seemed hard, and that made my dick want to play follow the leader.

I enjoyed being around her for many reasons besides her beauty, though. She was truly funny and lit up a room whenever she was in it. I loved listening to her talk. It put me in a good mood. Despite knowing nothing could come of these feelings, I was in no rush for her to leave tonight.

"Want a glass of wine before you go? I was about to open a bottle."

Her eyes moved to the side for a moment, and then she shrugged. "Sure. Why not? I guess we have a good excuse to celebrate tonight."

"The biggest excuse for me in nearly two years."

"I'm glad I could be part of it."

"Me, too, Wren."

Our eyes locked. I could get lost in hers. As soon as I caught myself lingering a little too long, I forced myself to look away.

She smiled. "I'd always heard webbed feet were genetic. I guess now I have proof."

"Can I see them?" I asked.

She looked down shyly. "My feet?"

"Yeah. I'm curious. Unless you'd rather not show me."

"No. I'm not ashamed of them."

She was wearing a dress, but she had on Chuck Taylors. She untied her shoe and slipped off her sock, displaying cute little toes with the nails painted light pink.

She lifted the two toes adjacent to her pinky. "See? It's just the left foot."

They were fused together, except for the very tips.

"That's wild. Now I'll have to pay special attention to Rafe's so I can compare."

She put her sock back on and slipped her foot back into her sneaker. Then she looked up at me.

The way she always looks at me. Deep into my eyes. It was a problem, mainly because of how much I liked it. It was fucked up that I got off on the fact that I knew I had an effect on her. The unspoken chemistry between us was as addictive as it was arousing. And I'd convinced myself that as long as I didn't entertain it in any way, it was acceptable to silently enjoy the feeling of wanting someone and having that feeling reciprocated.

Jesus Christ. Wasn't I supposed to open wine? I cleared my throat. "Let me get that wine."

I ventured over to the other side of the kitchen. Tonight was special, so I popped open the bottle of expensive cabernet I'd been saving for the right time. After pouring us each a glass, I carried them over to Wren.

"Thanks." She took a sip of hers. "How's Adriana, by the way?"

I froze. I'd never told Wren the name of my friend with benefits and had no clue why she'd just asked me that.

I narrowed my eyes. "How did you know her name?"

"I have my ways."

"There's nothing going on between me and her. It's meaningless." My lip twitched.

Her cheeks turned red. "But you're sleeping with her..."

Small beads of sweat formed on my forehead. "Actually, not for a while now."

The last time I'd seen Adriana was just after Wren had first come over for tea. And I hadn't seen her since.

I placed my glass on the counter and crossed my arms. "Seriously, though, how did you know her name?"

"Relax. A message just flashed on your phone while you were over there pouring the wine. It lit up, and I looked down at it. That's how I knew her name. Sorry, I was just being nosy."

My pulse calmed a bit. "You had me freaked out for a minute. I thought you'd had me followed or something." I winked.

"Oh, like you did me?" she cracked.

I chuckled. "Good one, I have to admit."

I grabbed the phone and looked at the message.

Adriana: I miss you. Which also means I miss your beautiful dick. It's been too long.

Fuck. I cringed. "I'm sorry you saw that."

"Why? I'm an adult. What does it matter?"

She had a point. Why *did* it matter? "It's crude." I shook my head. "That's just…her personality."

"So, this thing with Adriana… Is it good? I mean…the sex?" Her cheeks turned even redder.

"Why are we having this discussion again?" I asked.

She brushed the tip of her finger around the rim of her glass. "We're supposed to be friends. Friends have these types of discussions."

"I don't ask you about your sex life."

"I'd tell you what you wanted to know if you did. I'd tell you *anything* you wanted to know."

I swallowed. "Why do you want to know?"

"I guess it's just morbid curiosity."

"*Morbid.* Why?"

"Because I *don't* really want to know. But I still want to know." She laughed. "You know?"

I did *not* want to fucking know what she was doing with that Sam guy. That was for damn sure. I suddenly wanted to rip his head off, and I hadn't even met him. My feelings were a cross between protectiveness and raging jealousy, which was a bit surprising. I'd thought I'd accepted the fact that she was dating someone, but apparently I hadn't.

"Relax," she said. "I'll stop prying."

Tense silence filled the air. She changed the subject. "Do you still watch my performances on the channel?"

Every fucking night. "Sometimes."

"Is your favorite still 'The Swan'?"

"I think so, yeah."

"It always makes me emotional when I play it."

"I can see why. Every time I listen to your music, I feel like more and more trapped emotions are released."

"Wow," she whispered. "I'll take that as a compliment. That reminds me, have you been journaling?"

"I did it a few times, and then I stopped."

"You should go back to it."

"You're bossy."

"I care about you, Moody. That's all."

I tilted my head. "You haven't called me Moody in a while."

"Yeah, well, I feel like we've worked our way back to it." She smiled.

I smiled back.

I wanted to kiss her. And that really sucked.

She took a drink and put her glass down. "Oh, I wanted to tell you. I came across this article, and I wondered if it might be helpful when it comes to Rafe."

"Okay..."

"There's this therapist I follow online. He has his clients tell their stories in third person—like, their entire life story summarized. He doesn't want them to think about it too deeply. So it's sort of like journaling, a brain dump. But he wants them to use third person because he feels like if they hear their story play out as if it were someone else's life, it helps build self-compassion. That's something we all struggle with, self-compassion. At least I do."

"I do agree that people can be roughest on themselves. Forgiving people who've wronged you is hard, but it's nothing compared to forgiving yourself. I feel like I have a lot of personal experience when it comes to that struggle."

"What are you having trouble forgiving yourself for?" she asked.

Do you have all night? I certainly didn't want to open up that can of worms right now. I shook my head. "Not tonight. I'm in too good of a mood."

She nodded in understanding and didn't pry any further.

"So, Wren..." I said, eager to change the subject.

"Yes?"

"Why don't you tell me *your* story in the third person."

"Ah. I get it. So it's okay for *you* to pry but not me. Some things never change."

I smiled and nodded toward the living room. "Come on. Let's sit." I carried the bottle of wine over to the coffee table before lighting the fireplace. Wren made herself comfortable on the sofa.

"Be right back," I said, wanting to check in with Rafe.

I went to his room to peek in on him. He was playing video games and removed his headphones when he saw me standing in the doorway.

"You okay? You want dessert? You left the table before you could have any."

He shook his head no.

"You want to come hang out with Wren and me? We could watch a movie."

He shook his head again.

"Alright." I sighed.

I returned to the living room to take a seat across from Wren on the couch, making sure I wasn't sitting too close.

"Is he okay?" she asked.

"Yeah. He was just playing video games. I told him you were still here if he wanted to come downstairs and hang out with us."

"I'm sure he prefers to just play his game, like most teenagers."

I nodded. "Even if he's not joining us, I still think it's good for him to feel like this house is a bit more alive. Like if he did come out right now, he'd see more than just me sitting in that chair reading historical war fiction."

"War fiction? I didn't know that was your jam."

"Yeah. It's pretty much what I do at night. Read." *And watch you play cello.* "I even have reading glasses," I added. "Does that make me old?"

"No, glasses are hot on men." She laughed. "And men who read? That's even sexier."

I shrugged. "What one person finds old and boring, another finds sexy. Interesting."

"You're proof that someone can be all three of those things—old, boring, and sexy." She winked.

"Wiseass."

"What are some of your favorite books?" she asked.

"Are you looking for a recommendation?"

"Historical war fiction isn't my thing, so no. But I'm curious about what you like."

"Weren't you supposed to be telling me your story?"

She let out a long sigh. "I don't remember agreeing to that."

"You didn't, but I'd still like to hear it."

Seeming hesitant, she tucked a piece of her hair behind her ear. "Can I pour more wine first?"

"Allow me." I grabbed the bottle and poured us each another glass.

Wren cleared her throat. "Okay…"

I settled into my seat and gave her my full attention.

Chewing on her lip, she closed her eyes. Then she opened them and started. "Wren McCallister…had no idea where she really came from, nor did she care. Because where she was—safe in the home of Chuck and Eileen McCallister—was exactly where she was meant to be. Until the age of five, Wren's doting mother made sure her daughter lived a charmed life. Eileen gave Wren her undivided attention, whether it was accompanying her on playdates, baking cookies, or doing artwork together. Wren's perfect life came to a screeching halt one day when her mother, on the way home from grocery shopping, was struck and killed by a wrong-way driver." She closed her eyes for a moment.

Oh man. I'd known her mother died in a car accident but hadn't realized it was a wrong-way driver. I suddenly regretted asking her to tell me her story. I was just about to tell her she didn't have to continue when she started speaking again.

"Wren's life as she knew it ended that day. She no longer trusted that the universe had her back. It was no longer a safe place. From that day on, she lived on the edge of her seat, waiting for the next shoe to drop, the next tragedy. Wren became particularly paranoid that something would happen to her father. She refused to sleep anywhere but in his bed at night until the age of ten and felt extreme anxiety if he returned home late from work. Nevertheless, she still felt grateful to have Chuck McCallister for a dad. He was her entire world."

It struck me how similar her and Rafe's situations were. They'd both lost their mothers prematurely. The difference was that she had Chuck, a great dad. Rafe was stuck with *me*.

Wren took a long sip of her wine before she continued. "A few years after Eileen's death, Wren started learning to play the cello, and her love of music began. But even her musical talent couldn't save her from the dreaded teenage years. Like most parents, Chuck only had so much power over his daughter. Perhaps due to unconscious anger, Wren became rebellious, sneaking out at night and defying her father's rules. Chuck didn't deserve the worry Wren's actions caused him, but everything was out of his control. No matter what he did, Wren would find a way to go against him. Someday, as an adult, she'd want to go back and strangle her teenage self."

She paused, and her breathing became heavier.

"Are you okay?" I asked. "You should stop if it's too much."

"No," she whispered. "It's okay."

It seemed, though, like she was gearing up for the next part. I'd soon learn why.

"In a sad example of history repeating itself...like the woman who'd given her up, Wren became pregnant at age sixteen."

Shit. Feeling my heart in my mouth, I offered a nod of encouragement, prompting her to continue, even though I was a bit afraid to hear what happened next.

"Unlike her birth mother, who chose to give her baby up, Wren had decided she would raise her baby. But..." She swallowed. "Her pregnancy ended in miscarriage after three months. She didn't know how to feel—whether to be devastated or relieved. She often felt guilty for the latter. But the experience was a wake-up call, one that sent Wren into a life of solitude. She immersed herself further in the cello and stopped sneaking out. As much as Chuck no longer had to worry about her in one respect, he now worried in a different way. Because Wren was depressed. Everything—the failed pregnancy, the trauma from her mother's premature death—seemed to bombard her at once."

Once again, feeling terrible for opening the flood gates, I offered my hand for support. She took it and squeezed as she continued.

"Wren came out of her funk by the age of eighteen, befriending the boy next door, whom she grew to love and trust implicitly. Benjamin eventually moved away to attend college, leaving Wren behind and breaking up with her when he returned home that first Christmas. After that Wren would always dread Christmas, as it reminded her of being blindsided." She stared off for a moment. "Wren fell into a period of self-reflection after that, a time where she realized it was more important to love herself than be loved by someone else. That's not to say that she didn't hope to love another person again, just that she understood it wasn't the most important thing for survival. The phases of her life might have been very different, but her love of the cello and the support of her father remained constant. Despite her hardships, she's always known how lucky she is to have Chuck and her music."

She looked over at me, and I offered a smile, not sure if the story was over. But then she went on. "In her early twenties, after finishing college, Wren wanted a new challenge. So she decided to go to massage school to learn something that would make others feel good. She embarked on a new career and truly loved it." Her mouth spread into a smile. "One day, it led her to a mysterious man—the handsome and distinguished Dax Moody. He was more than just a client. He became a friend, and eventually Wren realized there was so much more to their meeting." She lowered her voice. "It was through Dax that Wren learned she had a brother, whose life—unbeknownst to her—had paralleled her own. Rafe, too, had lost his adoptive mother who loved him. He, too, had lost his entire world far too young. And in turn, he'd lost his voice in the same way Wren had figuratively after the loss of her unborn child."

Wow. Yeah.

"For the first time in her life, there was another human being whose well-being meant more to Wren than her own. She finally understood what her father might have felt when it came to her or what she might have felt for the child she never had. All she knew was that suddenly a stranger meant more to her than anything." Wren sighed. "And he doesn't even know it." She paused to look at me. "The rest is unwritten."

With that, she leaned back and let out an expansive breath, as if telling her story had taken a lot out of her.

"That was beautiful. Thank you for sharing all of that with me."

She sat up straighter. "Thank you for listening."

Even though I didn't want to, I pulled my hand back. "The best is yet to come for you. I know it."

"That really was my life in a nutshell. All of the important points." She wiped her eyes. "God, I didn't expect to get so emotional."

"It's understandable."

We sat and enjoyed more wine for a while, and I ended up opening a second bottle. Emotions still bubbled in my chest as I tried to grasp and appreciate all she'd been through. There was a lot I hadn't known about her—things that helped explain why she was such a strong person. I wanted to say something, but the words wouldn't come.

"I have a problem," she said.

"What's wrong?"

"I'm too buzzed to drive home."

I chuckled. "I would never let you drive home like this. I'd drive you myself, but I'm not that far behind you. I'll call you a ride."

She shook her head. "You can't."

"Why not?"

"I'm...afraid of getting into cars with strangers. I don't take cars or cabs for that reason."

My body went rigid. "Did something happen to make you feel that way?"

"A driver once hit on me. And I realized I had no power while in his vehicle. That scared the crap out of me. I haven't been able to forget it. So I choose not to get in anyone's car alone—unless I know the person, of course. I realize that's really odd, considering I'll go into strangers' houses. But something about being trapped in the car scares me." She chewed on her bottom lip. "Do you find that strange?"

"No. It makes total sense."

Her face flushed with embarrassment. "Would it be okay if I crashed here for the night?"

What am I supposed to say? "Of course."

"Are you *sure* that's okay?"

No, I'm not sure it will be okay at all. But I can't say no. "You're always welcome here. It's not like I don't have the space."

"Thank you." Wren breathed a sigh of relief.

"I'll sleep in one of the guest rooms," I told her. "You can have my room so you'll have privacy. It's the only room with an adjoining bathroom."

"I can't take your room, Dax."

"I insist. It's the least I can do after you got Rafe to speak today."

"I didn't do anything."

"Yes, you did. You're a light in his life, even if he doesn't know who you are yet."

"Well...I'm happy you feel that way."

Since she wasn't going anywhere, Wren and I put on a movie. It felt good to have someone to watch television with again. After Maren died, I'd stopped watching altogether; it always reminded me that she was no longer around to watch with me. It was one of the few things we'd enjoyed together toward the end—one of the few things that stopped our arguments. Why resolve a dispute when you can just drown it by bingeing an eight-episode documentary? She and I never got along better than when we were watching TV.

At nearly one in the morning, I took Wren up to my bedroom and gave her one of my T-shirts to sleep in. Then I ventured down to the kitchen and grabbed her a bottle of water and some Advil, in case she needed it in the morning. Rafe, who was sound asleep, had no clue she was spending the night. I'd have to explain why she was here in the morning.

When I went into the room where I'd be staying tonight, I noticed that the house felt different just because she was sleeping here. Different in a good way. *Alive.* I had to once again remind myself of the boundaries I'd set.

CHAPTER 10

Wren

Waking up in Dax's room was heaven. Not only was it the most comfortable bed I'd ever slept in, but everything smelled like him. Every inch of my body was sensitized.

Surprisingly, I didn't have a headache like I typically did when I drank. Instead, I felt rested, comfortable, and safe.

I couldn't believe I'd told him *everything* last night. I wasn't ashamed of my pregnancy—I'd been young and naïve—but it was still something I'd only told a few people. Now Dax was one of them. I worried he might see me differently now, but I hadn't gotten that impression from him.

My phone rang, startling me out of my thoughts. It was Sam.

Shit. Why do I feel so guilty?

Nothing had happened with Dax last night. But I supposed my thoughts toward him made me feel like I'd betrayed the guy I'd been dating, even if Sam wasn't technically my boyfriend. We'd never agreed to exclusivity.

My voice was groggy when I picked up. "Hey."

"What's going on? I just swung by your house to see if you wanted to grab breakfast, and your dad said you weren't home."

Sam knew about my relationship to Rafe, even if poor Rafe didn't. I'd had to tell Sam to explain why I'd been spending time here.

I ran my hand through my hair. "Yeah. I, uh, had a bit too much wine with dinner last night, so I decided to just sleep at Rafe's."

"Why didn't you call me to pick you up?"

That was a fair question. Even though Sam had been working at the restaurant when I'd made the decision to stay here, I could've waited for him to finish his shift.

"I didn't want to bother you, and I was asleep by the time you got off. My dad was working and wouldn't have been able to pick me up until after midnight. So I just crashed here."

"Wanna get a late breakfast? I'll swing by there and get you now."

I wasn't really in a rush to leave. "Maybe we can do dinner instead? I haven't showered yet, and I have some errands to run today."

"Okay, that's good, I guess. I have tonight off." He sighed. "Where did you sleep?"

I paused, unsure what to make of that question. "Dax gave me his room because it has a separate bathroom."

"He did, did he..."

My forehead wrinkled. "Why did you say it like that?"

"I don't trust that guy."

It's me you shouldn't trust. "I've known him for a while, Sam. There's nothing not to trust. He's just a guy

121

doing the best he can. He hasn't made a move, if that's what you're getting at." *Believe me, I've tried.*

"He'd better not."

While I couldn't blame Sam for being a bit suspect, his attitude was also annoying.

"So...I'll see you tonight, okay?" I said.

"Okay," he said, still sounding somewhat pissed.

After we hung up, I nestled back into Dax's sheets and buried myself in his scent under the covers. I couldn't even feel guilty again right now because this was too good. I didn't know if I'd ever have this opportunity again, so I decided to slip my hands down my panties and make myself feel even better than I already did.

For some reason, my mind gravitated to the text Dax had received last night. Except I pretended I was the one who'd sent it, telling him I "missed his dick." That was so tacky, but that's where my mind went.

I imagined him showing up at my bedroom after receiving the text. I ripped off his clothes before I knelt down and took him into my mouth. Suddenly there was a knock on the door. My hand froze.

"Hey, Wren. Everything okay in there?"

I cleared my throat and sat up. "It *was*, yeah."

"Did I wake you?"

"No."

"I wanted to see if you'd like to come down and have breakfast with us."

"I would love that. Can you give me like ten minutes? I just want to finish...uh, take a quick shower." *And finish your virtual blowjob so I can orgasm.*

"Yeah. Take your time. I'll have it ready in twenty."

I laughed to myself. If Dax only knew what he'd interrupted.

After I finished myself off and showered, I wrapped one of Dax's luxurious towels around my chest and returned to the bedroom to get dressed. On the way, I nosily opened Dax's bedside drawer. That was totally intrusive and wrong, but I couldn't help myself. This might be my only opportunity to snoop. Inside were some lemon drops, what I assumed were his old-man reading glasses in a hard case, and a box of condoms. *That lucky bitch, Adriana.* I also noticed the black journal with the fleur-de-lis on the front. I might have been nosy, but I was *not* an asshole. As much as I would've given anything to learn this mysterious man's deepest, darkest thoughts, I wasn't going to become privy to that information by stealing it.

Later that afternoon, back at my house, Dad had questions for me.

"So...why did you spend the night at Rafe's again?" he asked as he stirred his afternoon coffee. Dad always had fresh coffee on hand and drank it on and off all day.

"I told you, I had a bit too much to drink, and I didn't want to drive. You were working, so I couldn't call you."

"I take it you weren't drinking alone."

"Dax and I shared some wine, yeah."

"I figured as much." He smirked.

Feeling my face heat, I said, "We get along very well. We just talked. I told him a bit about my teenage years and all the stuff that happened back then, the lessons I've learned. It was therapeutic. I really like talking to him. I always have. But nothing is going on between us, if that's why you're smirking."

"That doesn't mean you're not towing the line."

"Dax has no intentions toward me. He's made that very clear."

Dad scoffed. "He desires you. He just doesn't think he should."

"What makes you say that?" I asked.

My dad knew nothing about the infamous final massage, or anything Dax had ever said acknowledging our chemistry.

"I sensed an energy between you the night he came to tell you about Rafe. You were flustered. It's clear he has an effect on you. And I caught the way he looked at you. Why wouldn't he be smitten?"

"Well, any attraction between us is a moot point. He won't touch me with a ten-foot pole because I'm Rafe's sister. He's too afraid of hurting Rafe—or hurting me, thus hurting Rafe. Dax and I will have to remain friends only, for Rafe's sake." I added under my breath, "He's got some woman he messes around with anyway."

My father took a sip of his coffee. "Does Sam know you spent the night there?"

Ugh. "Yes. He wasn't thrilled. He doesn't trust Dax, which is ridiculous because it wasn't even Dax's idea for me to stay the night. I sort of gave him no choice but to offer me a room because I refused to let him call me a car."

My father chuckled. "Be honest, Wren. You know you can't lie to me."

He was too perceptive. "What do you mean?"

"You knew damn well if you drank, you wouldn't be able to drive. You knew I was working second shift and couldn't pick you up. Although you could've certainly called me later, but you chose not to. You *wanted* to stay the night."

My father knew me better than anyone. "What do you want me to say?"

"You don't have to say anything because again...I know you."

"Any feelings I have for Dax are futile."

"You're underestimating the weakness of men if you think this guy doesn't have the capability to break his resolve. The more you do things like spend the night, the more you hang out together, the more likely that is to happen. I think you also need to decide if you want to put him in that position."

Talk about a guilt trip. But he was right. "I don't know what to think, Dad. Okay? Yes, I do have feelings for Dax. I have from the moment I met him—before I ever knew who Rafe was. But I also agree that nothing should happen between us. I just can't seem to help wanting to be around him." I looked away. "He has this...mix of strength and vulnerability. And when I'm with him, I always want to share more than usual. I'm obviously physically attracted to him, too."

"I hadn't noticed." Dad laughed.

CHAPTER 11

Wren

In the two weeks since the night I'd spent at Dax's, Rafe had started to talk more. It was mostly little comments here and there or answering simple questions, but that was a huge step in the right direction.

Dax was cautiously optimistic that things were finally turning around. Needless to say, Rafe's therapist and teachers were thrilled, even though they remained confused as to what to attribute the change to. They tossed around the word *spontaneous* a lot.

Rafe had come to see me as a family friend. One afternoon, I stopped by the house in Brookline to pick him up while Dax was at work. Rafe's school was closed today for staff meetings, so I'd offered to take him to a new bookstore that had opened in Cambridge. I'd noticed their large comic-book section and knew Rafe would love it.

He and I took the Red Line train to Harvard Square and walked the short distance to the bookstore. He chose two books, which I insisted on paying for, and I bought myself a nonfiction book. We picked up two hot chocolates from a café and took our new books to a nearby park. It was a little chilly but otherwise the perfect day for reading.

I wanted to take advantage of our time alone to try to get him to speak to me, so at one point while we sat on a bench, I interrupted his reading.

"I don't know if you know this, Rafe, but I lost my mother at a young age. I was five. So I understand what you're going through. I wanted you to know that. We have a lot of common interests, but I wasn't sure if you knew we had that in common, too."

He looked pensive. After a long moment of silence, though, he absolutely shocked me.

"But did you kill her?"

What? I blinked. "No. Of course not. She died in a car accident. Why would you ask that?"

He continued to stare straight ahead. "Because I killed mine."

My breath left me. "What are you talking about?" Maren had died of a brain aneurysm, so I couldn't begin to fathom why Rafe would say such a thing.

He began to tremble.

I placed my hand on his knee. "Rafe, you can tell me anything. Why did you say that?"

He turned to look at me. "The morning she died, I told her I hated her. I was being really mean because I was mad that she'd grounded me for something I did. The last thing I said to her was, 'I hate you.' Then she went to work, and she died." He buried his head in his hands. "I didn't mean to do it. But when I told her I hated her, it did something. I just know it."

He started to bawl into his hands. I felt profound sadness as I embraced him. How would I get him to understand he was wrong? Ultimately, I knew it was going to take more than me.

"Rafe, it doesn't work that way. You can't kill someone with words. You didn't even mean what you said."

He pulled away from me. "But what if she believed it?"

"People say things all the time when they're angry. Adults know that kids don't mean things like that when they say them. We know better."

We sat in silence for a moment.

"Is that why you went quiet?" I asked. "Because you believed your words could harm people?"

He wiped his eyes as he nodded.

My heart ached for him. "I can understand how you might've drawn that conclusion, Rafe. It was really bad timing. But it's not true."

"How do I know you're right?"

"You don't. But you have to have faith. And it might take time for you to believe it. Have you told your therapist about this?"

He shook his head. "No. I've only told you."

I sighed. "Thank you for opening up to me. But you need to let your therapist know, too, okay? You need to hear the truth from more than just me. I promise you didn't do anything wrong. Your mom wouldn't want you to feel guilty about it for the rest of your life, either. Your therapist will be able to explain that better than I can."

His hazel eyes glowed in the sunlight as he ran a hand through his rough curls. "What if I never believe what you're saying? What if I always believe it's my fault? No matter what you or my therapist says?"

"Belief is a choice. You can choose to believe you didn't harm your mom. You can build confidence in that choice until believing becomes knowing. That's what your therapist can help you with. But she can't help you if she doesn't have this vital piece of information."

He kept nodding. "Okay. I'll tell her."

I placed my hand gently on his arm. "Can I tell Dax about this? I know you don't open up to him a lot. Would it be easier if I filled him in so he can make sure you get the help you need?"

Rafe paused. "Yeah. That would be easier. I don't want to repeat this—not to him."

"Okay." I rustled his hair. "You're going to be okay. I promise." I took a deep breath, feeling grateful that he'd felt comfortable enough to make that admission.

More and more, I felt like the time was coming for me to tell him the truth about me. But we weren't there yet.

The following day, I sat across from Dax in his office. The view of the city from his window was spectacular. But my eyes were mainly focused on Dax as he pulled on his hair after I'd given him the news.

"Oh my God. This fucking explains so much, Wren."

I'd gone to see him in the middle of the workday so I could tell him about my talk with Rafe. Dax had to work late yesterday after Rafe and I returned from our outing. So I'd texted this morning to ask if I could meet him today because this was a conversation that couldn't wait any longer and needed to be in person.

"Magical thinking can be dangerous," I said. "All of this time you assumed he wasn't talking to you because he hated you. He was probably just afraid of his own words, unsure of what they were capable of."

Dax spun his watch around his wrist as he stared out the window. "That's scary to think he believed he'd said something that caused her death." He turned to me. "I can't thank you enough for getting him to talk about this."

I shrugged. "I didn't do much at all. I just told him I'd lost my mother at a young age, too. That sort of opened the door. I didn't see it coming."

"He's been comfortable with you for a while. You have that effect on people. If it weren't for you, I'm not sure he would've ever told me this. He has a connection with you that he probably can't understand because there's no explanation for it. It's innate."

That warmed my heart. "Well, whatever the reason, I'm glad the truth came out," I said.

"He told you it was okay to tell me?"

"Yes. I cleared it with him first."

Dax returned to his desk and tapped his pen. "I'm gonna call his therapist right now. Fill her in."

"Good idea." I nodded. "Anyway, I'd better get going and let you do that. I'm sure you also have to get back to work."

"Unfortunately, I do." He looked down at the stacks of papers on his desk. "I've got this deadline, and I'll be here through tonight. Shannon is staying late to keep Rafe company until I can get home. He's technically old enough to stay by himself, but I don't like him to be alone for long stretches, you know?"

"I don't blame you."

He tapped his pen again. "What are you up to the rest of the afternoon?"

"I'm off today. I'm meeting Sam for dinner downtown. Not doing much before that."

Dax opened his mouth as if he might say something, but then stopped. He seemed to think better of it.

Instead, he nodded and said, "Have fun."

Sam and I were finishing up dinner at Beantown Beerworks when my phone chimed. I looked down to find a text from Dax.

> Dax: Thank you again for taking the time to come see me today. I had a long talk with Rafe's therapist who's working on a new cognitive behavioral strategy. Also, you left your scarf on the chair in my office. I can take it home with me tonight if you want. You can pick it up the next time you're at the house. Let me know.

"Who's that?" Sam asked.

I looked up. "Dax."

He stopped chewing. "What does he want?"

I put my phone down. "I left my scarf at his office today."

"What were you doing at his office?"

"We needed to talk about Rafe."

He wiped his mouth. "Everything okay?"

"Yes. I just needed to fill him in on a conversation

Rafe and I had pertaining to his mom, something that helped explain why he's stayed silent for so long."

"So you went over to his office in the middle of the workday? It couldn't wait?"

My tone turned a little abrasive. "No, it couldn't wait. It was important. He had some time to meet with me, so I went."

Sam went quiet after that and seemed preoccupied for the rest of our meal. More and more, I knew I was just biding my time with him, and I shouldn't be stringing him along. I needed to end things. It wasn't fair to keep him around as a distraction from my desire for someone else. The only consolation was that I'd never promised Sam exclusivity. My heart certainly *wasn't* exclusively his.

Since Sam had taken the train to meet me, we went our separate ways after dinner. I headed toward the Orange Line train while he took the Blue Line back to his house in Winthrop.

I finally responded to Dax's text as I waited for the subway.

Wren: Are you still at the office?

Dax: Yeah. For about another hour.

Wren: Do you mind if I come grab my scarf before you leave?

Dax: Of course not. I'll be here.

Wren: Cool. Thanks. Your office is on my way home.

Two stops later, I got off at the station closest to Dax's building and walked the two blocks over.

After taking the elevator to the twentieth level, I noticed the lights were off in most of the offices on Dax's floor.

His door was slightly ajar.

"Knock, knock," I said before opening.

Dax tossed his glasses aside. "Hey."

"Did I almost get a glimpse of the old-man glasses?"

"Shit, yeah." He smiled. "I've needed my reading glasses for all this freaking paperwork."

Even though his eyes were red, he still looked as handsome as ever.

"You look tired," I said.

"Is that another way of saying I look like shit?"

"You could never look like shit," I answered.

"I'm so wiped, Wren. And on top of that, I can't stop thinking about Rafe."

"That's understandable. But he's on his way to getting better. That should provide some solace."

He rubbed his eyes. His stress was palpable. I couldn't help wanting to do what I do best—relieve some of it. "Close your eyes and take a deep breath," I suggested.

He did as I said. I walked behind him and began to massage his shoulders.

"You don't need to do that," he said in a low voice.

"It's on the house."

While this was nothing like my typical massage, I could still feel his body calming in response to my hands working his upper back. A long breath escaped him as he surrendered.

Dax hung his head forward and fully relaxed. "I forgot how fucking good it feels to be massaged by you," he murmured.

"You should've kept the façade going longer then," I teased. "Think of how many massages you could've had."

His body tensed.

I squeezed his shoulders harder. "I'm just kidding, Moody. Relax."

He exhaled, and once again let me do my thing. Of course, we were both getting something out of this. I'd missed touching him, and this was the only appropriate excuse I had. His arousing smell was overpowering.

After several minutes of working his shoulders and back, I forced myself to stop. While I didn't want to cease the contact, there was only so much I could do while he was seated and clothed. And honestly, I was burning up. Apparently, I was incapable of maintaining any semblance of professionalism when it came to this man.

"Thank you," he said. "That felt amazing."

I cleared my throat and walked back to the other side of the room. "You said you're almost done with work?"

"For tonight. I think so."

Lifting my scarf off the chair, I said, "Let me just grab this and get out of your way."

"Stay for a minute," he insisted. "Don't rush out."

That's what I was hoping you'd say. "Okay." I smiled, settling into the seat across from him.

"Did you have a nice dinner?" he asked.

"Yeah. The food was really good."

He licked the corner of his mouth. "I'm starving."

"You want me to pick you up something and bring it back here?"

"That's sweet of you, but it's okay. I'll get something on the way home. Where did you eat?"

"Sam and I went to Beantown Beerworks."

He fidgeted with his watch. "Are you and Sam...getting serious?"

Was this the question he'd wanted to ask earlier? While I knew things with Sam weren't going to last, I didn't want to come right out and say that, since it kind of pleased me that Dax seemed invested, perhaps jealous.

"We're not exclusive. So, no."

"Really. Is that your choice or his?"

"A serious relationship is not what I'm looking for right now."

"You only want something casual?"

"I'm not having sex with him, either, if that's what you mean by casual." *Ugh. Not sure why I blurted that out.*

"I wasn't fishing for that. But it's certainly...interesting."

"Why?"

"Why?" He scratched his chin. "I perhaps wrongly assumed that if you were spending regular time with someone..."

"You assumed I'm easy?" I teased.

His eyes narrowed. "Not at all. That's not what I meant."

"If I'm not sure I want something, I don't do it just to please someone else. When you really want something, you know it. You don't have to second guess."

He leaned back in his chair and examined my face. "You're not attracted to him..."

I decided to stop playing coy and just be honest. "With Sam... Honestly, I've enjoyed his company. But there's something missing, both physically and mentally. And I need to address it."

"You deserve to have it all. Never settle."

I couldn't help myself as I tilted my head. "Why do *you* settle?"

He started messing with his watch again. "You're talking about Adriana?"

"Yeah, unless there are more of them."

"No." He pretended to rub lint off his shirt. Then he looked up at me. "There's no one else. And like I told you, I haven't seen Adriana."

"Good."

He arched a brow. "That makes you happy?"

My pulse raced. "I don't even know her, but somehow I know she doesn't deserve you. She shouldn't have to chase you down like she does. She sounded desperate in that text. You should want her so much that she doesn't have to do that. I'm sure she's very beautiful and all that."

He paused a moment. "She's got nothing on you."

I shivered. That gave me the confidence to say, "She's got nothing on me? She's gotten to have you in a way I can't. That's a big thing she has on me."

He closed his eyes a moment and groaned. "Fuck, Wren."

"Anyway, you didn't answer me. Why do you settle?"

"Because..." He sighed. "Sometimes you just need a release without complications. But I agree that it's more enticing when something isn't easy. When it's unattainable." He stared into my eyes. "That's my fucking problem right now."

I felt the energy shift in his dark office.

"I think we have the same problem," I whispered.

He stared at me, and I could sense his walls starting to crumble. What he said next confirmed it.

"I told you I've been preoccupied because of Rafe and work. That's true. But I also haven't been able to stop thinking about you...since the other night. That's also part of why I can't focus."

My heart galloped. "Because of my story?"

"Hearing everything you've been through really had an effect on me, but it's more than that."

"Like..." I prodded.

"Like smelling you all over my bed the past several days. It's messed with my head. It's finally wearing off."

"Thinking about me is wearing off?"

"No. Your smell in my bed. I *wish* thinking about you was wearing off." He sighed deeply. "I don't know why I'm telling you this. It's inappropriate. I must be losing my mind."

My temperature rose. "Well, since we're being honest... I'll admit that I left my scarf here on purpose. I wanted an excuse to see you again. If you hadn't called me back, I was going to contact you so I could come get it."

"Shit." He looked up at the ceiling and laughed angrily. "This has to stop."

"Yeah, I suppose it does. Because nothing can happen between us. Yet you still think about me. What does that tell you?"

His eyes met mine again. "That I'm fucking selfish."

"No. It should tell you that we can only control so much. We can control actions but not feelings or desires. You can't help what you want."

"My priority needs to be Rafe. *Regardless* of what I want."

"Do you know what *I* want?"

He swallowed. "What?"

I took a moment to catch my breath. "You don't know? I thought I'd made it painfully obvious...to the point of making a damn fool of myself over and over."

He leaned into his knees and didn't say anything for the longest time, just rubbed his temples. Then he stood up, walked over to close the door, and turned the lock. After that he walked over to the window and stared out.

"What are you doing?" I asked.

He turned his head toward me. "Trying hard not to take you on my desk right now."

My heart pounded as he returned to his seat. My insides felt like they were about to explode. Taking a leap of faith, I walked over and sat on his lap, wrapping my legs around him. His breathing quickened, and I felt the heat of his cock awakening through his trousers as it throbbed beneath me.

"I'm going to fucking hell," he whispered.

"I'll see you there."

I waited. No way was I moving in to kiss him this time. I would never make that mistake again. If he wanted it, he was going to have to take it. I just stared into his eyes, an open invitation.

His eyes burned into mine. "You said you're jealous because Adriana's had me and you haven't." He swallowed. "You've fucking had me from the moment you first touched me. I haven't so much as thought about anyone else. I don't know how to make it stop." He wrapped his hands around my cheeks and brought me to his mouth. A groan escaped him, and I saw stars as the starvation I'd been managing for so long finally ended.

His kiss felt different than any other. The firmness. The wet hunger. The commanding way he held my face, the intensity of our breaths, the way his tongue circled mine rhythmically. Nothing else in the world mattered besides having his mouth on me, breathing in every bit of him, drowning in his taste. And when his tongue pushed deeper inside my mouth, it wasn't gentle. If the movement of his tongue was any indication, sex with Dax would be next-level.

"You're fucking perfect," he muttered over my lips.

I began to grind over him, the sensation so intense that I could've come at any moment if I'd let myself.

"I can't fuck you, Wren. I won't," he said, ripping his mouth away from mine. He urged me off him before getting up from the chair.

My tone was urgent. "What are you doing?"

"You can't do that to me anymore. The grinding thing." He ran his hand through his hair.

"Why?"

"Why?" He rubbed over his lips. "Because I'm about to lose it."

"That's what I want," I panted.

He walked toward me and backed me against his desk. "You wouldn't be ready for me right now if I really lost control."

Dax shoved a bunch of things to the side just before my ass landed against the desk. He lifted me, propping me up on it, and spread my legs apart as I lay back. He slid my panties down, practically ripping them, and positioned his head between my legs. The next thing I knew, his mouth was on me, his tongue lapping at my clit. The contact sent shockwaves through my body—the hottest, wettest ecstasy I'd ever felt. Pure, drunken adrenaline.

"When I said I was starving earlier—this is what I was referring to." He groaned.

Everything turned hazy as I writhed under him. I was transported somewhere else as his tongue explored my flesh, applying just the right amount of pressure. His low grunts vibrated through my body as I pressed myself against him.

Is this a dream? Because it couldn't be real. Dax Moody didn't have his mouth between my legs. He wasn't groaning as his tongue probed me, devouring me like I was his last meal.

My body fell all the way back as he slid me closer to him, spreading my legs wider and burying his whole face deeper. For a man who was hesitant to have me touch him, he was certainly not holding back right now. And I was thankful.

The room spun as I began to climax. It was the fastest I'd come in my life. As the muscles between my legs contracted, I gripped his hair and pressed his mouth harder against me. This almost felt like two orgasms in a row.

As I began to come down, he slid his tongue back and forth over my clit, as if to lick away the last remnants of what he'd done. He kissed gently upward, stopping on my abdomen. He breathed over the skin there as I lay limp for the longest time.

I eventually pushed myself up and hopped down from the desk, dropping to my knees to undo his belt. His pants could barely contain his erection. I wanted to taste him, too—give him even half the pleasure he'd given me.

But he placed his hand on my wrist, stopping me. A cold reality seeped in. It reminded me of when he'd grabbed my wrist that day on the massage table when I'd wanted to kiss him. He once again proved he was the one in control as he put an abrupt end to things.

Dax wiped the back of his hand along his mouth. "You need to go."

CHAPTER 12

Dax

In the days following my encounter with Wren in my office, I went back and forth between beating myself up for my actions and getting off on replaying them in my head.

I went down on Rafe's sister.

I went down on Rafe's sister and loved every second of it.

Of all the women in the world, that's who I'd chosen.

I was a sick fuck.

But she was the only woman I'd wanted from almost the moment I met her.

This madness needed to stop.

I'd just be going about my day, and then I'd remember how her flesh felt against my mouth, the way she tasted. I'd somehow justified it because I was the one pleasuring *her*, as if that meant I hadn't taken something I wasn't entitled to. But giving, not taking, somehow made what I'd done less unforgivable.

And then I'd practically kicked her out of my office. It had been so easy to imagine fucking her against the wall or on my desk. I'd been ready to explode, seconds away from burying myself inside of her. I suspected she would've let me do whatever I wanted. Because it was what *she* wanted. That scared the shit out of me. It might have seemed like I lost control when I went down on her, but I'd been absolutely aware of my limitations every second of the way. I'd made a clear decision the moment I lifted her onto my desk to give into temptation, but also not to let things go beyond giving her oral sex.

She probably took my telling her to leave as a rejection. But she couldn't have imagined how much I wanted her, all the things I wanted to do to her, the things I wanted her to do to me. I was more determined than ever, though, to stop anything else from happening before it was too late.

I needed to do something drastic. And that was going to start today.

One full week after the encounter, Wren still hadn't initiated contact. And I hadn't reached out to her. I knew she had to come around eventually since she'd want to see Rafe. But for now, I appreciated the space her absence afforded me.

Tonight was the first time in a while that I had plans to go out. My mission was to do my best to forget about Wren and this dilemma for one evening. Every year, Shannon threw a big New Orleans-themed party for her birthday. That was the perfect place to bring Keely, a woman I'd met on a dating app. I'd decided I needed to push myself to start dating again. That was the only thing I could come up with to distract me from what had happened with Wren.

Although it felt a little like penance, dating seemed like a logical idea. So did asking Keely to meet me at Shannon's party Friday night so things would remain casual in the event I wasn't feeling it. There would be lots of people around, so it seemed perfectly noncommittal.

As I stood across from my date that evening, the jury remained out. Keely was attractive enough, nice enough. But as I'd expected going into this, everything felt forced. Despite being here at this party, I couldn't seem to get Wren out of my head. At least Keely and I would have a good time at Shannon's, no matter what, even if the chemistry between us wasn't there. Rafe was here, too, and had disappeared into Shannon's TV room to play video games with Shannon's son, Bobby Jr., who was home from college for the occasion.

Redheaded Keely and I got to know each other a bit by the buffet table, which featured gumbo, beignets, and a mish-mash of other New Orleans-themed food.

As we noshed, Keely told me all about her position as an occupational therapist for the Boston schools, while I spoke a bit about my job and my appreciation for Shannon and all she did for Rafe and me.

At one point, my eyes wandered across the room, and I thought I was seeing things. Unfortunately, I wasn't.

She's here?

Right after Wren's eyes met mine, they turned to Keely.

"What the hell is Wren doing here?"

I didn't realize I'd said that aloud until Shannon answered from behind me.

"I invited her."

"How come you didn't tell me she was coming?"

Understandably confused, Shannon shrugged. "I didn't think you'd have an issue with it."

"I'm sorry." I shook my head. "You're right. I don't."

"Who's Wren?" Keely asked.

"She's..." *Right in front of my face.*

Wren's expression was serious as she stood before me.

Feigning a smile that probably looked like I'd been forced to eat dick, I said, "Hey, you."

She let out a tense breath. "Fancy meeting you here."

"Yeah. I didn't realize you'd be here." I swallowed.

"Where's that guy you're seeing?" Shannon asked. "I told you to feel free to bring a guest."

"Sam and I aren't seeing each other anymore."

"Really?" I said.

"Yeah." She turned to me. "I developed feelings for someone else. And I didn't think it was fair to waste his time anymore."

I swallowed hard.

She then turned to Keely. "Are you Dax's date?"

"Yes."

Wren nodded. "You must be Adriana?"

Ugh.

"No, I'm Keely." She looked over at me. "Who's Adriana?"

"Sorry. I guess I can't keep track," Wren said. She abruptly walked away.

Shit. What have I done?

"Who is that girl?" Keely asked.

145

"She's a friend," I answered, my eyes still fixed on Wren's back as she disappeared into the kitchen. "Will you excuse me a moment?"

When I walked into the kitchen, Wren was leaning against the counter with her hand on her chest as if she needed it to contain her heart.

I felt like absolute shit. "Wren..."

"Don't say anything." She walked over to the water cooler and grabbed a paper cup. "You don't owe me an explanation."

"Yes, I do. I would've never brought a date if I knew you'd be here."

"You're *dating* now? I thought you only *fucked* women. Well, any woman but me, apparently—you just fuck me with your tongue," she seethed. "Now, a week later, you're dating someone new? You seem to have moved on pretty quickly from whatever happened between us."

"What happened between us is precisely *why* I brought her."

She shook her head slowly. "I was looking forward to seeing you here tonight. I feel like such a fucking idiot."

My stomach was in knots. "I'm not proud of the decision I made the other night with you. So I forced myself to find a distraction because I badly need one. I don't..." I took a moment to catch my breath. "I don't want to hurt you."

"Well, you just did."

We both looked over to find Shannon in the kitchen. She'd likely heard everything.

"I'm sorry, Shannon," Wren said. "I have to leave."

"No worries, honey." Shannon glared at me, looking both confused and disappointed.

We watched as Wren stormed out of the kitchen. Shannon followed me back out to the living room. Keely had disappeared from her spot by the buffet table.

"Where's Keely?" I asked, though I wasn't really concerned about it now.

"She left. That's what I came into the kitchen to tell you. Wanna tell me what the hell is going on?"

Thank God Rafe was still in the TV room and hadn't witnessed this awkwardness. That could've been disastrous.

"You haven't figured it out?" I asked.

"No, I have. I just want you to know you can talk to me. And I'm sorry if I caused a problem by inviting Wren."

"No, you didn't. It was fine." I looked toward the door. "I need to go find her."

"I take it you don't mean Keely."

"No."

"Go." She waved me off. "Rafe is fine here with us."

"Are you sure?"

"Yes, I'm sure."

"I owe you one," I said as I headed toward the door.

"Just add it to the tab," Shannon joked.

I rushed out, and as soon as I hit the cold air outside, I took out my phone and texted Wren.

Dax: Where are you? We need to talk.

A few minutes passed, and I began to doubt she was going to respond. But then a text finally came in.

Wren: I'm heading home.

Dax: Can you meet me at my house? Or I can come to wherever you are. Whatever you prefer.

When she didn't answer after a full minute, I typed again.

Dax: You don't owe me anything, but I'd really appreciate the opportunity to better explain my actions.

The dots moved around for a while before she finally answered.

Wren: Fine.

Her car was parked in front of my house when I pulled up. She got out and rubbed her hands over her arms.

"It's cold," I said. "Let's get you inside." My heart nearly stopped, though, when I noticed she was sniffling. "Are you crying?"

"I'm feeling very emotional tonight, and before your head gets all big, it's not for the reason you think."

Rushing to the door, I opened it. "What's going on, Wren?"

She followed me inside. "I went to the party to tell you something important. And seeing you there with her rattled me."

I'd been so shocked earlier that I hadn't fully appreciated how goddamn stunning Wren looked in the emerald green dress she wore. It had subtle sparkles and fit her perfect little body to a tee. Her blue eyes shined under the lights in my foyer. She took my breath away.

"Come here." I pulled her into my arms, the only thing that felt right. Taking a deep breath of her scent, I spoke into her hair, "I'm sorry. I've been doing everything in my power to forget what happened between us. I can't forgive myself for my weakness. I thought if I could just force myself to take that woman out tonight, maybe I could somehow shift the direction of my life and pretend I hadn't royally fucked up with you. I never imagined you'd be there." I wanted to stay here in this spot with her wrapped in my arms, but she pulled away.

"It wasn't like you looked at me and made my legs magically open, Dax. I wanted it, too. I wanted more... But you told me to leave before that could happen. So stop blaming yourself for what we did. It is what it is."

Her words made me feel a little better, but I didn't deserve a shred of the peace of mind she offered.

"What do you need to tell me?" I asked.

Her chest heaved. "I found out today that I got the teaching position in France."

Perhaps excitement should have been my first reaction. Instead, my stomach sank. "What?" I feigned happiness. "You did? That's...great, right?"

"It's a two-year contract."

Two years? "They make you commit to that?"

"Well, no one's going to arrest me if I'm unhappy and want to leave. But I sign a two-year contract, during which I'm not supposed to leave or go work for another school."

This is really happening. She's leaving. A mix of panic and relief bombarded me. My mouth opened and closed a few times. "I don't even know what to say. I guess we knew this could happen, but it still seems a little surreal. This is what you want, isn't it?"

She wiped the corner of her eye. "It's funny... I thought I did. Until I actually got it. Now I'm kind of freaking out."

"Why?"

"I'm excited about the prospect of travel, but I don't want to leave my dad. I don't want to leave Rafe," she whispered. "Or you."

My chest hurt. "You're gonna take it, though, right?"

She looked at her feet a moment. "I think so, yeah."

Good. This was good, right? I should've been relieved that she wasn't going to let anything between us sway her decision. The feeling in my chest certainly wasn't relief, though. It felt like I'd been gutted.

But I wasn't going to keep her from something she'd always dreamed of—traveling overseas. And now she'd have the chance to live there for a while, something I hadn't done myself. Not only would this be a once-in-a-lifetime opportunity, but it would give her much-needed space from me. That felt more imperative than ever.

"I feel lost, torn between two different sets of feelings...happiness and sadness," she said.

Yeah, I can relate. "Well, I'm glad you realize turning this down isn't an option. You're gonna be scared. Leaving what you know is gonna feel foreign. But you won't regret it."

What she said next surprised me.

"I want to tell him, Dax."

It took me a second to understand. "You want to tell Rafe the truth?"

She nodded. "Not right now, but before I leave. I've been doing a lot of thinking about this. By the time I come back, he's going to be almost sixteen. I don't want him going all that time not knowing. It will give him more context for why I need to keep in touch with him while I'm away. I feel like he's in a better place now and can handle it. What do you think?"

I rubbed the scruff on my chin as I processed that. I couldn't think of a reason not to tell him, especially since he'd been doing so much better over the past month.

"I think you're right. If your gut is telling you this is the right time, I think we should tell him."

"I'm glad you agree."

I nodded. I just had no idea how he was going to react. I sucked some air in. "When do you leave?"

"They want me there by June first. I'll probably leave at the end of May to get acclimated to the area. I would be teaching a summer program initially and then going right into the main fall semester after that."

Less than three months. That hit me like a sucker punch.

"I'll let you decide when you feel the time is right to have the conversation," I said.

"I was gonna tell him a couple of weeks before I leave. So that way there's some time where I'm still here, if he has questions."

"I'll support you in whatever decision you make. And Shannon and I will be here for him if it takes him some time to process."

Wren stared into my eyes. "We need to talk about us, too."

A rock settled in my stomach.

"I haven't been able to think of anything but you in a week and a half," she confessed.

Rather than admit I'd had the same problem, I asked, "When did you end things with Sam?"

"I don't even know that there was anything to end because we weren't exclusive. But I went to see him right after I left your office that night."

I nodded, hating myself for the trace of sick pride I felt upon hearing that—as if I were the Cunnilingus King, ruining her for all other men.

"After what I experienced with you, I knew I had to act," she continued. "It made no sense to string him along anymore. If I took anything away from what happened with us, it's that I deserve to feel that kind of fire with someone. Even if you and I can't be together, you showed me what it's like. And I definitely didn't have that experience with Sam." She looked into my eyes. "It wasn't just what you did to me on your desk. It's how I feel every minute I'm with you, Dax. Even if we're just talking. I..."

Her words trailed off, but she didn't have to explain further. I knew *exactly* what she meant. I took a few steps closer. "I know because you saw me with a woman tonight, you think I don't care about what happened between us. But it's just the opposite. I feel every bit of what you do, if not more."

"So fucking someone new was the solution to handling it?"

"I promise you, I had no intention of sleeping with her. It wasn't about that. It was about me running like hell from what's been happening between us." I raked my fingers through my hair. "There are so many reasons I'm wrong for you, Wren. Even if you weren't Rafe's sister, I wouldn't be right for you. That's important for you to understand, too. I have a lot of shit I haven't dealt with. You deserve someone who can open his heart to you without baggage and issues to work through." I sighed. "My sexual attraction to you and my admiration for you are not an excuse to overlook that harsh truth. I'm the wrong man for you. I think your new adventure is badly needed, and it will put some space between us."

"You think I'm so addicted to you that the only thing that can stop it is an ocean between us?"

"No. I'm the one who needs the ocean because I'm addicted to *you*." Those words felt like a weight off my chest. "I'm fucking addicted to you," I repeated. "I can't stop tasting you on my tongue. But if that were the only problem, maybe I could handle it. It's not just physical. I can't stop listening to your music—I've been doing that since the moment I discovered it. Almost every night. Did you know that? And I can't stop replaying our conversations because they make me think about life. They make me want to write in that fucking journal and do things I've never imagined myself doing. You have a way of making me feel better about myself, even when I don't deserve it. I can't stop thinking about *you*." I lowered my voice. "And it really has to stop. Because I don't want to ruin your life... or Rafe's. The kid is traumatized enough. This is what I do. I hurt people." Feeling my walls crumbling, I got choked up. "I was a terrible husband, Wren."

"What do you mean?" She blinked. "Were you unfaithful?"

"No. But I didn't give my wife the type of affection she deserved. I loved Maren, but..." I paused. This was hard to admit. "I don't think I was *in love* with her when

I made the decision to marry her. The biggest sin of my existence will always be that I wasted those two years of her life while she was married to me. She could've been with someone who truly deserved her. I thought I could grow to be that man. I wanted to love her in that deep, soul-crushing way."

I'd thought I didn't have it in me until these powerful feelings had formed for Wren. But I would not be admitting *that* to her tonight.

"So you see..." I said. "I sure as hell don't deserve a second chance if she didn't get one. That would be too fucked up for words. *I'm* too fucked up for words. And I'd be dangerous for you."

She shook her head. "You don't fucking scare me, Moody."

I let out a long, frustrated breath. "You're calling me Moody again. You must not hate me anymore."

"I wish I hated you. I wish I didn't..." She hesitated.

Me, too, Wren. Me, too. I *felt* the rest of that statement. There were endless ways to end that sentence.

I wish I didn't.

I wish I didn't want to pin you against the wall right now.

I wish I didn't care so damn much about you.

My phone chimed.

Shannon: Rafe is more than welcome to spend the night here. He can sleep in Mikey's old room. We have plenty of clothes that will fit him, too. He's still having a good time gaming. Shall I just bring him back in the morning?

Shit. Rafe coming back home tonight might have been the one thing to keep me out of trouble. I wasn't going to stop him from having a good time, though, just because I couldn't trust myself with Wren.

> **Dax:** That would be great. Thank you. I'm glad he's having a good time. I owe you another one.

> **Shannon:** I won't ask you what you'll be doing with the free time.

I sighed. Wasn't even gonna touch that.

"Is that Keely?" She rolled her eyes.

"No. It's Shannon. Rafe is going to spend the night there. He's having a good time gaming."

Our eyes locked.

"Do you want me to leave?" she asked.

"Do I think you should leave? Yes. Do I *want* you to leave?" I shook my head. "No."

Her mouth curved into a smile. "Can I ask you a favor?"

"Yeah."

"Will you give me tonight?"

My heart raced. "Give you what exactly?"

"An overnight with you. Just to spend time together. Nothing more. Now that I know I'm leaving, time with you is very important to me."

"Do you really think an overnight is smart?"

"This isn't about sex. Because believe it or not, and especially now that I'm leaving, I think that would be a bad idea. I don't want you to feel guilty. You have enough to worry about." She sighed. "But this is probably the one time Rafe will be away until I'm gone. I don't want to leave you tonight."

"Time alone with you in this house sounds very fucking dangerous to me."

Wren shrugged. "So maybe I want to flirt with danger a little. But I won't let us cross that line." She flashed a wicked grin. "Tow the line maybe, but not cross it."

Her smile lit up her face and warmed my cold soul.

Giving my inhibitions a rest, I reached out and looped her fingers with mine. "I do want you here with me tonight."

"I'll stay in the guest room this time. I insist. We'll have a slumber party first, though." She laughed. "But I have a strange request."

I raised my brow. "Okay?"

"I want to see you reading your book in your chair with your old-man glasses."

I bent my head back in laughter. "Why?"

"Because I've imagined it, and I want to see it just once. I want to watch you read."

"What are you gonna do while I'm reading?"

"Just watch you." She started to walk away.

"Where are you going?"

"Up to your room to put on something more comfortable."

While she was upstairs, I leaned against the counter, pulling on my hair. I needed my fucking head checked for agreeing to this little *slumber party*. Pretty sure I was kidding myself if I actually believed nothing was gonna happen tonight. But I also felt invigorated. I loved having her here.

She came back downstairs wearing one of my blue and orange Syracuse T-shirts that came practically down to her knees. My dick rose to attention at the sight of her breasts pressing against it. Seeing her in my shirt was so goddamn hot.

"I didn't know you went to Syracuse," she said.

"I did." I smiled. "You look better than I ever did in that shirt."

"Your turn," she said. "Go get into your comfy night clothes. I'll make some tea and snacks for us."

I needed to not overthink tonight and enjoy it for what it was: a night in with one of my favorite people. *Self-care and all that shit.*

After changing, I came downstairs to find Wren fishing through the cabinets, taking stuff out and making the kind of mess this house was in desperate need of. This was life. *She* was life. I loved her chaos, and for a brief moment I wished this were my reality, that I could have her here every day like this. That thought was immediately followed by relief that she was fleeing the country so I didn't have a chance to tarnish her.

"Where are your glasses?" she asked.

"You mean for wine?"

"No. Your *eyeglasses,* old man."

I chuckled. "Don't worry. They're in my briefcase over there by the kitchen table."

She gave me a once-over. "I like your ensemble."

I looked down at myself. I'd put on a white tee and gray sweatpants. "You said to get comfortable. This is what I lounge around in."

"See, I would never know that if I weren't spending the night." She winked. "I'm making us some junk food. I don't cook. Have we talked about that?"

"No. But I don't, either. I guess we can figure out how to heat stuff in the oven together."

Wren prepared a medley of things that were mostly from the freezer: pizza bagel bites, chicken nuggets, and sweet potato fries. She made two plates.

We took them to the living room and ate together on the floor by the fire. It was pretty amazing how this night, which had started as an awkward first date with a stranger, had turned into a pleasant surprise.

We played music, and Wren told me some stories about her childhood growing up in Boston. She listened with great interest as I talked about my business and explained how I invested millions of dollars of other people's money every day, like a constant game of Monopoly. I soaked in every laugh, every smile. I felt twenty years old again, like being around her had tapped into my younger, more carefree self—the person I was before I lost my family, lost my wife, *lost myself.* For the first time in a long time, if only for one night, my troubles seemed lightyears away.

CHAPTER 13

Wren

The sight of Dax in his glasses was even better than I'd anticipated. As he sat there humoring me, reading his book, I sat by his feet with my legs crossed. I grabbed a blanket as the fire roared and opened a novel I'd chosen off his shelf: *The Things We Cannot Say*. Even though historical fiction wasn't my normal cup of tea, I wanted to spend this quiet time with him, joining him in one of his favorite hobbies. Hanging out like this was something I'd always fantasized about.

It was getting late. I knew this night would be over in a flash, but I wanted to cherish every second of it. "Will you tell me your story, Dax?"

He took his glasses off. "My story..."

"Yeah. Remember how I told you mine? Will you tell me yours in third person?"

I knew that was a tall order. But if not tonight, then when would I have a chance to hear it? My chest tightened at that thought.

He closed his book. "I thought tonight was supposed to be about fun..."

I shook my head. "You don't have to if you don't want to. I don't want to upset you or ruin the mood. I would just love to know more about Moody. You've only told me bits and pieces, and I want to know everything."

To my surprise, he set his book aside and got up from the chair. "I might need some wine, then."

My hopes were officially up. *Did he just agree?*

"Frankly, I'm surprised we've made it this far without wine," I teased.

He ventured into the kitchen, returning with a bottle of red and two glasses.

"You're the only one who could get me to do this, you know that?" He sighed. "You're gonna have to bear with me because I don't think I can tell my story as seamlessly as you told yours. I might have many more pauses."

"That's perfectly fine." I smiled. "There are no rules."

He settled into his chair, and I once again sat by his feet.

"Okay…" He took a long drink before he started. "So… Dax Moody was the oldest son of three boys born to Alexander and Mona Moody. His childhood was pretty uneventful. There was nothing particularly bad or traumatic, which he's grateful for. His life in the Catskills—New Paltz, New York, to be exact—was quite privileged. His family was wealthy, and Dax never wanted for anything. But his father was unloving, constantly working. And while his mother did the best she could to hold the family together, she seemed to live in fear of her husband. Mona always did whatever Alexander wanted, even if it was against her best judgment. She didn't seem to have a mind of her own or a backbone. Dax was fairly close to his brothers, Mitch and Stephen. The three of them had each other's backs—or so Dax thought at the time."

He took a moment, seeming to ponder what to say next. I waited until he finally continued.

"Dax had one girlfriend throughout high school but broke her heart when he ended things soon after they went to separate colleges. He wanted a fresh start at Syracuse and hadn't wanted to hold either of them back. It was probably the most mature decision he'd ever made, though she never forgave him for it. Kayla became depressed and eventually started taking pills. She'd call Dax from school in Pennsylvania in a drug-induced haze, swearing a lot and blaming him for her depression. Thank God she eventually got clean after college. But Dax would often blame himself for the years she was hooked on drugs. If something had happened to her, he would've never forgiven himself."

He turned to me, his face reflecting shame. I reached for his hand to offer support.

"It seemed whenever Dax made a decision in his own best interest, he was made to feel guilty for it. After Syracuse, his father expected him to return home to work for the family business. Moody Cement was the largest cement company in all of the Catskills. But instead, Dax decided to go to Boston University for his MBA. Anything he could do to put off the inevitability of being *cemented*—for lack of a better word—into the family business. Dax's father had always assumed his three sons would run the company together. While in grad school, when Dax broke the news that he didn't want to run Moody Cement with his brothers, his father disowned him." Dax shook his head slowly, seeming lost in his memories.

Then his eyes darkened. "Surprisingly, Alexander was also able to turn his other sons against Dax. That was the part Dax never saw coming. On some level, he knew he'd lose his father, and his mother by default, if he chose to follow his dreams. But he never thought he'd lose his brothers, too." He paused. "As Dax struggled to excel in school so he could someday make a name for himself in the financial sector, he fell into a deep depression, and probably for the first time could relate to the betrayal Kayla felt after he ended their relationship." He held his head in his hands. "The pressure was too much for Dax, and he started experimenting with recreational drugs." He looked down at me. "But by the grace of God, he caught himself before it spiraled. Actually, his roommate, an amazing guy named Tyler Brinkman, had a lot to do with helping him see that things were getting out of control. Dax took a leave of absence from grad school and entered a rehab facility, managing to clean up his act before it ruined him."

I let go of the breath I'd been holding.

"Dax returned to grad school in full force, got a great job after graduation, and by his late twenties, he'd become one of the top venture capitalists in the city, working at one point under the apprenticeship of Maren Wade at Stryker Investments." Dax smiled. "His boss was a remarkable woman. Not only did she run a company, she was a single mom to a boy she'd adopted when he was eight. It wasn't until Dax left that job to take a position at another firm that Maren and he became close on a personal level. She seemed enamored with him, and he felt lucky to be on the receiving end of that admiration." He stared out into the fire. "Maren gave him the kind of love he didn't have from his family anymore. She respected his ambitions, made him feel wanted and protected. Deep down, Dax knew he wasn't in love with Maren the way you need to be to commit to spending your life with someone. But he wanted so badly to reciprocate her feelings. He didn't want to lose her. So when she suggested they go to Las Vegas one weekend and tie the knot, Dax agreed. After all, he couldn't imagine a life without her in it. At the time, though, he hadn't yet realized that a marriage meant more than just mutual respect and admiration or a feeling of security. In order to really work, there had to be passion." He exhaled. "He will never forgive himself for not realizing that sooner, for not giving her the type of love she deserved, and for wasting her precious time. He will spend the rest of his life making up for that tragic mistake, ensuring that Rafe, the son she loved so much, never wants for anything."

Dax closed his eyes, and I felt like maybe this was getting to be too much for him. "You can stop," I assured him.

"No. It's okay," he muttered before taking a deep breath and continuing. "After his wife died suddenly, Dax felt lost, totally consumed by guilt and feeling an emptiness he'd never experienced before. Nothing compared to it, not even the abandonment of his own family. One day, he decided to look into Rafe's past, so he could potentially find someone who might love the boy in a way Dax felt he was too broken to be capable of. That search led him to discover that Rafe had an older, biological sister." He smiled. "Dax crafted a plan to get to know her by pretending to be one of her clients, fooling her into believing he simply wanted a massage. Wren wasn't the only one fooled, though. The biggest trick Dax played was on himself. Because from almost the moment she looked into his eyes, he felt different. He felt something he'd never felt before: a magnetic pull to another human being. Whether he was listening to her hypnotizing cello or having an honest conversation, Wren made him feel human again. But the great irony? Wren was the one woman Dax couldn't pursue. He'd made a promise never to hurt Maren's son. And he intended to keep that promise. And anyway, there were many other reasons he wasn't right for her. But understanding that didn't stop him from dreaming of her at night. Thus, his life remained a conundrum." He turned to me. "The rest is unwritten," he whispered, repeating the line I'd used when I ended my story.

Overcome with emotion, I stood and moved to sit with him, wrapping my hands around his face and looking into his eyes. "Thank you for sharing that with me. No one has ever made me feel the way you do. It's scary, and at the same time, I understand everything you've said. But we all deserve a second chance, Dax. You're no different just because you've made some mistakes. And you're no more responsible for what happened to Maren than Rafe was. You're doing the best you can every day, and I respect you so much for that." My eyes watered. "Thank you for taking care of my brother. Thank you for finding me and giving me the gift of knowing him. And the gift of knowing you. You might feel like your life has been less than perfect, but you're one of the most influential people in *my* life."

His eyes seared into mine. "You deserve the world, beautiful girl. I hope over the next two years you take it by storm."

Dax pulled me to him, enveloping my mouth with his. I wasn't expecting him to kiss me tonight, but I was so glad he did. We seemed to fall into it so naturally. *Like a magnet.* This kiss felt different from our first. It wasn't as fast and frantic. It was firm and passionate. Because it was slower, I felt it in every fiber of my being, as if with each second, he was pouring his soul into mine.

His sweatpants did nothing to contain his erection, and I couldn't help moving on top of him and bearing down on the heat beneath me, even if just for a minute. I wanted to feel him inside of me more than I'd ever wanted anything, but I knew I had to stop egging him on. As my father had said, "*Men only have so much control.*" And something told me if we both lost control tonight, I'd become even more addicted than I already was. No way could I get on that plane and leave him. It'd be hard enough as things were. But I also realized the night was still young. I didn't trust myself.

As we pulled away to catch our breath, I forced myself off of him and returned to my spot on the floor.

"Can I ask you a favor?" he asked, rubbing his fingers over his lips, still plump from my kiss.

"Sure."

"Will you play the cello for me once before you leave?"

"Like a private show?"

"Yeah. Live, in person."

"Of course. I don't do that for just anyone, but I'll do it for you." *I'd do anything you asked me to, and that's the problem.*

We stayed up and talked until we could no longer deny that it was, in fact, the middle of the night. I never wanted this evening to end.

"I can stay in one of the guest rooms," I insisted.

"You didn't like my room?"

"I loved your room. But it's not necessary. I can take one of the other rooms this time."

Dax and I headed upstairs, and he turned on the lights in one of his two spare bedrooms. The décor had a feminine vibe, and I knew that Maren must've designed it.

I looked around. "I have everything I need in here." *Except for you.*

Dax looked conflicted. Like maybe he didn't want me to stay the night? Was he still having doubts?

"What's wrong?" I asked.

He bit his lip. "I want you in my bed."

"This room is really fine," I insisted.

"With *me*, Wren," he clarified.

Chills ran down my spine. That's what I wanted, of course, but I didn't understand his sudden change in stance. "Don't you think that's a bad idea?"

"I do. I think it's a very bad fucking idea. But I want to lie with you anyway, hold you for just one night. I feel like this is my only chance."

I inched toward him. "I want nothing more than to lie with you tonight."

He offered his hand. "Let's go, then."

As Dax led me down the hall to his bedroom, it felt surreal. I had no idea what to expect, but I was grateful to get to hold him, at the very least.

Once inside his dimly lit room, Dax removed his watch and placed it on the end table. I sat at the edge of the bed, unexpectedly nervous.

"Don't worry. I won't bite you in your sleep," he said.

"Damn. I was counting on it," I teased, despite my jitters.

When had the roles reversed, making him the confident one and me the ball of nerves? He pulled down the comforter and sheets, and I lay down. He followed suit and faced me.

As my head hit the pillow, I confessed, "I know you said you could smell me on your sheets, but all I could smell was *you* the last time I slept here. It kept me up—in a painfully good way. But nothing compares to this...lying next to you."

His voice was low. "What were you thinking about when you smelled me on the sheets?"

I stroked his cheek. "I just kept pretending you were with me."

"How does one do that...*pretend* I'm with you? Did you grab the pillow or something and call it Moody?"

I ran the tip of my finger along his chin. "You really want to know what I did?"

"Yeah, I do," he said seductively.

"I touched myself thinking about you. When you came to the door to tell me about breakfast, you interrupted."

"Fuck, don't tell me that." He buried his face in the pillow. "I should've come in instead."

"I've touched myself a lot thinking about you these last several months," I confessed.

"You're not the only one. I've nearly taken my dick off thinking about you."

Curling into my pillow, I said, "I have another confession."

He placed his hand on my cheek and brushed his thumb along my skin. "Well, tonight seems to be the night for that. Anything goes. Tell me."

"The first time I massaged you, my panties were wet."

He shut his eyes. "Jesus."

"That hadn't happened to me before."

"I might never recover from hearing you admit that."

I chuckled. "That's when I knew I was in trouble with you."

"I jerked off in the shower upstairs before I came back down to face you that day. But I never imagined that you felt that way the first time."

"How could I not? You're the most beautiful man I've ever seen."

He caressed my hair. "I'm so fucking attracted to you. You blow me away every time I look at you." He lowered his hand and tugged at the material of the T-shirt I wore. "And I love you in my shirt."

I *love you* in my shirt. Hearing the words *I love you* come out of his mouth gave me goose bumps for a split second before my brain registered the context. I knew, on some level, that I might have been falling in love with Dax. I couldn't imagine hearing him say those three words to me. But I'd take *I love you in my shirt* over nothing.

I'd promised myself I wasn't going to do anything to tempt him, but it was incredibly difficult to lie so close to him, to feel his breath on my body, and not want to feel him everywhere. I couldn't help it. I leaned in and pressed my lips against his, relishing the low groan that produced. I loved his taste. And I wanted so much more than this. My body ached for it.

I lowered my hand and wrapped it around his swollen cock, feeling it instantly move through his pants.

His body stiffened. "I don't think you should do that," he whispered over my lips.

I removed my hand. "You've gone down on me, and I can't even touch you?"

"I *do* want you to touch me. Very badly." He moved back an inch. "But I have this fucked-up idea that it's okay if I touch you, as long as you don't touch me."

"Which is ironic because didn't this whole thing start with me touching you?"

"I suppose it did."

I let out a frustrated sigh. "Can I kiss you again, if I can't touch you?"

"Yes. Of course." He pulled me close, taking my lips again and slipping his tongue inside.

We kissed for several minutes, and my panties were drenched.

"If I'd known I was going to spend the night here, I would've brought a spare pair of underwear, maybe three."

His breathing quickened. "Can I feel how wet you are?"

I nodded, desperate for his touch.

Dax lowered his hand and slipped it inside my panties. He closed his eyes and began moving two of his fingers in and out of me slowly. My clit throbbed as he gently fucked me with his hand. He looked dazed, almost in a trance, with his mouth agape, as if he were trying to imagine his fingers were his cock and we were having sex.

As much as I loved looking at his face, I closed my eyes and did the same, imagining he was deep inside me. But I knew his cock would fill me so much better than his fingers. I opened my eyes when I felt his hand leave me.

Don't stop. Panting, I asked, "Is everything okay?"

He nodded and took his fingers into his mouth to lick

my arousal off of them. If that wasn't the hottest thing I'd ever seen...

He licked his lips. "I'm sorry I'm so goddamn weak."

"*You're* weak? I would let you do anything you wanted to me right now."

"Fuck." He gritted his teeth. "Don't say that."

"If you won't let me touch you, then let me watch you touch yourself, Dax...while you touch me."

His chest rose and fell as he considered my proposition. He took a deep breath in. I watched intently as he lowered his hand to the band of his sweatpants. He pushed the material down and his beautiful, gigantic cock sprung out. While I'd imagined what it looked like, the reality definitely surpassed all expectations. It seemed this perfect-looking man had a perfect-looking cock to match, with girth as impressive as its length, and beautiful, veiny skin. My mouth watered. Not being allowed to taste or touch him was pure torture.

He wrapped his hand around it in a firm grip and began to pump. He reached his other hand underneath my shirt and began massaging my breast. I worked to slip my panties off and tossed them to the side before taking my fingers to my clit and circling them over the tender flesh.

Dax jerked off faster as his eyes stayed fixed to the sight of me pleasuring myself. We couldn't get enough of watching each other.

"That's so fucking hot," he rasped. "I need to taste you again."

He lowered himself between my legs and began devouring me. *God, yes. Thank you.* Even though I could no longer see straight, I felt his arm moving and knew he was still jerking off. The thought of that, combined with the incredible feeling of his tongue fucking me, was definitely too much to bear. Threading my fingers through his hair, I came hard against his mouth, letting out a shriek of pleasure that echoed through his bedroom.

Almost immediately after, a loud groan escaped him, vibrating against my clit. That's when I felt the rush of wet heat—his load coating my lower leg. With his mouth still between my thighs, I could feel his panting gradually ease. He stayed in that position for a while as I massaged his scalp.

"Don't move," he finally said. "I'll get something to clean this."

Cold air replaced his warmth as he slipped out of bed and returned with a washcloth and towel.

I leaned up to watch him cleaning the cum off of my calf.

"I'm sorry," he said.

"Sorry for what? I loved it."

He left to discard the towels before returning to the spot across from me.

"Do you feel more relaxed?" I smiled.

"I didn't expect to take it that far. But you want to know the truth?"

I threaded my fingers through his hair. "Yeah."

"I normally do calm down after I come. But with you...I only want more. Like I'm ready for more right this second, which is scary as shit to me. It's like I can't be fucking tamed."

I can only imagine how good the sex would be. I knew he would cave if I kept taunting him. That was my gut feeling. But my gut also told me to stop. I needed to protect my heart, and the last thing he needed was more guilt. So rather than pushing the envelope even further, I decided—for once—to do the right thing.

"I think you wore me out," I lied. "Let's sleep, okay?"

He nodded, not looking tired in the least. I turned around, facing my back to him, and he wrapped his arms around me. So tightly. Now it seemed the joke was on me. Lying here in his arms was more powerful than sex could ever be. Here in this intimate place, all of the feelings I'd ever had for him rose to the surface. I felt safe. I felt protected. I felt loved, even if he didn't exactly love me.

Dax didn't realize that all he had to do was whisper in my ear to stay in Boston, and I'd never leave.

CHAPTER 14

Dax

The weeks leading up to Wren's departure went by extraordinarily fast. It was hard to believe it was now mid-May and she'd be leaving in only a couple of weeks. Based on our interactions since the sleepover, you'd never know that had happened. We hadn't been alone together since, and that was the way things needed to be. We'd enjoyed that evening together as if it were our last night on Earth; I'd never forget it. But the priority right now needed to be Rafe.

Over the past couple of months, he had continued to improve. Once his therapist became aware of the reason for Rafe's mutism, she'd been able to get through to him in a way she hadn't before. With the new cognitive-behavioral-therapy approach, he was now back to talking almost normally. He still might not initiate many conversations, but he'd been able to fully participate at school, and was no longer intentionally staying silent when spoken to.

Wren had been coming over regularly to visit Rafe, making the most of the time before she had to leave. My one job, when I happened to be around during her visits, was to continue to pretend her moving to France wasn't killing me inside. Despite the fact that we'd been keeping our distance, she remained constantly on my mind.

Today, in particular, two weeks before she was set to leave, was a huge day for all of us. Wren would be coming over to tell Rafe the truth—who she really was. We'd chosen a Saturday afternoon for the big talk, and although Shannon didn't normally work weekends, she'd come over to offer her support. The talk wouldn't fall exclusively on Wren's shoulders. It would be a team effort.

We had a few minutes before Wren was set to arrive, and Rafe was upstairs in his room with no idea of what was about to hit him. Shannon brewed some coffee while I sat in a kitchen chair, bouncing my legs. I was a ball of nerves, unsure of how this was going to play out.

"You okay?" she asked.

"Yeah. Just a little anxious for him, even though I know this is a wonderful thing."

She cocked her head. "Just anxious for *him*?"

"What do you mean?"

"Wren is leaving in a couple of weeks. How do you feel about that?"

"It doesn't matter how I feel about it," I balked.

"I never asked you what happened the night of my party because it's none of my business. But I can tell something's changed in you since then." She paused. "You obviously have feelings for her."

There was no point in denying it. Shannon could see right through me. I sighed. "I'm definitely going to miss her. But I'm not going to mess up this opportunity for Wren. She knows I have feelings for her. But she also knows I'm not going to do anything about them."

"Because of Rafe..."

"Of course, because of Rafe."

That was the absolute truth. Because if it weren't for Rafe, despite all of my other fears, I would've chanced it. I would've moved toward being with Wren. It would have been my absolute pleasure to explore where things went between us. But since nothing could happen, it was best that she was leaving.

Shannon frowned. "I wish things were different. Because I've not seen you light up around anyone like you do around her. But I totally understand the dilemma."

The doorbell rang. *Saved by the bell.* "That's her," I said as I got up out of my seat to answer the door. My heart raced, fueled by a combination of what was to come with Rafe, and the anticipation of seeing her, which always made my heart do crazy things.

I opened the door to find Wren looking just as tense as I felt. She wore her signature ripped jeans with that familiar black-and-white-striped, off-the-shoulder shirt.

"Hey, you. How ya doing?"

She exhaled. "I'm good. A little nervous. You?"

"Same."

She followed me into the house.

"Wanna sit and have some coffee first? Shannon brought beignets."

She held out her palm. "I'm too anxious to eat or drink. But thank you."

"Okay."

She walked into the kitchen. "Hey, Shannon."

MOODY

"Hey, honey." Shannon sprinkled powdered sugar on the beignets. "How are you doing?"

"I'm hanging in there. Had a busy morning. I'm trying to get ahead of the game with packing. It's hard to figure out what to bring for two years, and what to keep home. I know I can buy stuff when I'm there, but I just want to take everything with me." She glanced over at me.

"I'm sure," Shannon said as she flashed me a look.

"Who's gonna lead the conversation?" Wren asked me.

"I'll start and explain my part in how things played out. This won't all be on you." I placed my hand on her shoulder. "You're shivering."

"I'm more nervous than I thought I'd be. What if he feels like I tricked him all this time, pretending to be a friend?"

"Come here." I took her into my arms and held her tightly.

I couldn't bring myself to look over at Shannon, who must have taken great amusement in the gesture.

"I've got you. It's gonna be okay," I whispered into Wren's hair. "He's gonna understand, even if it's not immediate."

After several seconds, she pulled away. "Let's call him down now, if you don't mind."

"Okay. I'll go get him." My own jitters rose to the surface with each step I took up the stairs.

Rafe's door was slightly ajar. I knocked a few times before opening. Per usual, his room looked like a cyclone had hit it, with clothes and wrappers everywhere.

"Hey, dude. I want to talk to you about something. Wren is here, too. Can you come down to the kitchen?"

He took his earbuds out. "Am I in trouble?"

"No. Not at all. Just something we need to talk about."

He shrugged. "Okay."

I headed back down to the kitchen and found Shannon and Wren sitting together on one side of the table. I pulled up a chair for Rafe.

When he finally entered the kitchen, he sat next to me.

"Hey, buddy." Wren smiled at him from across the table.

"Hey," Rafe said, looking around and seeming understandably confused.

I circled my thumbs and pushed out the first sentence. "There's...something really important I need to tell you." I paused. "It involves Wren."

He looked over at her, then back at me. "What's going on?"

"You know how she's leaving for France. We wanted to make sure we had a chance to talk about something before then."

He drew in his brows. "Okay..."

"Rafe..." I turned to him in my seat. "I know you and I haven't always connected, particularly when I first married your mom and moved in. It was a bit of a rude awakening for you, and when we lost her, you were stuck with me, a virtual stranger. It might've seemed like I was the enemy for a while, but I'm proud of how our relationship has evolved since then. I want you to know that I've always only wanted the best for you and always will."

He chewed his lip, continuing to give me his undivided attention. Wren's face was turning redder by the second.

"After you lost your mom," I said, "I felt helpless, because even though I knew I'd always be here for you, I never felt like I was enough. You deserved so much more, so I thought it would be a good idea to try to find your... biological relatives."

Rafe's expression was stoic.

"I want to make it clear that my actions in no way had anything to do with wanting someone else to take care of you. That's my responsibility. I just wanted to see if I could brighten up your life a bit, in case there were people who didn't know about you and might have wanted to."

"What do you mean?" he interrupted. "You found my birth mother?"

"The investigator I hired did." I forced myself to take a breath. "She wasn't in a place in her life to meet you. She still has a lot of issues. But we learned through her that she'd also given up another child...more than a decade before you were born. A daughter." I paused. "And I located her." I looked across the table at Wren. "That's what led me to Wren. I know you've assumed all this time that she was my friend. And she is." I looked into his eyes. "But she's also your sister."

He immediately looked over at her, but his expression was hard to read. If anything, it was pure shock.

I gave Wren a supportive nod, which was her cue to speak.

"I'm your sister, Rafe," she said shakily. "It was never our intention to keep this from you for very long. Dax needed some time to learn about me to make sure I would be a good influence in your life. He didn't tell me right away, either, because he wanted to be very careful to make sure neither one of us got hurt. So I didn't know who you were when we first met."

He blinked several times. "When did you find out?"

"Right around the time I started coming over more often, back in February."

Rafe looked away. "I can't believe this."

Wren's eyes glistened. "I know it's a lot to take in. It was for me, too. But in a good way. I never thought I'd have a sibling. Finding out about you was the best news ever."

"Wait…" he said. "You're still leaving, right?"

She nodded slowly. "Yes, I am. That's part of why I wanted to make sure you knew now, so you'd understand why I need to keep in close contact with you while I'm away. I don't want you to feel like I'm abandoning you. I will never abandon you, Rafe. I'll only be a plane ride away if you need me. And it's only for two years. You'll blink, you'll be almost sixteen, and I'll be back. I realize the timing is not great. And please don't take my leaving personally. This adventure is just one I need to take right now."

Rafe finally looked over at me again. "I don't know what to say."

"It's going to take some time for you to absorb this. You don't have to say anything," I assured him. "We just needed you to know."

Shannon remained quiet. I was about to open my mouth, but Wren took the helm again.

"It took me some time to process, too." She let out a quivering breath. "I know the past couple of years have been so tough for you. It's not my intention to make your life more complicated. I want to make it better. I hope you'll let me. And I hope, once it sinks in, that this is happy news for you."

She started to tear up, and I wanted so badly to reach across the table and hug her. I was fully responsible for anything negative that might come out of this. Everything was still in limbo because I couldn't gauge how Rafe was feeling about it.

"I did sense something weird when it came to you," Rafe finally told her.

She wiped her nose with her forearm and laughed. "Well, I'm a weird person, so..."

"I don't know how to explain it but...it finally makes sense now." He nodded. "*You* finally make sense."

Wren visibly relaxed. "I love you, Rafe. I want you to know that I've loved you from the moment I found out you were my brother." Her lip trembled. "Are you okay? Do you have any questions for me?"

He shook his head, seeming dazed. "Not right now. Maybe later I will."

All our eyes were on him. My heart felt heavy, but in a good way, in a relieved way.

He finally turned to me. "May I be excused?"

"Of course."

As he left the room, the three of us sat in silence for probably a full minute until Shannon broke the ice.

She smiled. "Well...I think that went...okay?"

I reached across the table for Wren's hand. Shannon's eyes landed on our intertwined fingers.

"I think it went as well as we could've hoped," I said. "He didn't seem upset that we'd kept it from him—that's a good thing. And I'd say his shocked reaction overall was to be expected."

"Yeah. I know that shocked feeling, thanks to you, Moody." Wren chuckled. "Kidding."

I reluctantly let go of her hand. "It's gonna be alright."

Shannon insisted on bringing out the beignets and poured coffee for us. Wren said she'd stop into Rafe's room on her way out. But before she had the chance, he came downstairs again. We turned to him as he stood in the entrance to the kitchen.

My eyes widened. "Hey."

He looked over at Wren. "I wanted to see if she was still here."

She put her beignet down and brushed the powdered sugar off her hands. "I am, buddy."

Rafe walked over to Wren—and hugged her. The trapped air I'd been holding in me since this morning felt like it finally released. Seeing them embrace felt surreal. It was...everything. *Thank you, God.*

"Thank you, Rafe," she whispered as she held on to him. "Thank you."

"I didn't want you to think I was mad. I'm not. I'm happy," he told her.

She shut her eyes tightly. "That means the world to me."

After a moment, they just stared at each other. I assumed Rafe might have been looking for signs of himself in her face. Whatever it was, it was simply awesome. The relief I felt was overwhelming. For a minute, I could breathe freely. Then the thought that Wren would be gone soon popped into my head, and I felt like I was choking all over again.

In the week after breaking the news to him, Wren took Rafe out for one-on-one time twice. They'd gone to the museum and to another bookstore she discovered. She was trying to make the most of the short time she had left here—one week and a day to be exact. *Not that I'm counting.* Other than that, Wren had been busy packing her stuff and getting ready to move. In the meantime, I'd done my best to immerse myself in work.

It was about 6 PM on a Friday night when Wren paid an unexpected visit to the house. I'd just gotten home from work and was about to pour myself a drink after a long day.

"Hey. I wasn't expecting you," I said as I opened the door, my heart hammering at the sight of her in a dress.

"I know. I was passing through Brookline on my way back from an appointment in Watertown. I thought I'd stop by and see Rafe."

"Damn. I'm sorry. Rafe went home with Shannon tonight. Bobby Jr. is home for the weekend, and Rafe wanted to do some gaming."

"Oh." She looked down at her feet. "I probably should've called first anyway." When she looked up at me, there was sadness in her eyes. I wished I could kiss it away.

"You okay?"

She shook her head. "Not really."

"Come inside. Come here." I pulled her into a hug. "Talk to me."

She spoke into my chest. "Am I making a mistake by leaving?" She looked up at me. "So much can happen in two years. Something could happen to my dad. And I'm missing those years with Rafe…"

Last-minute doubts sucked, but as scared as I was for her to leave, I was more afraid of her staying. I paused to settle myself. My advice needed to be objective and separate from my feelings or fears. "Only you can make that decision," I told her. "But I would say fear is never a good gauge. If the only reasons you have for not going are based on a fear of bad things that haven't happened, or that might happen, I'd say you should probably disregard them."

She wiped her eyes. "Yeah, I know you're right. I'm just getting a bit chicken now that the date is looming. I suppose I could also regret *not going* for the rest of my life."

"That's right."

I wanted her to stay, but I knew being alone together was a bad idea. We'd had our one night. Towing the line was over. But in a matter of days, she'd be gone… I thought up a compromise. "Are you hungry?"

Her expression brightened. "Yeah. A little."

"There's this Indian restaurant that just opened in town. I've been dying to try it. A friend owns it, actually. How about we go? It's within walking distance. It's a nice night for a walk."

She smiled. "That would be great, Moody."

The restaurant was only four blocks from my house. When we got there, they put us in a private corner. It helped to know the owner, especially since it was a packed Friday night, and we had no reservation.

The mood during dinner was fairly light, considering how things had started. We split an order of chicken tikka masala and aloo palak. The naan bread was warm and buttery, and the mango lassi drinks were delicious.

During the meal, Wren told me a bit about the area where she would be living—outside of Paris in Versailles. She'd been brushing up on her French, which she'd had two semesters of in college.

After a couple of hours, the line to get into the place was out the door, so we felt bad hogging the table. My dilemma continued because I didn't want to take her back to the house, but I wasn't ready to let her go yet.

"It's a nice night. Wanna take a walk?" I suggested.

"I feel like I could stand to walk off all this tikka." She smiled. "So, sure. Although...I don't know how far I can go in these shoes. I almost never wear heels, but for some reason I decided to be bold today."

Crap. "We don't have to walk, then."

"No, I want to," she insisted. "Let's just see how I do. I'll let you know if my feet start to hurt."

We left the restaurant and strolled through the center of town. After only a couple of blocks, I noticed her limping a little. That didn't take long.

"Okay, you're clearly not comfortable in those shoes. We should head back toward my house. Or if you prefer, I can go and come back with my car."

"No. I'll be okay." The sadness in her eyes when she showed up at my house tonight had returned. "I don't want to leave you. If we go back to my car, I need to go home. Because I know I shouldn't go inside with you. So we need to keep walking."

That broke my heart. She was willing to hurt her freaking feet just to spend time with me. But her feelings echoed my own. If her feet weren't hurting, I wouldn't have cared if we walked to downtown Boston and back tonight. After several seconds of ruminating, I got a brilliant idea.

"You know what? There's a park not terribly far from here where we can sit and talk. We just have to get you there."

She perked up. "Let's go."

"I'm not letting you walk in those shoes anymore, though."

"What do you suggest?" She laughed. "That I go barefoot on the grimy sidewalk?"

Without thinking any further, I wrapped my arms around her and scooped her up, causing her to squeal in laughter.

"You've always swept me off my feet, Moody. But *this* is taking it to a whole new level."

"You're even lighter than I thought." I winked.

"Seriously, thank you."

As I carried her, I tried not to look in her eyes, knowing if I did, I'd be tempted to take her mouth. My heart was going a mile a minute the entire walk to the park.

When we arrived, I put her down in front of one of the benches.

"Remind me to wear these shoes again if it means getting a free ride like that."

"Don't get *carried* away," I teased.

We leaned our backs against the bench and looked up at the evening sky. The park was empty, so we had it all to ourselves.

"Thanks again for taking me out," she said. "Pretty sad that our first actual date is under these circumstances." She looked at me to gauge my reaction. "I'm kidding. I know it wasn't a date—even if it felt like it."

For some reason, that realization hit me in the feels. We'd been through a lot together. Yet until tonight, we'd never actually been *out* together. That seemed crazy. And no, this wasn't a date. It was more. Everything with her felt like more.

"I guess everything's been ass backwards with us, huh?" I said.

There was that sadness in her eyes again. "Can I be honest about something?" she asked.

"Of course."

"Even though we've been keeping our distance these last couple of weeks, I'm still struggling with my feelings for you. It's a bigger part of my not wanting to leave than I might be letting on."

That wasn't something I wanted to hear. She deserved my honesty, too. But if I told her I was also struggling, it would only add fuel to the fire of her doubt. When I didn't say anything, she continued.

"I keep thinking about our night together, how it felt to sleep next to you in your bed. I don't know that there's any place I could travel that beats that." She took a slow breath in and let it out. "I know why I have to ignore these feelings, but it feels very unnatural."

I looked up at the dark night sky and then turned to her. "I've been struggling, too." It felt good to let it out, even if I didn't plan on elaborating.

She kept looking at me like she was waiting for more, more of an explanation of my feelings. I could've told her I'd never felt about anyone the way I felt about her. That she's the only person I felt comfortable opening up to. How I dreaded worrying about whether or not she'd be safe in a new, strange place so far away. But I had to continue to remind myself that Rafe's well-being and mental health took priority. Wren getting to live her life and not being tied down right now took priority. And protecting her from my inability to be a good long-term partner also fell somewhere into the equation.

She interrupted my thoughts. "Promise me something, Moody."

I raised my brow. "I guess I have to know what it is first."

"Promise me you won't waste your time anymore with someone who doesn't deserve you—like that bimbo who messaged about your dick." She rolled her eyes. "It's hard for me to accept that my leaving will mark the end of whatever this is between us." She let out a shaky breath. "Was it a relationship? A fling? Playing with fire? I don't even know, but I *do* know it will be over soon. So I'm really grateful for this extra time with you tonight. And I want to make sure you know that you *do* deserve love, Dax. I don't care what your family's actions led you to believe. Or what you feel like you deserve because you made some mistakes in your marriage and never had the chance to make things right. You're not responsible for what happened to Maren, either."

Her words weren't quite enough to permeate the thick cloud of self-loathing I'd built around myself. But I appreciated that she tried. "I hear you." I nodded. "I wish it could sink in easier. I wish I could promise you I'll eventually see myself the way you do. But I can promise you I'll try."

She reached for my hand. I brought her fingers to my mouth and kissed them. I just couldn't help it.

"I'm sure you'll meet someone there…" I paused to acknowledge the hurt in my chest. "And I don't know, maybe you'll fall in love. That's what they do in France, right?" I forced a smile. "I guess what I want you to promise *me* is that you won't let what happened between us fuck that up for you. I want you to forget about me. Maybe that sounds egotistical to assume I carry that much weight in your head and in your heart. But I feel it. I somehow feel what you feel for me. I know you truly care about me. Quite frankly, I don't know if anyone else in this world cares about me the same way." It was hard to say what came next. "I want you to try to release it. Because I don't want it to be a barrier to your happiness."

Her eyes turned glossy with tears. "You *are* my happiness right now. And my greatest pain. It sucks. But I wouldn't trade a second of our secret."

"Neither would I," I said.

She inhaled deeply and stood up from the bench. "We actually *should* get going."

What? "Already?"

"Yeah. I changed my mind. I think it's better." She shook her head. "Because I feel like I'm falling for you all over again tonight. I need to go home and undo some of that."

I felt her words deep in my chest. "*My happiness… and my greatest pain.*" Every second spent with her always made me want her more. And any progress I'd thought I'd made in forgetting these feelings was erased any time I was around her again. It was a hamster wheel of incessant wanting.

"Well, then…" I stood. "Your carriage awaits, Ms. Mc-Callister." I scooped her up off her feet.

I carried her all the way back to where her car was parked outside my house. The walk with her in my arms was serene yet emotional. No words were necessary.

It felt like goodbye.

Once we got back to my house, we stood facing each other on the sidewalk in front of her car.

"What time is your flight on the twenty-ninth?" I asked.

"It's at 8 PM, but I have to be there a few hours earlier. My dad is actually going to be gone that day because he has to help my grandmother move into an assisted-living facility up in New Hampshire. It was just bad timing. So I'll say goodbye to him in the morning and take the train to the airport."

That didn't sit right with me. She was leaving for two years, and no one was going to see her off? No fucking way.

"I'll take you."

She blinked. "Are you sure?"

"Of course. Traffic can be a bitch at that time with everyone heading into the city to go out on Saturday night, so I'll come over to your place a little early. We'll get you to the airport in plenty of time."

She looked like she was ready to cry. "That means a lot, Moody. Thank you."

"Believe me, after everything? It's the *least* I can do."

CHAPTER 15

Wren

On the Friday evening before my departure day, my emotions were all over the place. I tried to bury them by putting all of my energy into packing.

Dax was working late, so he wasn't home when I arrived at his house to say goodbye to Rafe.

Shannon answered the door.

"Hey, Shannon." I hugged her.

She squeezed me. "I sure am gonna miss you, Wren. It won't be the same."

"I'm gonna miss you, too." I knelt to pet Winston, and he rolled onto his side for me to rub his belly. "And figures, this guy is finally starting to like me right when I have to leave. I'll miss you the most, you fluffernutter."

Shannon always looked like she was holding back saying something. She knew about Dax and me, so it was always a little awkward around her. But I was glad Dax had her as a sounding board, happy that she was someone he could trust and talk to.

I looked toward the stairs. "Is Rafe in his room?"

"Yeah. He knows you're coming to say goodbye."

I headed upstairs and knocked on Rafe's door, which was open.

He removed his earbuds. "Hey."

The room smelled like Cheetos and sweaty socks. I moved some notebooks to the side and sat at the edge of his bed. "How are you?"

He shrugged. "Okay…"

"I can't believe I have to say goodbye to you tonight."

He frowned. "I know."

"We're gonna talk on Zoom a lot, okay? I'll turn my camera around some of the time and show you France. It'll be like you're there with me."

"That'll be cool."

"Are you sure you're okay?" I asked him.

He shrugged, his expression sullen. "I guess. It just sucks that you're leaving."

"I know," I whispered.

"When do you come back?"

"Well, I don't have an exact day. I don't know how I'll feel in two years, but I'm pretty sure I'll be coming home the first chance I get. So maybe around two years from next week? Mark your calendar now." I smiled. "I hope it's okay that I asked my dad to come visit you for me from time to time, since I can't be here in person."

"That's fine. Your dad's nice."

"Promise me you'll be good for Dax. He's trying. I know you don't always get along with him, but he cares so much about you."

"He's alright," Rafe muttered.

I chuckled. *Yeah, he is.*

I looked over at a sketch on his desk. I couldn't believe my eyes. He'd drawn the spitting image of Dax in pencil.

I went over to it, lifting the paper. "Did you do this?"

"Yeah."

The angular jaw, the perfect nose, the magnetic eyes... It was spot on.

"Rafe, this is unbelievable."

He tried to downplay it. "It's okay, I guess."

"How did I not realize you could draw like this?"

"I don't show many people."

"Dax has never seen this?"

"No."

"You need to show him."

"No way. I don't want him to know I drew him."

"Why not?"

"Because it's creepy."

"It's not creepy at all."

"I've drawn you, too."

My mouth curved into a smile. "No way. Can I see?"

He walked over to his desk and opened a folder that contained drawings of several people, many of whom I assumed were classmates. Then he turned to a sketch of me. Just like the one of Dax, it was strikingly lifelike. It was like looking in the mirror.

"Oh my God. You've got to let me have this. I want to put it in a frame and hang it in my apartment in France."

He shrugged. "Take it, if you want."

I looked through all of the illustrations. There was even one of Shannon. Then I returned to my favorite—the one of Dax. I looked back and forth between that one and the drawing of me, feeling overwhelmed with love. Once again, doubts about leaving crept in. Everything I loved was here. Rafe. My dad. Dax.

Dax.

I loved Dax. I knew it in my heart, but this was the first time I'd admitted it to myself.

I held up the drawing of Dax. "Can I have this one, too?"

"Why would you want that?" he asked.

Fair question. "I just think it's really good."

"Yeah. Okay. Whatever. Just don't show it to him."

"I won't." I tucked the two drawings into an empty manila folder Rafe had laying on his desk.

I sat again on the edge of his bed. "I think we should have a regular time every week to talk. What's good for you?"

"I have to check my schedule."

"Are you serious?"

"No." He laughed.

I loved this kid. He'd come such a long way—from not talking at all to a total ball buster.

After spending two hours hanging out with him, I finally hugged my brother goodbye, one of the hardest things I'd ever done. My gut told me this was only the tip of the iceberg, though; and tomorrow would be even harder.

Nothing could've prepared me for how I felt the following afternoon—the day of my departure. After a long and tearful goodbye with my father before he left for New Hampshire this morning, I'd been alone and basically panicking.

All of my stuff was packed, but I felt frozen and unable to perform simple tasks. Case in point, I'd taken off my toenail polish last night and had spent forty-five minutes of precious time today trying to decide on a new color. Then when I finally selected one, my hands were trembling, so I couldn't even paint my toes. Thank goodness I didn't have any more packing to do in this state of mind. I would've never finished.

My phone rang. It was Dax.

"Hey," I burst into tears upon answering.

"Hey, I—" He paused. "Are you crying?"

The phone shook in my hands. "I don't know what's wrong with me, Dax. I'm freaking out."

"Take a deep breath."

"I've been unable to make the simplest decisions, ever since I said goodbye to my dad." I sniffled. "And have I mentioned I've never even flown before? Now is not the opportune time to discover I have a fear of flying."

He stepped right into action. "I'll come over now. Okay?"

"Yes," I said without hesitation, as if he'd thrown me a life raft.

"I'll be there in twenty minutes."

I hung up and cried even harder. I slid to the ground and sat in the same spot against the wall until the doorbell rang.

I forced myself up to answer the door.

The sight of Dax standing there made my heart flutter.

"C'mere," he said, taking me into his strong arms.

"I don't know what's wrong with me," I cried.

Dax caressed my hair. "You're scared. That's all." He pulled back to look at me. "Despite your fear, you *do* want this, right?"

I want it, but I want you more. I nodded. "I do want it. I just wasn't expecting it to feel like this."

He looked down, noticing droplets of red paint on a couple of my toes—my attempt at a pedicure.

His eyes went wide. "Is your toe bleeding?"

"No. I tried to paint my toenails, but my hands were shaking so I couldn't finish."

"Where's the nail polish?"

"In my room."

He took my hand and led me up the stairs. "Come on."

Dazed and confused, I followed him into my bedroom. He spotted the nail polish on my desk and grabbed it.

"Lie down," he said.

I sat on my bed and leaned against the headboard. Dax sat farther down the bed with his back against the wall at my feet. He pulled my legs over his and opened the bottle. I watched in awe as he carefully began painting my toes. It was the most tender, precious thing anyone had ever done for me.

"Have you ever done this before?" I asked.

"Never." He smiled.

"You're not bad."

"Well, when you open your spa someday and need a manicurist, you can let me know." He winked.

"That would be a sight for sore eyes." I laughed—the first time I'd laughed all day. "Thank you for coming to my rescue, Moody."

He painted a few more strokes. "I'm not gonna lie. I've been struggling all morning, too."

"Yeah," I whispered.

The rest of the painting session was quiet. I sat back, trying to tame my nerves while watching this beautiful man concentrate.

After finishing my last nail, he closed the bottle and blew on my toes. It was adorable and made me love him even more—though I couldn't tell him that. He then massaged the balls of my feet.

"Is this a role reversal, you massaging me?"

"Just trying to calm you down."

"It feels good. Thank you."

He kneaded the bottom of my foot. "You're all packed and ready to go?"

"Yeah. Thankfully I had the foresight to get it done early, given how scatterbrained I feel right now."

He applied a bit more pressure. "You have the right to feel however you feel."

"Like my heart is being ripped out?"

"Even that." He stopped massaging and looked up at me. I could see the sadness in his expression.

"I can see it in your eyes, Moody. Even if you're trying to be tough about this, your eyes don't lie. And honestly, I can *feel* it. I can feel how much you don't want me to go, even if you can't say it. I think it's why I'm so fucked up. I'm sorry. I know I'm supposed to be strong and not talk about us anymore..."

He shook his head. "It's okay. Say what you want."

I might've taken that liberty a little too far, but I took him at his word.

"I want to feel you inside me," I murmured. "It's all I want."

He shut his eyes as if my words stung.

It wasn't fair of me to have blurted that when I damn well knew *why* we couldn't go there. But I couldn't hold it in. I ached for him. If this was the last moment of our secret, I had to let him know. My voice was barely audible. "I'm sorry."

"No. Don't be. You've apologized enough for an issue that's not yours to bear alone. There's nothing more I want..." He hesitated. "...than to be inside of you right now. I want you so fucking much it hurts."

"What if we give in just this once? Then never speak of it again once I leave. He'll never have to know."

He let out a slightly angry laugh. "That would be the death of me."

I thought it was going to end there, but then he spoke again.

"But pretty sure I'm willing to die if it means getting to have you even once." His eyes burned into mine as his chest rose and fell.

When his words actually registered, every inch of my body became engulfed in arousal. Any further analytical thinking I might have done ended the moment he lifted me onto him, wrapping his arms around me and kissing me with everything he had.

"I've never needed anything more than I need you right now, Wren."

This is really happening.

He flipped me around to lie under him. My body was on fire. I'd dreamed so many times of being in this position, pinned beneath him. Gripping his hair, I pulled him into my body, and he pressed his lips to mine. We fell into a passionate kiss, breaths ragged, limbs writhing, totally lost in each other with no fucks left to give.

I wrapped my legs around his back as he pressed his cock against my clit through his jeans, grinding against me as I bucked my hips.

"Fuck me, Dax," I begged. "Please. I need you inside me."

He nodded. "Not gonna stop it this time."

A second later, I felt his hand slide my pants down before he lowered my panties. I worked to unbuckle his belt as fast as humanly possible and pushed his jeans lower. He suddenly froze as he panted against my neck. "I don't have anything, Wren."

I reached over to my side-table drawer and fumbled around until I found one of the condoms that had been in there for...let's just say, a long time. I'd certainly learned from my past mistakes and always had condoms in my possession, even if I wasn't currently sexually active. You never knew when you'd need them.

"I've got you," I said, handing him the condom.

I watched with great interest as he took it and ripped the package open before sliding it over his engorged cock.

He hovered over me. "Promise you won't hate me for this."

My eyes must have looked like daggers. "I'll hate you if you stop."

He lowered himself down. "I'm so fucking weak," he groaned before spreading my legs and sinking inside. It burned as he stretched me. But no amount of fleeting pain could surpass the intense pleasure of feeling him enter me. He closed his eyes briefly the moment he was balls deep.

Then he began moving in and out, fucking me rhythmically the way I'd always dreamed about. And it was ecstasy. I had no idea just how badly I'd needed it until he was actually inside me. Now I couldn't imagine how I was planning to have lived life without ever having experienced this.

"Please don't stop," I begged when he paused.

"I just need a second," he gasped.

I watched his face as he tried to compose himself and regain control.

A few moments later, he resumed thrusting, harder than before. The bed kept banging against the wall, and he looked into my eyes the entire time. I loved it. I wasn't used to that during sex. It seemed like he was trying to see inside my soul, maybe needing to burn this experience into his memory.

Because this was the first and last time. We both knew it. That fact was just as unnerving as it was beautiful.

His thick cock filled me in a way I'd never been filled before. I pulsed around him, digging my teeth into his shoulder as I struggled to contain my orgasm; I was ready to explode at any moment.

"You're incredible," he muttered as he moved his cock out slowly before thrusting all the way in again. "I wish I could stay inside you forever, but I need to come, Wren."

"Fuck me as hard as you can, one last time before you let go."

"You sure?" He panted.

"Yes. I want to feel you tomorrow when we're not together anymore."

Dax smiled over my lips and took my words to heart as he sped up his movements, pounding into me with even greater force. I'd never been fucked so hard; I thought the bed might break. Each raspy breath that escaped him matched the rhythm of his thrusts, and every nerve ending in my body tingled. I struggled to prolong this for as long as possible, yet I screamed in pleasure at one point, so close to losing it. He must have thought he'd hurt me.

He slowed. "Are you okay?"

"Yes."

"Am I being too rough?"

"No. Keep going. Don't stop."

I kissed him harder and gripped his hair, never wanting to let him go, dreading the end of this. But the clock was ticking. There wouldn't be time for an encore.

"I love you. I love you. I love you," I thought to myself with each thrust. And then I just couldn't hold it in. My eyes widened as I felt my orgasm beginning to ricochet through me. Dax must have felt it, too, because his body shook shortly thereafter, as if he'd been waiting for the moment he could let go. I felt the heat of his cum fill me through the condom, and he pumped into me with greater force, pushing out the remainder of his load as he groaned, his voice echoing through my room—a beautiful sound I'd never forget.

It would haunt me forever.

CHAPTER 16

Dax

The guilt I'd expected never came as I lay next to her. I kept waiting for regret to seep in, too, but no part of me regretted what just happened. No part of me wished I could take it back. Lying here felt like the aftermath of a beautiful storm, where you might have been expecting destruction, but instead there was nothing but the sun peeking out again—a deep appreciation for what I'd experienced.

I did wish she wasn't leaving, that I could hold her until the sun went down tonight and never let her go. But nope, not guilt. Maybe it would come later, and I would deal with it then.

"You look lost in thought," she said, running her fingers through my hair. "Are you okay?"

"Yeah. I am." I kissed her neck. "You?"

"I'm remarkably calm," she said. "It seems *you* were what I needed all along."

"I know the feeling." I leaned in to kiss her, cherishing the feel of her naked body pressed against mine. "I'll never forget this."

She ran her finger along my chin. "You know what I realized?"

"What?"

"I never played for you. I promised I would before I left." She slipped out from under the covers.

I admired her beautiful body as she walked to the corner of the room and took her cello out of the case. She pulled up a chair and positioned herself behind the instrument.

I sat up, leaning against the headboard. "Well, this is certainly not how I'd imagined it, but you won't hear me complaining."

She launched into "The Swan," the song she knew was my favorite. As always, I became lost in the hypnotic trance of her musical talent. Her playing naked, just for me, was beautiful—another part of this day I'd never forget. It was quite literally our swan song.

The strange tension in my chest grew with every minute that passed as she continued to play. I knew this was *it*. This was the feeling I'd thought I'd never feel, that I hadn't thought I was capable of. This was what I'd wanted to feel for Maren but couldn't. It wasn't something you could create or control. It was utter passion and intoxication. Utter wanting. And utter pain with the knowledge that I couldn't have Wren, despite my feelings.

Making love to her had pushed me even closer to the edge, yet I was still not able to take the leap. The longing seemed unbearable now. Would it eventually fade? I didn't know.

When she stopped playing, I got up from the bed, still naked myself, and knelt before her. I rested my cheek against her abdomen and kissed her skin. She threaded her fingers through my hair, and we just sat. I wondered if she could sense all of the feelings inside of me.

"I'll never forget this day," she said.

"Me neither, beautiful. Me neither." I finally lifted my head and cupped her cheek.

She looked over at the clock. "We have to leave. I want you again. And again. But there's no time left."

I stood. "Maybe it's better that we've run out of time. It's probably the only way we'd stop."

She nodded. She turned to put her cello back into the case and then picked up her clothes off the floor. I stopped her for a moment and pulled her to me, placing a firm kiss on her lips and cherishing the silkiness of her skin so I never forgot what it felt like. She sighed into my mouth, and after a minute, I let her go. I watched as she got dressed, and I reluctantly did the same.

The mood soon switched from emotional to downright morose. I wanted time to stand still, and I also wanted these minutes of sweet torture to pass so we could be put out of our misery.

We barely said a word as I packed her suitcases into my trunk. A postal service truck was parked across the street, which reminded me that today was business as usual for seemingly everyone else but us. I told myself the current quiet was better than if she were in tears or upset like earlier.

Traffic, as expected, was a bitch. I put on some classical music and held her hand the entire way to Logan Airport. The feeling of dread grew with each mile that passed. I kept second-guessing everything—as if there was a decision to make. There wasn't. A relationship with Rafe's sister would never be an option. Inevitably hurting her and him would *never* be an option. So I needed to stop the voice in my head that kept telling me I was making a huge mistake in letting her go, that there was still time to tell her how I felt, turn around, and take her home.

The voice retreated in defeat as the signs for the airport gates began to appear.

"I'll park and go in with you?" I suggested.

"I would prefer it if you didn't," she said. "That would only make things harder at this point."

I nodded. Prolonging this goodbye wasn't going to help either of us. After I pulled up to the airport drop-off area and parked, I reached into my glove compartment and took out a rectangular box. I handed it to her. "Keep this in your travel bag. Be very careful with it, but don't open it until you get to your apartment in France."

Her eyes watered. "Okay."

Forcing myself out, I walked around to her side and opened the passenger door before heading to the back of the car to lift her bags out of the trunk.

As we faced each other on the curb, I wiped the tear forming in her eye.

"Promise me something, Moody," she said.

"Anything."

"Promise you won't beat yourself up for what we did today, after it all sinks in later. Because it will."

I wrapped my hands around her face and looked into her eyes. "I will never regret what we did today. You hear me? Never." I held her close and felt her heart thundering against my chest. "Jesus, your heart."

"Better than the alternative." She sniffled. "I feel like if it stops beating it would break."

I made myself step back. "You'll feel better once you're there."

"I really hope so." She looked down at the time. "I have to go." She shook her head as she stared down at her shoes. "Not saying goodbye. Too painful. Just gonna walk away."

"I understand, beautiful. No goodbye." Tears welled in my eyes.

Wren laughed through her tears. "Thanks again for painting my toenails."

I forced a smile, fighting like hell not to cry.

She moved out of my reach, but I couldn't let her go without one last kiss. I stopped her, took her mouth in mine, and breathed her in one last time, hoping to burn everything about her into memory. This wonderful thing we'd experienced over the past eight months had just come to an end.

This time, when she broke away from me, I let her go. As she moved toward the airport sliding doors, my heart was in a chokehold.

The doors opened for her, and I watched her walk away until she was out of sight.

PART TWO

Two-and-a-half years later

CHAPTER 17

Wren

L ife in Versailles had been everything I'd hoped for and
more. Rich in history and known for the 17th-centu-
ry palace of Versailles, built by Louis the XIV, Versailles
was today a touristy residential area not far from Paris.
My apartment was less than a mile from the school where
I taught music to middle-school students. Middle school
here was known as le collége. Students of this age were
great to teach, always so curious, and not yet old enough
that they weren't easily impressed.

Over the past two-and-a-half years, I'd made many
new friends, casually dated some handsome French men,
and eaten the most amazing food. I'd connected with my
students and been invited into their homes many times for
fabulous dinners—always with amazing bread. But probably the best thing that happened during my time overseas
was the bond I'd developed with my brother. Rafe and I
had video-chatted once a week on Sunday evenings. He
was sixteen now, thriving in school, and he had a girlfriend. From what he'd told me, his relationship with Dax

was still a work in progress, but it was leaps and bounds better than it had been when I'd first met them. And Shannon was also still a big part of their lives.

So why, after more than two years, wasn't I back in the States as planned? I guess you could say it was fear of reality. My dad really wanted me to come home, but he hadn't pressured me. And other than him and Rafe, there wasn't anything back in Boston waiting for me. Dad had visited me here recently, which took the edge off of missing him and added to the feeling of not being in such a rush to go back. While I knew I had to return to the States at some point, I hadn't been as eager as I once imagined I'd be. At the moment, I was buying a little more time here. Maybe I'd stay another year. Maybe I'd change my mind and come home in six months. The point was, I had options and flexibility. The school where I worked had agreed to keep me on indefinitely, though I was now working out of my contract. My apartment lease was also month to month.

Honestly, though, above everything, there was one major reason I hadn't rushed to go home. And that was Dax.

I hated to admit that I was still hung up on him after all this time. I wished I were a stronger person, but I wasn't. About six months ago, Rafe had told me Dax's relationship with a woman named Morgan seemed to be getting serious. She'd been spending the night at their house a lot on weekends, he said. My response to such news, or anything Rafe ever had to say about Dax, was always nonchalant, so as not to tip him off in any way.

Of course, Rafe had no reason to think telling me about Dax's girlfriend would have been earth-shattering news, since he'd never known about Dax and me. And I couldn't ask him not to give me information, so I just died a little inside anytime Rafe mentioned something. But it was all to be expected. What was Dax supposed to do? Remain celibate for the rest of his life? He and I had agreed to end things, and to go on with our lives. None of this should've come as a surprise after more than two damn years.

Dax and I had kept in occasional contact for a while, mostly via email at the beginning. I'd even told him when I'd started dating. But our communications had faded over time. My information now came through Rafe. And it worked both ways. I knew Rafe probably passed information back to Dax as well.

Things were as they should be. So, again, the news of his relationship getting serious shouldn't have been a big deal, but it was. It was all I'd been able to think about. And it was the thing that kept me here.

I knew I'd face the fire back in Boston eventually, but I wasn't ready.

The day I'd arrived in Versailles two-and-a-half years ago, the first thing I did when I got to my apartment was open the box Dax had given me at the airport. Given the shape, I'd suspected maybe it was a necklace. Boy, was I wrong. Inside was a boatload of French currency that equated to twenty-thousand US dollars, along with a note.

*I knew you would never agree to take this unless
I snuck it on board with you at the last minute.
This should cover your groceries for two years.
If you feel even remotely guilty for accepting it,*

*don't. Consider this compensation for the joy
you brought me every single second we were
together. You can't put a price on that. I want
to take the edge off of any stress you might be
feeling about supporting yourself while you're
there. I know they're not paying you a ton, and
I promise this is just a drop in the bucket for me.
So let me do this for you. Thank you.*

*Also, I hope you arrived safely and are already
loving it there.*

XO Dax

*P.S. I'm missing your 25th birthday on June 3.
You never mentioned it, but Rafe told me. If it
helps, consider this an early birthday gift.*

That box of cash had already been stashed in Dax's
glove compartment when he arrived at my house to take
me to the airport. So when he'd written that note, he'd had
no idea what would transpire between us—that we would
lose control and have sex in the eleventh hour. I still cherished the memory of what would always be our sacred secret.

When I'd first moved away, Dax would leave comments on some of my RenCello videos. That's how I knew
he still watched. And that made playing all the more emotional for me. But the comments had stopped about a year
ago. And I sensed he wasn't watching at all anymore. Maybe that had coincided with meeting *her*, though I couldn't
be sure.

I hadn't expected to keep in contact with Dax indefinitely. We both knew that would make it too hard to cut the cord. And now that I knew his and Rafe's relationship had flourished in my absence, I was more certain than ever that we'd made the right decision. But the *right* decision isn't always in line with your heart's deepest desires. My heart still beat faster whenever Rafe said Dax's name, or whenever I snuck a peek at Rafe's drawing of him. It was now tucked away in a notebook in my drawer. I didn't have a single photo of Dax besides that drawing. Two-and-a-half years had gone by without seeing his face, but my heart's reaction to the memory of it hadn't waned.

One Tuesday afternoon, my good friend Micheline had come over for tea after I got home from teaching. She lived in the apartment a couple of doors down.

"Are we going out to dinner tonight?" she asked.

"Sure. 6 PM?" I winked, knowing that was way too early for her.

"I'll just be waking up from my nap at six." She laughed.

The very first time Micheline and I made plans to go out, shortly after we'd met, I'd suggested meeting at six in the evening. She'd informed me that standard dinnertime in France was more like 8 PM. Back home, Dad and I were always done eating by seven. At first, eating after eight had seemed so late, but I'd since gotten used to it.

When she'd finished her tea, Micheline kissed me on both cheeks. "I'll meet you back here later?"

"Sounds good."

I watched as she left, her long, black hair swaying from the breeze that came in through the open apartment windows.

Since I had some time to kill before dinner, I decided to sit out on my balcony with a book. I'd been reading more since moving here, and I preferred thrillers lately. Sitting out on the balcony gave me an elevated view of the street below, and I loved listening to the kids playing and music in the distance from a neighbor who practiced bagpipes down the road. Sometimes I'd take my cello out and play alongside him, but today I'd just enjoy the bagpipes from afar with my book.

Just as I'd settled into the chair, my phone rang. I looked down at the screen to find it was Rafe calling.

Rafe?

There were a couple of things wrong with this scenario. Number one, he and I only ever talked via video chat. Number two, we mainly spoke on Sundays, aside from last week on Thanksgiving. It was not like him to call me in the middle of the week. *Something's happened back home.*

My heart sank as I answered. "Rafe? Is everything okay?"

He let out a deep breath. "Not really."

I placed my hand over my heart. "What's wrong?"

There was a long, uncomfortable silence. My terror grew as my mind raced to imagine what might have happened.

"Why did you never tell me about you and Dax?" Rafe finally asked.

Shock closed my throat. I tried to catch my breath for a moment. "What?" My stomach churned, and my vision went blurry. "What are you talking about?"

"You and Dax," he repeated slowly, as if I hadn't heard him the first time.

My heart pounded as I went back inside the apartment. "What about me and Dax?"

"You're gonna make me say it?"

"Well, I need to know what you're talking about."

"You were a thing. You had sex. All that shit. What the fuck? How the hell did I not know?"

The room started to spin. How the hell *did* he know? Did Dax tell him? No way he did. No way in hell.

I kept my questions as generic as possible. "Where are you getting this information?"

"First admit it, and then I'll tell you."

Tears sprung to my eyes. I was frozen. I couldn't lie to him, but I didn't want to betray Dax, either.

I raised my voice. "I'm not saying a damn thing until you tell me where you got this information, Rafe."

"I read his journal."

Oh. Oh my heart. "Why?" My voice trembled. "Why would you do that?"

"I swear, I didn't mean to. I went to his bedside drawer to steal a condom before I went over to Kelsey's house. I saw this cigar box. I was going to snag a cigar and smoke it. But there were no cigars inside. There was just a notebook in there. I opened to one of the pages to see what it was, and the first thing I saw was your name. So I kept reading. I read the whole damn thing."

All I could think to say was, "You're having sex?"

"Are you seriously trying to change the subject on me?"

"I'm sorry." I shut my eyes tightly. "I'm so sorry, Rafe."

"Sorry for what?"

His question confused me. I had lots of reasons to be sorry. Especially since I didn't know how explicit the journal was. I needed to assume the worst in that regard. He knew we'd had sex. Couldn't get much worse than that, I suppose.

The phone shook in my hand. "What happened between Dax and me started before I knew who you were. I just...fell for him really hard. It had nothing to do with his role in your life. We connected as individuals. But we thought it best not to continue things because we didn't want to hurt you."

"He was in love with you."

My heart did somersaults. "What...what are you talking about?"

"The last entry in the journal was the day you left. He wrote about how much he loved you, how it was killing him to let you go. But he had to." He paused. "He never wrote anything again after that day. That was the last entry."

I shut my eyes and breathed into the phone for several seconds. I didn't want this information as the result of such a violation of privacy. But if there was one thing I wanted to know, it was that. *Dax loved me?* I'd always imagined that he cared deeply for me, but I would have never categorized it as love. I loved *him*. That was for certain. To know those feelings were returned was mind-blowing.

But then the guilt set in, because neither Rafe nor I was supposed to be privy to this information. I shook my head. "Don't tell me anything else. Neither of us has a right to know what he wrote in there."

Rafe sounded panicked. "He can't *ever* know I read it, Wren. He'd kill me."

"He was so scared to hurt you, Rafe. I can't stress that enough. You were always our priority. That's why we ended things as soon as I—"

"Wait, is that why you left and went to France?"

I swallowed.

Was it? On some level? I would've stayed if Dax had asked me to. If things were different. I'd wanted this European adventure, but not as much as I'd wanted Dax. Since I couldn't have him, being apart was easier than having to face that.

"I wanted this experience. But separating from Dax at the time was a benefit of my leaving. It kept some distance between us once we'd decided to end things."

He was silent for a long time.

"Tell me what you're thinking, Rafe."

"I don't know what to think, to be honest. It's fucked up. It's not like it hurts me or anything. I just find it... weird." He paused. "Did you love him, too?"

Too.

I didn't have to think about my answer. "I did love him, yes. But I never told him."

"Why not?"

"Because it wouldn't have mattered. He wouldn't have considered being with me because, again, he was too afraid to hurt you." I exhaled. "So was I."

"Why would it have hurt me, though?"

"Because he sees you as a son. He's responsible for your well-being. And I'm your sister. If something had gone wrong between him and me, we'd have to remain in each other's lives. It would've made things awkward for everyone."

"But you're in each other's lives anyway. Now you have to see him with someone else when you come back. That's not awkward? That's gonna suck for you. When I told you about Morgan, I didn't know about you and him. I wouldn't have said anything to upset you if I knew."

"I know," I whispered. "It's okay." I shook my head. "Anyway, it's over between him and me, so it doesn't matter what you tell me."

"You don't care about him anymore?"

I tried to downplay it. "Like I said, it doesn't matter, Rafe. It's been over two-and-a-half years."

"How could you love someone just a couple of years ago and not care about them anymore?"

"Rafe..." I sniffled. I'd tried to stop the tears from falling. But I couldn't.

"You liar. You *do* still love him." Rafe exhaled. "Holy shit."

"He's moved on, Rafe. We both have."

"*You* haven't," he shouted.

"I still have feelings for him, yes. But it doesn't matter."

"Stop saying it doesn't matter and using me as an excuse. Don't forget, I read everything in that journal. You can't lie to me. I know what happened. I know *everything*."

Jesus Christ. How graphic was that journal? I was too damn afraid to ask. But if he said he knew *everything*, I suppose it was pointless to downplay things any longer.

"I think you should come home," he said.

A flash of panic hit. "Why?"

"Because things are getting serious between him and Morgan. If he marries her, it's gonna be too late."

A wave of nausea overtook me. "If he's happy, I don't want to disrupt that."

Dax had been through so much. He deserved peace. He deserved happiness. He didn't deserve me coming in and complicating his life just because I was jealous.

"He's only with her because he thinks he can never have you," my brother said.

Hope filled me until I realized that wasn't necessarily true. Rafe didn't know that. He was making an assumption based on Dax's feelings from over two years ago, feelings that had likely long expired.

"People can change, Rafe. His feelings for her could be stronger than his feelings for me. You said he didn't write anything after the day I left. You don't know how he's feeling now. He might care about her more than he ever cared about me."

"Well, he didn't feel the need to write it all down. So how special can it be?"

I hated that his point made sense to me. My voice was barely audible as I wiped my eyes. "Rafe..."

"Whatever. Ignore me. Ignore all of this if you want. But I had to tell you. Because I can't tell him I know. I don't want him to ever know I read it."

As much as Dax cared for Rafe, my brother was always a little afraid of him. A part of Rafe always felt like Dax had no reason to stick around and care for him. So he never wanted to mess things up. It was something he'd had to work on in therapy—his fear of abandonment. I could understand his worry about upsetting Dax, even if it was unfounded.

"What is it I'm supposed to be doing if I go back, Rafe? Breaking up his relationship? I would never want to cause trouble for him. You're not telling him you violated his privacy, so he won't know you know. He'd never consider leaving someone he currently cares about for someone from the past he believes he can't be with. Think about it, Rafe."

"Well, if he really cares about her, you coming home shouldn't matter, right?"

"Exactly. Which is why I should just stay here for now."

"Maybe I want you to come home. Have you ever thought about that?"

My heart felt ready to burst. "Really? That's a different story. You've never said that before. You want me to come back?"

"Well, yeah, it would be nice. I barely knew you were my sister, and then you left. I feel closer to you now than I did then, but it's not the same as you being here. It would be nice to see you before I, like, go away to college after next year. Then that's another four years apart."

I hadn't thought about that. If my brother was asking me to come home, that was a gamechanger for me. I needed to at least consider it. "I didn't know you felt so strongly about it," I told him. "I thought you were okay with me being here."

"I *am* okay with it. But...I also miss you. I'm not exactly gonna be mad if you come back."

I smiled. "Well, okay, you've given me a lot to think about."

"Yeah, unfortunately, I have a lot to think about, too, after that shit I read. I wish I could erase it from my head."

I cringed. "Please try. You were never meant to read his private thoughts. No one should read anyone else's journal—not while the person is still alive, anyway." I swallowed. "Also, when did you start having sex?"

He sighed. "It's new."

"Does Dax know?"

"He had the sex talk with me when he found out I was dating Kelsey. So I think he might know. But I haven't told him I actually did it."

I felt he was too young at sixteen, but it would've been hypocritical of me to criticize him since I'd had sex by that age.

"Well, I'm glad you're being careful. Please use protection each and every time. You have no idea the trouble you could get into. Promise me you'll always be careful, Rafe."

"I will."

Someday I'd tell him what had happened to me as a teenager. But this conversation had already been *a lot*.

CHAPTER 18

Dax

Morgan and I were making dinner together on a Thursday evening when she started talking about weekend plans. Well, technically, she was the one making dinner; I was trying my best to stay out of her way as I set the table.

"What are you thinking for this Saturday?" she asked.

"I'm open."

"The Turner's Modern World exhibit is starting at the Museum of Fine Arts. We should check that out, then grab lunch."

I set a glass down. "That sounds like a plan to me."

"Do you think Rafe would want to go?"

"I doubt it. He's been doing his own thing lately."

"The girlfriend?" She grinned.

"Yeah. Still not sure how I feel about that whole thing. But at least he seems less grumpy lately."

"Well, a pretty girl will do that."

"Yeah, I can relate." I winked.

She smiled up at me as she sprinkled brown sugar over the sweet potatoes. "Everything okay at work today?"

"Yeah. I'm dealing with this new client. Owner of a startup. The guy is kind of a pain in the ass."

"Is that why you asked me to pick up wine on the way here tonight?"

"That's *exactly* why I asked you to pick up wine."

A couple of nights a week Morgan would come over after work for dinner. She mostly stayed the night on weekends but went back to her place on weeknights. Shannon appreciated the break from having to deal with dinner on the nights my girlfriend came over. Like Shannon, Morgan was an amazing cook.

I'd met Morgan at a bookstore. She and I had reached for the same copy of *The Young Lions* at the same time. We'd struck up a conversation, and for the first time in a while, I'd truly enjoyed a woman's company. We went out for dinner that night, and the rest was history. That was ten months ago now.

Morgan had just made partner at the patent law firm where she worked in downtown Boston, so things were going really well for her. In some ways, she reminded me of Maren: successful, smart, driven. Like my late wife, Morgan was also tall with long, blond hair. She was beautiful. And I felt lucky to have met her, considering I hadn't been trying to meet anyone at the time. It just happened.

After everything that went down with Wren, it had taken more than a year and a half for me to find the mental headspace to even think about dating again. I'd chosen to focus that first year after Wren left Boston on building my relationship with Rafe. As he got older and more involved with his friends, though, I came to the conclusion that I needed to get a life. While my relationship with Morgan was unexpected, it seemed to have come at just the right time. I was happier than I'd been in a while.

About a year ago, a couple of months before Morgan came into my life, I'd forced myself to move on from the idea of Wren. I'd made a decision to stop watching her cello videos and stop living in the past. Tuning in to the Ren-Cello channel on a regular basis hadn't been healthy—as much I'd loved...*her music*. I couldn't do that to myself anymore. That mental shift had taken willpower, but it opened the door to new possibilities for me. It was probably no coincidence that I'd met Morgan soon thereafter.

I found myself grateful for a lot lately—grateful that my relationship with Rafe was stronger than it had been in the past, grateful that Shannon still stuck around and put up with my ass, grateful for a relationship with a great woman who had a good head on her shoulders. My life was going well.

"Want to call Rafe down for dinner?" Morgan said.

"Sure."

I placed the last napkin on the table and headed to his room. Per usual, Rafe was listening to something, probably blowing his eardrums out.

"Rafe..." I signaled for him to remove the earbuds. "Dinner..."

"Yeah. Coming," he mumbled.

Morgan had set the sweet potatoes and lamb chops on the kitchen table when I returned. She'd also made a side of asparagus. Even though I had a formal dining room, most nights we ate in the kitchen. She'd poured two glasses of red and had a water set on the table next to Rafe's plate.

"How was school today, Rafe?" she asked.

"Fine," he muttered.

"School's always fine," I said. "He never has much to say about it."

"What do you want me to say?" he snapped.

"Anything more than fine?"

"I did crappy on my calculus test. How about that?"

"Shit. The one you needed at least a B on to get a C in the class?"

"Yep." He stuffed his mouth with potatoes.

"When will you find out the grade?"

"Should be posted tomorrow," he said, shoveling more potato into his mouth.

"Maybe you need to cut back a bit on the running practice."

"Nope." He spoke with his mouth full. "Not gonna happen. Sorry."

Running was Rafe's life. It was the only sport he'd ever showed interest in. I worried he'd been pushing himself so hard that it took away from academics. Being the top runner in the school, he was on target for a scholarship if he could keep his grades up a bit. He'd chosen to take honors classes because that looked better on paper, but I feared some of them were too advanced for him.

After cleaning his plate in less than ten minutes, as per usual, Rafe had no interest in sticking around. He took his dirty dish to the sink and rinsed it before putting it in the dishwasher.

"Thanks for dinner, Morgan. It was really good."

"Of course, honey."

"Thanks for the compelling dinner conversation as always," I chided.

Rafe walked backwards out of the kitchen. "I have homework. You wanna do it for me? Then I could stick around and talk."

"Okay. Get outta here." I yelled after him. "And make sure you put your dirty clothes in the wash tonight, please. Don't throw them around the room so Shannon has to go on a scavenger hunt to find them."

He disappeared down the hall.

I shook my head and chuckled. "Thanks for dinner," I said, turning back to Morgan. "It was delicious."

"You're welcome." She reached across the table for my hand. "If you weren't so stressed, I'd let you pay me back tonight."

I suppose I could've contested that and suggested she sleep over. But I *was* damn tired and wanted to hit the sack. There would be plenty of time to make it up to her this weekend.

Just as I'd gotten up to help Morgan clear the table, the doorbell rang. I wasn't expecting anyone. Maybe Shannon had forgotten her purse? That had happened once or twice over the years. Winston barked and scurried after me to the door. Without checking the peephole, I opened it.

In that moment, as the frigid late-January air blew into the house, it felt like someone had knocked the freaking wind out of me.

I stared at her in shock, without saying anything, for I don't know how long. Enough seconds that she had to be the first to speak as Winston barked and circled around her.

"Are you gonna say anything, Moody, or are you just going to stand there like you saw a ghost?"

Wren stood before me, looking...*different. God, why does she look so different?* Not in a bad way, but in a way that made me realize how much damn time had passed since I'd laid eyes on her. Her copper hair was longer than I'd ever seen it, past her shoulders. I never knew how silky and wavy it was because she'd always worn it short. She looked amazing.

"Wren..." I blinked as if to make sure I wasn't seeing things. "What are you doing here?"

"Good to see you, too."

She finally bent and gave Winston the attention he'd been begging for. Wren wrapped her arms around him and smelled his fur. Winston seemed to love every minute of their embrace as he panted and wagged his tail.

Yeah, Fluffernutter. I can imagine.

"You remembered me!" she cooed. "Thank you, buddy. I missed you, too." She finally stood up and faced me again.

I shook my head. "Sorry, I should've said it was good to see you before asking what you were doing here. That was asinine of me. I'm just...a little shocked." I leaned in to hug her and felt her stiffen. My body, on the other hand, seemed to come alive in a way that it hadn't since the last time she was in my arms. Her familiar, flowery scent was intoxicating as ever. I hoped she couldn't feel how fast my heart was beating.

"It's okay." She laughed, her breath grazing the skin of my neck.

Fuck.

"I know I caught you off guard." She pulled away from me as cold air billowed from her mouth. "Are you gonna invite me in or...?"

God, is she still not even in the house? "Jesus. Of course!" I waved my hand, urging her inside. "I don't know where my head is. Come in."

My heart sank to the pit of my gut in anticipation of having to introduce her to Morgan.

"Does Rafe know you're in Boston?" I asked.

She looked around and lowered her voice. "No. I wanted to surprise him."

"When did you get back?"

"I got in late last night. I was jetlagged and slept most of the day away."

"Are you back home permanently now or just visiting?"

"I decided to come back for good."

My stomach churned. Of course, I was happy she was back—for Rafe—but I wasn't prepared. Not in the least.

"The last he told me, you were considering staying a bit longer. That's why I'm so surprised."

"Yeah." She shrugged. "I changed my mind."

I swallowed the lump in my throat.

"I assume he's home?" she asked.

"Who?" I asked in a daze.

"Rafe..."

"Oh. Right." I laughed. "He's upstairs." *Jesus. Get your fucking shit together.*

It was one thing to block someone's existence out of your mind when you were an ocean apart. But having her in front of me like this was something entirely different. I hadn't forgotten a damn thing, apparently. It was like my feelings had been hiding all this time and decided to jump out in this moment, as if this were my surprise party.

"Dax, who's here?"

Here we go.

Morgan appeared behind me. I couldn't even turn to face her for fear she'd know something was off just by looking at my face.

Wren forced a huge smile and said, "You must be Morgan. Rafe's told me all about you."

He has?

Morgan's eyes narrowed. "You're not Rafe's girl-friend, are you?"

Wren laughed nervously. "No, I'm his sister."

"I was gonna say. You don't look sixteen!" She laughed. "Oh, gosh. What a surprise. Wren, right?"

She nodded. "Yes."

"You're back from Europe, then...obviously."

"I decided to move back, yes. He has no idea. I'm here to surprise him."

Morgan clapped her hands together. "He's going to be elated."

Did we just have a mild earthquake in freaking Massachusetts, or is that my head causing the room to sway?

Since Morgan entered the room, Wren hadn't looked at me once. I knew this because I hadn't taken my eyes off her. The food I'd just eaten felt like it was going to come back up.

Wren finally glanced over at me long enough to ask, "Mind if I head upstairs?"

"Of course not. He's doing his homework. He's gonna freak out when he sees you...in a good way."

Not the bad way in which I'm currently freaking out.

"Okay. I'm gonna go see him."

My eyes followed as she ran up the stairs, the beat of her footsteps matching the thundering inside my chest.

Wren hadn't even made it to the top yet when Morgan said, "Wow, she's cute."

How the hell am I supposed to respond to that?

I didn't have to because Rafe's jovial screech from upstairs filled the air. Morgan and I turned to each other, and despite everything, I couldn't help the wide smile that spread across my face. I was so damn happy he had his sister back, even if it would take some getting used to for me, to say the least.

I listened to them talking and laughing for a moment before Morgan snapped me out of my thoughts.

"Gosh, you know who she'd be perfect for?"

"Huh?"

"Dylan. I think Wren would be perfect for him. Don't you?"

Dylan Valeri was an associate who worked under Morgan at her law firm. He was about Wren's age, an uncomfortably great-looking guy, and a decent dude. Actually, he was a truly nice guy whom I'd had many conversations with. He had a damn good head on his shoulders and his shit together. Sadly, if it didn't fuck me up inside to think about them together, I might've thought to set them up, too. Instead, I currently wanted to skin him alive.

She interrupted my thoughts. "How old is she?"

I paused. "Around twenty-seven. Maybe almost twenty-eight."

Like I don't know exactly when she'll be turning twenty-eight—on June third.

"That's perfect. He's twenty-eight. We'll have to invite them over for dinner at the same time or something."

Could this situation get any worse? Would I eventually tell Morgan about Wren and me? It would be easier for everyone involved if she didn't know. The fewer people who knew, the better. But how could I keep something like that a secret from someone I expected honesty from in return?

I could still hear Rafe and Wren talking upstairs. Deciding to give them privacy, I walked over to the sink and began cleaning some of the dishes.

"Those are already clean," Morgan called out. "I just had them drying over to the side."

"Oh. Sorry. Guess that's what happens when I try to help."

She came over and rubbed my back. "Are you okay?"

"I'm fine."

"You seem a little flustered. Are you concerned about Wren being back in his life?"

"Of course not." My eyes narrowed. "Why would I be concerned?"

"I wondered if she wasn't a good influence on him or something. I know they hadn't had a lot of time together before she left." She examined my face. "You just seem off since she showed up."

"No." I shook my head. "Wren is great. My mood has nothing to do with her."

"Okay." Morgan smiled and poured water into the tea kettle. On evenings when she didn't spend the night, she typically made tea before heading home.

We were sitting at the table about ten minutes later when Rafe and Wren entered the kitchen.

Rafe was beaming. "I can't believe she surprised me. You didn't know about this, right?"

I shook my head. "No, I was just as surprised as you," I said. "I've never heard you yell like that. You must be pretty damn happy to have your sister back."

"I'm happy to *be* back." Wren grinned, looking over at Rafe.

Again, she was looking anywhere but at me. I couldn't fucking blame her. She'd walked right into the fire tonight. I also felt terrible that I couldn't have the type of conversation with Wren that I wanted to. There was so much I wanted to ask her. My hands were tied at the moment, though.

"Are you single, Wren?" Morgan asked, interrupting my rumination.

Great. I began bouncing my knee under the table.

Wren hesitated. "I am. Not much chance to meet anyone straight off the plane from France." She laughed nervously before glancing over at me.

I attempted to telepathically apologize with my eyes for Morgan's intrusive question.

"That's true, huh? You just got here. Wasn't sure if there was someone back in France." Morgan laughed. "Anyway, I'd love to have you over for dinner and invite a friend of mine. He's around your age. Super good-looking, successful...a great catch."

Eyes wide, Wren just nodded and smiled.

I balled my fist. The whole thing was awkward as fuck.

Wren turned to Rafe. "I'm still jetlagged, so I'm gonna head home. I'll come by tomorrow night and pick you up for dinner. You can bring your girlfriend if you want."

"Yeah. I want you to meet her," Rafe said.

Wren looked over at Morgan. "It was really nice to meet you, Morgan."

Clueless Morgan flashed a smile. "You, too!"

Wren finally looked at me for more than a few seconds. "Good to see you again, Dax." I noticed the hint of sadness in her eyes. I'd known this wasn't easy for her, but now I could actually *see* it.

Not being able to tell her I was sorry for putting her in this position was killing me. I would never have chosen for her to meet Morgan on her first damn night back. Actually, I might have tried to avoid that meeting for as long as humanly possible. But maybe, in a way, this was better. Like ripping the Band-Aid off.

I noticed Rafe looking intently at his sister. Did he notice something was off, too? Then he turned and looked straight at me. I inwardly panicked for a millisecond before reminding myself that he didn't know anything. It was just my rattled nerves playing tricks on me.

CHAPTER 19

Wren

"**I**t was *the most* awkward moment," I told my father during lunch the following day.

"Dax must have been shitting a brick. I feel a little bad for the poor bastard. He's just trying to do the right thing, move on with his life. Then you blow in like a storm."

When my father came to visit me in Europe, one night over drinks on my balcony I'd confessed to him what happened between Dax and me. I'd wanted my dad to know why I hesitated to come back to the US immediately when the two years were up. While he hadn't been surprised by what I told him, he'd told me he felt sad that I was still harboring feelings for Dax.

Maybe a girl talking about her sex life with her dad wasn't a popular thing, but I always felt lucky that I could tell Chuck anything. Under the current circumstances, I was grateful to have at least one person who understood why things were so messed up for me right now. I'd also told Dad of Rafe's revelation about reading Dax's journal.

"The worst part is his girlfriend mentioned setting me up with some guy she works with." I dropped my head into my hands a moment.

Dad's eyes widened with a hint of amusement. "What did Dax do when she said that?"

"I don't know. I hardly looked at him. I couldn't. It just…hurt too much."

My phone chimed, and my heart did a flip when I saw his name pop up.

> Dax: Hey. I'm sorry for any awkwardness last night. I was a little shocked, which is why I acted like a fool when I answered the door. It was so good to see you. You look great. And you seem happy to be back. I know you're picking up Rafe later for dinner. I was wondering if you had time to meet up beforehand. Not at the house. I'm working from home today but can clock out early and meet you somewhere. No worries if you can't.

Goose bumps covered my arms. *You fucking idiot*, I told my body. It hadn't gotten the message that there was no point in getting excited to see Dax anymore.

"It's him," I told my dad. "He wants to talk later this afternoon. He feels bad that things were so awkward last night."

Dad smiled. "I figured you'd hear from him."

I texted back the only thing I could muster.

> Wren: Sure.

The dots danced as he typed.

Dax: Are you at your house? I can swing by and pick you up.

Wren: Yes.

Dax: Say 4?

Wren: Sounds good.

I went to my room and debated what to wear, then swore at myself for caring. Why did it matter? Dax was with Morgan. As expected, she was beautiful. Blond, which seemed to be his type—other than the blip with me. I knew from Rafe already that she was a lawyer—smart, successful, and a little older than Dax by a year or two. That was also his type—older, shit together. The opposite of me.

When Dax came to the door, I let my father answer as I finished putting my eye makeup on in the downstairs bathroom. I suppose it was natural to want your sort-of ex to eat his heart out.

Dax was standing next to my father when I emerged from the bathroom. He swallowed as his eyes traveled up and down my body. I might've worn a sexy, super-short romper for the occasion. I would probably always crave this kind of silent admiration from him since it was all I had left now.

"Sorry to make you wait."

"No worries." He smiled. "You look nice."

"Thanks. So do you," I said, fidgeting with my hands.

My father looked between us, unable to hide the enjoyment peeking through his grin. *Glad we're entertaining you, Dad.*

"Where are you going?" my father asked.

Dax's eyes were still fixed on mine when he answered. "There's a new tapas restaurant not far from here in Jamaica Plain. I was thinking it might be nice to try it. Unless you're saving your appetite for dinner with Rafe later. We can just grab a drink."

I shrugged. "I'm good with anything." A few seconds of awkward silence passed. "Let me grab my jacket."

After doing so, I followed Dax out the door. We didn't speak as he opened the passenger side of his Porsche to let me in. It felt different sitting in this seat because it was *her* seat now. In fact, I looked down to find a stray blond hair on the leather.

He got in next to me, and rather than starting the car, Dax leaned his head back on the seat and let out a long breath.

"When did you tell your father we slept together?"

I gulped. "Did he say something to you?"

"No. But he knows. I sensed it. When did you tell him?"

"When he came to visit me in Europe a few months ago," I admitted. "How could you tell?"

"It was the look he gave me—a cross between amusement and warning. He used to come visit Rafe, as you know, so I've seen him a few times while you were away. He's *never* looked at me like that before."

I sighed. My father was never one to hide his feelings very well. "Are you mad that I told him?"

Dax stared out the window. "No. How could I be? In retrospect, I remember you saying you tell your father everything." He laughed angrily. "But fuck, a warning would've been nice. I would want to kill me if I were him, Wren."

"He's not mad. Dad thinks you're a good guy. He understands why everything went down the way it did."

Dax looked back at me. "You grew your hair out. I've never seen you with long hair before."

"You stopped watching my videos."

His smile faded. "How did you know?"

"Because you would've known I'd grown my hair out if you'd seen the latest ones. But you also stopped commenting a while back. I just sensed you were gone." My eyes started to well up. *Holy shit. What's wrong with me?* He hadn't even turned on the car and I was already emotional?

"Fuck," he whispered.

"I'm sorry. I don't know why I'm—"

"Don't you dare apologize. You have every right to be upset right now."

I wiped my eyes. "Anyway... It's not a big deal that you stopped watching. I just..." I looked at him. "...Felt your absence."

He turned his body toward me. "Wren, I had to force myself to stop. Because every time I watched you, I got really caught up in it." He closed his eyes a moment. "All I wanted to do at night for much of that first year was watch you play. It was unhealthy."

I fought back more tears as my old wounds burst open. "Did you stop when you met Morgan?"

He swallowed. "It was around the same time, yeah. I'm sorry you had to meet her like that last night."

"You have nothing to be sorry for. You're doing exactly what you should be. I want you to be happy, Dax. That's all I've ever wanted. We decided a long time ago that it wasn't going to work between us. So none of this is a surprise. I just need to get used to it."

He stared down at the steering wheel. "What made you come back when you did? Rafe had told me you'd decided to stay out there indefinitely. Then suddenly you're back. What changed?"

Well, I found out you loved me, and I needed to see you again. Now I feel lost. I cleared my throat. "It was just time. Rafe said he wished I'd come back, and he reminded me that soon he'd be going away to college, which will mean four more years of being apart the majority of the time. That swayed my decision."

"That makes sense." He nodded. "Was France everything you hoped it would be?"

"It really was." I smiled. "I was homesick, of course, in the beginning. I missed you a lot—more than I let on through our correspondence. But time went by, and eventually I became acclimated to my new life there. You know from our early emails that I was dating. But nothing lasted. I tried to move on, though. And I always expected you would, too." I paused. "What we had was special, even if it had to be short-lived. But if we can't be together, I still want you to be happy. It seems you are...with Morgan."

He searched my eyes, not quite seeming to buy what I was selling. "I guess we have to try to find a new normal, whatever that is."

"Yeah," I whispered. "New normal."

He tapped the steering wheel. "I should probably start this fucking car, huh? I'm not even thinking straight, yet again. Haven't been since last night."

"Yeah. We should go—especially considering my father has been at the window the entire time."

He looked over at the house. "Shit, you're right." He squinted. "You don't happen to notice a shotgun in his hand, do you?"

We shared a much-needed laugh before Dax finally started the car and pulled away from the curb.

At one point, he glanced over at me. "I don't know if Rafe mentioned that he won the state running championship? He also broke the school record for best time."

I nodded. "Yes. I'm so proud of him."

"Did he mention I'm throwing him a party next weekend?"

"He didn't."

"I invited his team over, along with the coaches. I'm just doing a big, catered barbecue. I know he'd love it if you were there."

As awkward as it would be to see Morgan again, I couldn't miss Rafe's party. "Okay. Thanks for the invite. I'll definitely be there."

"Good." He flashed a smile, and it took me back for a moment. My heart clenched. My mind went to the time he'd carried me home—our first and last date.

When we got to the restaurant, we were somehow able to bury the tension between us as we summarized the past two-and-a-half years for each other. I told him about the people I'd met, like my friend Micheline. Detailed my quirky little neighborhood and the delicious foods I'd enjoyed. I even described the two men I'd dated most seriously, Alec, an artist who lived in my building, and Pierre, a chef I'd met at a farmers' market in Paris. Neither brief relationship went anywhere, but each man now had a small part in the story of my life.

Dax recalled for me how much his relationship with Rafe had grown. While things weren't perfect, the situation was a lot better. As painful as it was, I asked him about how he'd met Morgan, and he told me the story of how they'd reached for the same book in a bookstore. While that left me a little nauseated, Morgan seemed perfect for him—on paper, at least. Dax seemed happy with her, but I hadn't been around them long enough to know whether that was really the case.

When our conversation had run its course, some of the earlier awkwardness seeped back in. We sat across from each other, out of words to form a shield for the tension between us.

I looked down at my phone. "I actually have to head back. I'm supposed to be picking Rafe up for dinner in an hour."

"Of course. That's right. We can go."

As we left the restaurant, we carried that quiet tension with us back to my house. I couldn't tell you how many times Dax fiddled with the radio and temperature gauges.

After he parked, he got out to meet me at the passenger side. He slipped his hands in his pockets as we stood facing each other on the curb. "So we'll see you next Saturday for Rafe's party, then?"

We. He and Rafe or he and Morgan? "Yes. I wouldn't miss it."

"Cool."

He reached out to give me a hug, but I took a step back.

His smile faded. "I'm sorry. I—"

"No need to apologize. I just think it's better if we don't...do that." I let out a shaky breath, surprised by my self-protective mechanism. "You know, the whole new-normal thing," I added.

"Of course," he said, looking regretful. "I didn't mean to cross the line."

"You didn't."

He wasn't the problem. It was *me*. The last time he hugged me—when I'd arrived at his door—was torture, and I didn't want to feel that painful longing again.

"Alright." He nodded, looking down at the ground for a few seconds before forcing a smile. "Have fun tonight with Rafe."

"We will."

I turned around and didn't look back. Dad had been watching us from the window again—fortunately sans shotgun.

The following weekend, I sat in my car outside Dax's house. I could see a tent set up in the yard and teenage boys milling about on the lawn. It took several minutes before I could garner the strength to get out and join the party.

Just as I exited the vehicle, Rafe spotted me walking toward the house.

"Hey!" He ran to me.

"How's the party going?" I smiled.

"Good." He raked his hand through his curly hair.

"At first I thought Dax was crazy for doing this outside in early February, but you got lucky," I said. "It's actually not that freezing today."

"Yeah, the big tent has heaters, though, so you don't even feel like you're outside under there."

I'd forgotten money could pretty much buy anything, including plenty of heat in the dead of winter.

"Are you okay being here?" Rafe asked, his eyes serious.

I loved him for caring enough to ask, but I didn't want him to worry. "Of course. Things are fine." I smacked his arm playfully. "Didn't I tell you Dax and I worked everything out when he and I met up last week?"

"No, you didn't say too much about that."

"Well, we're working toward a...new normal. So you don't have to worry about me. I can handle this."

He shrugged. "Alright. If you say so."

I waved him off. "Go hang out with your friends. I'll catch up with you."

"Okay." He gave me a hug, and the contact relaxed me a bit.

That is, until I made my way over to the big tent and spotted Morgan with her arms wrapped around Dax as he flipped burgers. He wore a Syracuse beanie and black parka vest. He had only gotten hotter with age. At thirty-five, he looked better than ever. *A freaking zaddy.*

He flinched when he spotted me, causing her to release him.

It's showtime. Commence fake smile. One foot in front of the other. "I thought you said this was catered. Since when do you flip burgers?" I teased as I approached.

"Well, I had all of the side dishes brought in, but I figured for an authentic barbecue, you actually have to cook the meat on site."

"Hope you're hungry, Wren," Morgan said. "We have burgers, shrimp, chicken wings, hot dogs, sausage..."

I've had Dax's sausage. Did you know that, Morgan?

She was still clueless, and that was probably a good thing. I'd hate to imagine what this experience would be like if she knew the truth. Once again, I forced a smile. "I'm sure these boys will take care of all the food, no problem. I've seen the way Rafe eats now. He wasn't like that before I left."

"You noticed that, huh?" Dax nodded. "Do you know my grocery bill has doubled in the past year? The kid goes through a gallon of milk every other day."

"He's a growing man now, I suppose." I laughed.

When I spotted a smiling Shannon walking toward us, I breathed a sigh of relief. She'd taken the day off last week when I'd picked up Rafe for dinner, so this was the first time I'd seen her since arriving in Boston.

She opened her arms wide. "Wren! I heard you were back. It's so wonderful to see you!"

"You, too, Shannon!" I gave her a hug.

She looked me over. "I almost didn't recognize you with the long hair."

"I know. I stopped cutting it a while back."

"I love it," she said.

"Thank you."

"But you have such a pretty face, it wouldn't matter if you had no hair at all," she said.

"That's very true," Morgan agreed.

Oh boy. I couldn't help glancing over at Dax, who understandably chose not to chime in about how pretty I was. Instead, he'd returned his focus to the grill, flipping the burgers and adding some hot dogs to one side of them.

"It's kind of nice to be here and not have to do any work for once." Shannon winked.

Dax looked up from the grill. "I bet."

"I know this is a party for high schoolers, so I assume there's no booze?" she asked.

Morgan held her arms up in the air. "Are you kidding? How do you have a party for high schoolers without any booze to help the adults get through it? I have a secret stash in this cooler right here. What can I get you, Shannon?"

"Any white wine?"

"You got it." Morgan turned to me. "Would you like some wine, too? I also have beer and wine coolers."

"White wine would be great."

Morgan grabbed a couple of red Solo cups and poured us each some Chardonnay. I guess she was officially the hostess of this party.

"Want to take these over to that table and sit?" Shannon asked me.

"Sure," I said, grateful for the excuse to leave this particular spot.

Shannon chose a table right next to one of the heaters. After we sat down, she said, "I love the story of how you surprised Rafe."

"Yeah. It was fun to do that."

"I know he missed you."

"He actually told me he wished I'd come home. I'd been planning to stay maybe another six months, but once he said that, I had to come back."

"Your relationship with him has only grown since you went away."

"It's kind of hard to believe, but I have to agree."

She looked over her shoulder and lowered her voice. "And you deserve an Academy Award for putting on a smile over there." A look of concern crossed her face.

Shannon and I had never discussed my past with Dax, but I knew he'd told her everything. She was his confidante, and it was a relief to know someone understood my struggle right now.

"It's not easy, but I need to adapt to this new normal. For Rafe." I sipped my wine. "And Dax is happy, right? That's what matters to me."

Her eyes narrowed. "Do you really feel that way, Wren? You can be honest with me. Anything Dax says to me stays with me. And I will offer you the same discretion if you'd like to vent right now. No matter what you're telling me, I know seeing him with her can't be easy."

I felt a weight lift from my shoulders. "You're right." I let out the breath I'd been holding. "It's not easy at all."

She pursed her lips sympathetically. "I figured as much."

Running my finger along my Solo cup, I asked, "Do you like her? Morgan?"

She sighed and looked toward where Dax was grilling. "I will say this," she told me softly. "I do think he's happy. He's very calm around her. But you see, that's not necessarily a positive sign. When things were happening between you two a few years ago, he was the opposite of calm. He was tense, dysregulated...but I don't see that as a bad thing. I feel like when you're passionate about someone, you're not *calm* at all. You're bouncing off the walls from adrenaline. You're calm when you've...settled." She waved her hand. "Anyway, my opinion doesn't mean anything in the end. And I certainly have not expressed my opinion to him. Lately I try not to interfere in his personal life unless he asks me for advice or brings up the subject himself."

I tilted my head. "You didn't answer my question about whether you liked her, though."

She once again looked over to where Morgan was talking and laughing in the distance. "I think she's okay. That's how I feel. I don't have a strong opinion one way or the other. She's respectful to me. But..." She hesitated. "A couple of things have rubbed me the wrong way."

I leaned in. "Like what?"

"I'll give you an example," she said. "I happened to be cleaning up one night when I heard her talking to him about taking Maren's photo down. You know, the one in the foyer where she's wearing the wedding dress. He immediately refused. I was proud of him for not considering it. I mean, how disrespectful would that be to Rafe? That's his mother. The only mother he ever knew. Why would anyone want to take her photo down?"

My blood felt like it was boiling. "What was her rationale? Why did she want him to do that?"

"Well, she said something like, 'The house needs a new aura.' That enough time had gone by and if he wanted to start anew, he needed to let go of the past."

I shook my head. "That's insane to me, Shannon. Maren is dead. How could Morgan possibly feel threatened by her—because that's what it's really about."

"Of course, it is. I know. It's insane to me, too." She sighed. "But like I said, he seems happy overall, and I haven't wanted to rock the boat."

Morgan was still glued to Dax's side as he continued to grill. I allowed myself a few seconds to look, then forced myself to turn away. When I looked back over at Shannon, I realized she'd been watching me watching them.

"I'm just gonna say one last thing before we change the subject to France because I want to hear all about your travels," she said.

"Okay..."

"I wish things were different, Wren. What he felt for you was genuine. But I also understand the dilemma you faced. I probably would've made the same choice if I were him, as difficult as it was. And I think you did the right thing in leaving when you did to put some space between you. But again, I wish things were different because I think you're absolutely fantastic."

I looked down. "You're gonna make me cry."

She placed her hand on my arm. "Aw, I'm sorry. I didn't mean to do that."

I took a deep breath and then spent the next half hour or so recapping my time in France for Shannon while the tent filled with teenage boys who came to devour the food that had been laid out. The caterer had brought in two different types of potato salad, pasta salad, green salad, fresh corn on the cob, and the most delicious coleslaw I'd ever tasted. For dessert, there was a massive cake with a running track on top.

Dax remained at the grill most of the afternoon, taking special orders from the boys.

After we ate, Shannon left because she had plans with her husband, so for the first time all day, I found myself sitting alone.

That didn't last long, though, because a few minutes later, a gorgeous man appeared in the seat next to me. He had blond hair, blue eyes, and sparkling teeth. The heater blew some of his amazing scent toward me.

"You must be Wren." He held out his hand. "Morgan's told me all about you. I'm Dylan."

CHAPTER 20

Dax

The demand at the grill had finally waned, though I wished I still had stuff to make. At least then I could've immersed myself in something other than sitting here, struggling not to look over at Wren.

Much to my chagrin, Morgan had invited her work associate, Dylan Valeri, to the barbecue without telling me first. It's not like I would've told her he couldn't come, but at least I would've had a warning that this would be happening today—a warning that I'd have to watch him fawn all over Wren.

Selfishly, I'd hoped Morgan had forgotten about setting them up. I knew her intentions were good, but I didn't need a front-row seat.

I caught myself. *Look what I'm saying.* Why should I be spared watching Wren with another man when she couldn't avoid having to see me with Morgan? This was exactly what I deserved.

Morgan leaned into me as she looked across at them. "They seem to be getting along, huh?"

I stabbed the fork a little too hard into my cake. "It would seem that way, yes."

"I'm glad I thought to invite him."

I ground my teeth. "Yeah. You didn't mention he was coming."

"I know. I'm sorry. I totally forgot to tell you. That was okay, right?"

"Of course," I muttered.

They did appear to be getting along. Wren had laughed more than once at something he'd said, and her body language seemed to indicate she might like him. She'd twirled her hair a couple of times.

My stomach felt uneasy. It wasn't that I didn't want her to be happy. I just didn't want to witness it.

I thought I was getting a handle on it until Wren and Dylan stood up and went for a walk around the grounds. My pulse raced as they disappeared into the trees. Apparently, *not* seeing them but knowing they were together was worse than having to watch. But Wren deserved happiness. She deserved the world. And if she was going to date someone, I'd rather it be someone like Dylan who had his shit together than someone who wasn't worthy of her. I needed to try to be okay with this, even if I wished I could give Dylan an atomic wedgie right now and suffocate him with his own underwear.

Morgan interrupted my thoughts. "I'm gonna get another drink. Want something?"

"Hmm?" I blinked out of my trance.

"A drink. Do you want one?"

"Sure. Grab me a Sam Adams."

"You got it."

Guilt crept in. My girlfriend was unaware of the turmoil in my head, which was a good thing, but I continued to feel uneasy about not having had a chance to talk to Wren all day. It seemed wrong not to acknowledge that I knew coming here wasn't easy for her. Though, perhaps, that wasn't necessary anymore; she seemed to be doing just fine.

Morgan returned with my beer, and I vowed to refocus my attention where it belonged, on my girlfriend—not my ex-lover who was currently enjoying the company of another man.

Sometime later, Wren and Dylan reappeared and returned to their seats at the table.

Morgan squeezed my shoulder. "Let's go over there and chat."

"I think I'll stay here and enjoy my beer, if you don't mind. It's been a long day."

"You don't want to be rude. Have you said hello to Dylan yet?"

I sighed. "Actually, I haven't."

She tilted her head toward their table. "Come on."

I got up and followed her to where they were sitting, hoping it wouldn't make Wren uncomfortable.

"Hey, you guys," Morgan said.

"Hey." Dylan smiled and turned to me. "Great party, Dax. I can't believe Rafe won the whole damn championship."

"Yeah. The kid's pretty amazing."

He turned to Wren. "You must be so proud of your brother."

"I am." She smiled. "So proud."

Though Wren wouldn't make eye contact with me, I tried to make conversation with her. "Shannon was talking your ear off there for a while earlier, huh?"

"Yeah." She breathed out. "We had a lot of catching up to do."

"I would imagine," I said, certain I must have come up a few times.

"Wren was telling me the amazing story of how you used a private investigator to find her," Dylan said. "Talk about a gift to Rafe."

"Yeah," I said. "I got lucky. It was definitely...fate."

My eyes locked with Wren's for a moment, and I knew what she was thinking: that fate was pretty fucked up sometimes. I *really* wished I had a moment to speak to her privately.

An hour later, Dylan announced that he had to leave for a family event, and Wren walked him to his car.

I still hadn't had a chance to talk to her alone since Morgan had been glued to my side. The sun was going down, and many of the teenagers who had converged upon my house were starting to leave.

When Morgan disappeared into the house. I went to see if I could find Wren—to at least say goodbye. I wasn't even sure whether she was still here. Holding my beer, I walked around to the front of the house where a few boys were getting into cars and taking off. I spotted Wren talking to Rafe on the front lawn.

I walked over to them. "Did you have a good time, Rafe?"

"Yeah. Thanks again. It was really awesome."

"You're welcome." I patted his shoulder. "You deserved it."

Rafe looked between us, and as if he could read my mind, he turned and walked off without saying anything else. It was a little odd, but I was grateful for the moment to be alone with Wren.

"I haven't had a single chance to speak to you all day," I said.

Her smile seemed strained. "Did you need to speak to me about something?"

My heart clenched. "No, Wren. Nothing specific."

"You did a fabulous job with this party. Truly."

I nodded. "So...you likely figured out that Morgan invited Dylan here because of you."

"Yes. That didn't take rocket science."

"I had nothing to do with that." I felt the need to clarify.

"I didn't think you did."

"He's a...really good guy." I looked down into my beer bottle a moment. "I just wanted you to know that if you wanna see him...it won't bother me."

Her eyes narrowed. "I didn't realize I needed your permission."

My eyes widened. She'd taken my comment the wrong way. "You don't."

"Well, that's good. Because you certainly didn't ask my permission before subjecting me to watching another woman all over you today."

Shit. This was *not* going the way I'd hoped. I opened my mouth to respond, but she spoke before I could get the words out.

"But this is the new normal, right?" Wren looked up at the sky and shook her head, seeming to catch herself. "God. I'm sorry. You don't deserve my attitude. Today was just…a lot."

"Fuck. I know, Wren," I whispered. "Believe me, I know. There's no need to—"

"There you are!"

We turned to find Morgan strutting toward us.

Wren pulled her shoulders back and forced a smile. "Hey! I was just telling Dax what an amazing party this was."

"Yeah. We got lucky with the weather not being too bad." Morgan smirked. "Can I be nosy, Wren?"

Wren blinked uncomfortably. "Sure."

"I saw you and Dylan exchange numbers before he left. What did you think of him?"

Wren glanced at me for a millisecond and nodded. "He's a nice guy. We might grab a drink sometime."

And there it was. The answer to my burning question.

"Handsome, too, right?" Morgan winked.

"Very." Wren smiled.

The beer turned in my stomach.

"Well, then my job is done." Morgan beamed.

"Thank you for thinking of me," Wren said.

"Of course. You're Rafe's sister. You're family."

I took a long sip.

"Yeah." Wren glared at me. "This one's basically my daddy."

I nearly choked on my beer.

Morgan laughed, but she had no idea how sick that joke was.

Wren's face turned red. "Kidding, of course."

I swallowed.

"Well..." Wren said. "I have to get going." She turned to Morgan. "Thank you both for a wonderful time."

"Thank *you* for coming," Morgan said as she rubbed my arm.

Wren's eyes went to Morgan's hand for a moment.

Then she turned around, got in her car, and left.

A few nights later at dinner, Morgan dropped a bomb.

"Dylan told me he and Wren have a date set for this weekend."

I'd been bracing for this, but I still dropped my fork, perhaps a little too loudly. "Oh?"

"Yeah. I think it's great." She examined my face. "You don't?"

"Why would you say that?"

"I don't know. You just don't seem that happy about me setting them up."

I looked away, and my eyes landed on Rafe across the table. He was staring at me. That made lying all the more difficult. But telling the truth—*I'm jealous*—wasn't an option.

"You're imagining it," I assured her.

"I thought maybe you felt protective of her or something because she's Rafe's sister. You know I wouldn't hook her up with anyone unless I was a hundred-percent sure he was a good guy. Which Dylan is."

I resumed eating with a nod. "You're absolutely right. Dylan is great."

"Okay." She breathed a sigh of relief. "Anyway... I think it's cool they're going out."

"No one's gonna ask *me* what I think of Dylan?" Rafe asked.

We turned to him in unison.

"I'm sorry, honey," Morgan said. "You're right. You met him at the party. What did you think?"

Rafe spoke with his mouth full of pasta. "I think he's a tool."

I couldn't help but snort. Rafe resumed eating without any further explanation. And Morgan must have been too surprised to continue her questioning. She just looked between us with her mouth hanging open.

Later that night, lying in bed, I had an uncontrollable urge to text Wren. I didn't even know what I wanted to say to her. I held the phone in my hand, and my finger hovered over her name for what felt like minutes on end. I eventually shoved my phone in my side-table drawer and slammed it shut. Unfortunately, that didn't make the urge go away.

There was nothing I could say to her that wouldn't come off as inappropriate. Acknowledging that I knew about her date with Dylan—no. Giving my opinion about it? Also no. Telling her I was thinking about her? Big no. Texting her at all: inappropriate.

Yet the need continued. So I opened my laptop and did something I hadn't done in ages. I logged on to the website that housed her RenCello account. I felt like an addict who'd relapsed after a long period of sobriety. But relapsing through her music was far better than saying or doing something I'd regret. This kept my fucked-up feelings *my* problem, not anyone else's.

Wren had uploaded a new performance. I looked at the date and realized it had been posted the night of the barbecue. It was a cello version of the Amy Winehouse song, "Love is a Losing Game."

CHAPTER 21

Wren

G osh, where is he?

I'd taken the trolley into the city to meet Rafe at Boston University for a college tour. I'd been looking forward to it since I knew this area pretty well. It was close to my own alma mater, Boston College of Music. After the tour, I'd planned to take him out to dinner at one of my favorite haunts in Kenmore Square.

We were supposed to meet in front of the student union at three. But it was 3:15, and he wasn't here yet. I supposed fifteen minutes wasn't that late—especially for a teenager—but I was starting to feel paranoid that maybe I'd screwed up the time. I'd been known to do that.

Then I heard a voice from behind me. "Wren? What are you doing here?"

I turned to face the source of the sound—Dax, not Rafe—my heart awakening at the sight of his handsome face. It had been almost a month since I'd seen him at Rafe's party, and that had seemed like forever. Dax looked so damn hot in a black wool coat and scarf, his hair blowing a bit in the wind. He took my breath away; every time I looked at Dax was like the first. I wished I could've run into his arms.

"What are *you* doing here?" I asked. "I'm meeting Rafe for a tour of BU."

His eyes narrowed. "He told me to meet him here at three to do the same, but I got stuck in traffic coming from downtown."

"He didn't mention you were coming with us," I said.

Dax scratched his chin. "He told me it would be just him and me."

I blew a breath up into my forehead. "The question is...why is he not here and we are?"

"That's a damn good question. Let me call him." Dax took out his phone and scrolled. A moment later, he said, "Rafe! Where are you?" He ran his hand through his hair. "You're kidding. I took off the rest of the day for this. I canceled two important meetings. Your sister is here, too. Her time is equally as precious." Dax paced. "You need to be more responsible." He exhaled. "Alright. Alright. Go." Then he paused. "What?" He laughed. "Okay. Goodbye." He pressed end and shoved the phone back in his pocket.

I crossed my arms. "What the hell happened?"

He rolled his eyes. "He says he forgot he asked both of us to come. Apparently, he *also* forgot that he has some important bonus practice his coach added to the schedule to prep for the next season. He was apologetic, but he needs to be more responsible with other people's time."

"Why were you laughing at the end there?"

"Oh..." He chuckled. "Because he said, 'It's not like you don't work enough. Take my sister out to lunch and chill.'"

I'm gonna kill him. I forced myself to take a breath. "Well, that explains the delay."

Dax let out a long breath. "Anyway...I'm sorry he messed up. Is there somewhere else you should be right now?"

"No. Like you, I took the afternoon off. I had a couple of massage appointments this morning, but nothing for the rest of the day."

"You want to take Rafe up on his suggestion? Get out of here and get something to eat?"

My stomach did a flip at the prospect of spending time with Dax. It would be platonic, but I'd craved his attention and missed being alone with him.

"Why not?" I shrugged. "I'm starving."

"Me, too." He smiled. "I know just the place."

"Where's that?" I asked as we took off walking. "Because I was going to suggest something. This area is sort of my domain."

"Have you ever been to The Tavern?"

My mouth dropped. "That's where I was going to suggest! It's one of my favorite places."

"They have the best beer."

"I know," I said. "They brew their own. And the food is great."

"Well, great minds think alike." He winked.

When we arrived at the bar and grill, Dax held the door open, and the smell of beer and fried food immediately hit me. As we waited to be seated, I thought about this being only the second time Dax and I had been out together. After the hostess checked us in, I felt the heat of his body behind me as we walked to the table.

As I perused the menu, I looked up to find him staring at me.

My cheeks burned. "What? You're looking at me funny."

He set his menu down. "It's still hard sometimes for me to believe you're back."

"Were you hoping I'd stay away?"

"Of course not."

The waitress came by and took our drink order.

After she left, I laughed. "I won't ever forget the look on your face when I showed up at your door that night."

He smiled. "What did it look like?"

"Like a deer in headlights." I winked.

"I'm sorry if I acted like an idiot. It was surreal to see you right in front of me when the last time we were together before that..." He paused.

"You were inside me," I finished.

His eyes widened. "Yeah," he whispered.

Feeling heat wash over me, I closed my menu. "Well, at least Morgan doesn't suspect anything."

"No. She doesn't. She really likes you."

"You're not ever going to tell her, are you?"

He was silent a moment. "I haven't figured that out."

"I don't think you should. It wouldn't serve any purpose."

"I feel guilty hiding it, but I do think it would hurt her."

"Exactly. Better that she doesn't know. Anything you did before you met her doesn't matter. You don't list all the other women you've slept with, right?"

His expression turned serious. "You were more to me than just someone I slept with, Wren."

Feeling ready to crawl out of my skin, I looked around. "Where the hell are our drinks?"

The waitress finally appeared with the sampler of beers we'd ordered. She set two trays carefully on the table.

I lifted one of the small glasses. "Cheers."

Dax lifted his own. "Cheers."

I decided to add a little toast. "To college tours that turn into awkward meals with your ex." I downed almost all of the first one. "That should make this a bit easier." I winked, but noticed he wasn't laughing. I frowned. "I'm just kidding, Dax."

"I get it. It's easy to want to numb it all..." He took a long drink and slammed the glass down. "Speaking of things I need to numb, I know you've been out with Dylan a couple of times recently."

I nodded, licking the remaining beer off my lips. "Does that bother you?"

His ears turned a little red. "It's complicated, right? It's not that I don't want you dating a good guy. But it's always gonna hurt to see you with someone else. That's just the way it is. Doesn't mean I don't want you to be happy. Please don't ever think that. Like I told you before, Dylan is a great guy."

"He *is* a really nice guy. He checks all the boxes for sure. And he really seems to like me."

Dax swallowed hard. "Well, good then."

I raised my brow. "Is it?"

He wiped his forehead. "Why wouldn't it be?"

Because I still love you. "I don't know," I muttered.

The tension in the air dissipated slightly when the waitress came to take our food order. Dax ordered a buffalo chicken burger while I opted for lobster mac and cheese.

"Is Morgan moving in with you anytime soon?" I asked as the waitress retreated.

Dax began shredding his napkin. "We were talking about that happening after Rafe goes to college. But the subject hasn't come up recently."

I felt jealousy burning in my throat. "Does Rafe like her?"

"He seems to. It's obviously hard since she's the first person I've dated seriously since Maren."

"Right..." I muttered.

His mouth opened and closed a few times. "I didn't mean..." He shook his head. "I meant the first serious person he *knows* about."

"I understood what you meant." I looked up at the ceiling to compose myself.

He slammed his glass down again. "Fuck this awkwardness, Wren. Talk to me. Tell me what's going on in your head right now."

"What do you want me to say?"

"I just want you to be honest with me."

I laughed angrily. "No, you don't."

"Yes, I do."

After several seconds passed, I finally said, "Every day..." My voice trembled. "...Is a struggle to force myself to move on, Dax. That's all there is to it. I'm not ever going to feel nothing when I look at you. It's not about getting rid of these feelings. It's about learning to live with them."

He took a deep breath and nodded slowly. "I thought..." He hesitated. "I thought I'd done a good job of getting rid of my feelings. Or at least burying them deep—until the moment you showed up at my door. Everything rose to the surface again. As if no time had passed."

My chest constricted. "Is hearing that supposed to make me feel better?"

"It's just the truth." He took a long gulp of beer and changed the subject. "Are you liking your new massage job?"

I shrugged. "It's going okay, but I'm applying for some music-teacher positions. The experience I garnered overseas now qualifies me for a teaching position here, though there are less than a handful across the state."

"That's amazing. You never mentioned that."

I folded my hands together. "Well, there's a lot we haven't discussed in recent years."

"I should clarify that *Rafe* never mentioned that was your plan. I tried not to grill him too much while you were away. Anytime he's offered any information about you, though, I've cherished it."

"I can relate to that."

"I was never sure if he'd told you about Morgan. But you obviously knew."

I nodded. "Knowing about her made it easier to be prepared when I came back."

"You know...she kept pressuring me to get on social media. But I never listened. I was afraid if I did, she'd tag me in everything, and you'd see me with her. I didn't want to upset you."

"You must assume I think very highly of you." I raised an eyebrow. "I'm joking." I smiled. "I can appreciate why you did that."

His eyes seared into mine. "I sensed how uncomfortable you were that first night you came back."

"I'd rather deal with the discomfort than not see you at all, though. You disappearing from my life is not what I want, especially since Rafe is our common denominator. I just have to get used to things the way they are. That hasn't happened yet."

"We need time." He exhaled. "Speaking of time...*this* time with you right now is a nice surprise."

I knew my brother had arranged this on purpose. But he didn't know Dax like I did. Dax wasn't going to cheat on his girlfriend, or bend on the decision he'd made when it came to us. I wasn't even sure it would change things if he knew Rafe had read the journal. Dax felt it was wrong to be with me. That unwavering belief had been the final nail in our coffin before I left for Europe.

Our food came, and we managed to move on to lighter topics during the meal.

After my plate was clean, I took a long sip of the last sampler from the beer flight. "This is starting to hit me."

He chuckled. "Me, too."

"Unfortunately..." I wiped my mouth. "The more I drink, the more I feel like grilling you again. That's the last thing I should be doing because the things I want to know are also things I *don't* want to know."

He nodded. "I feel like we've always had the kind of relationship where we've been honest with each other, even if it hurt."

I searched his eyes. "You seem happy...but are you?"

He shredded a bit more of his napkin. "I've come a long way since you first met me. I'm not as miserable. Rafe and I finally have the kind of relationship I'd hoped for. Things aren't perfect, but I'm proud of where I am."

"Things with Morgan aren't perfect?" I tilted my head.

"Things with Morgan are good. But nothing's perfect."

We were perfect. At least it felt that way. "Do you see yourself marrying her?"

He was quiet a moment. "She would like that."

"Would you?" My heart accelerated.

"I don't see the need to get married ever again."

"But you'd do it for her?"

He chewed on his lip. "We're not there yet."

Yet. "She'd do it in a heartbeat, if you asked," I said.

"You're probably right."

"You're holding back and giving me the bare minimum right now because you don't want to hurt me."

"Can you blame me?"

"I can handle it. I can handle all of it, Dax. If I could handle leaving for Europe after the best sex of my life with a man I..." I stopped to choose my words carefully. "...Cared deeply for, I can handle anything."

"I'm not sure *I* can handle knowing everything, Wren."

I tilted my head. "Dylan, you mean?"

"I was jealous when I had to watch you with him at Rafe's party."

"I could see it on your face." I laughed a little. "It gave me satisfaction because at least I knew I wasn't the only one experiencing it."

He nodded and looked away.

"Are you okay?" I asked.

"What do you mean?"

"I mean, are you doing okay in general? Is there anything that's happened in your life you haven't told me?"

He smiled. "That reminds me of when you asked that question when we first met. To this day you're still the only person who's ever asked if I'm okay."

"Are you?"

He slowly shook his head. "No."

My eyes widened in shock. "No?"

"No, I'm not. Not since you came back." The napkin was now fully shredded. He pushed the pieces to the side. "I watched your channel the other night. It was the first time I tuned in again since I made the decision to stop. I felt like a recovering addict who suddenly went on a bender."

"What made you do that?"

"It was the alternative to texting you when I knew that would be wrong."

My heart filled with hope, and I wanted to punch it. "You wanted to text me?"

"It just felt weird seeing you and not being able to..."

"I never said you couldn't text me."

"I know." He looked around the room and finally back at me. "I was afraid of what that would lead to. I was trying to do the right thing. Watching your channel was a compromise." He smiled. "But listening to you play again was awesome."

"Glad to have you back—even if it was just for one night."

"You played that Amy Winehouse song, and it was posted the night of the party. I wondered if..."

"If I'd chosen it because of you? Cocky, aren't you?" I winked.

I wasn't going to admit it, even if it was obvious my song selection was no coincidence. I never imagined he'd log in again after he'd stopped. But deep down, I still yearned for his attention as much as ever.

I changed the subject. "Has anything new happened in regards to the situation with your family? Have you heard from them at all?" I asked.

He took a sip of his beer. "That's a whole 'nother can of worms."

"Why?"

"I haven't heard from them, no. But Morgan seems to think I'll regret it if I don't try to work things out, with at least my brothers. She's been trying to convince me to call them. That's been a point of contention between us lately."

"Never mind what she thinks. How do you feel?"

"My gut says that's not the right thing to do. Of course, I'll always regret losing them, but how can you forgive people who haven't accepted any blame? Or even tried to ask for your forgiveness?"

I nodded. "I agree with you, Dax. You didn't do anything wrong by pursuing your dreams. You don't owe them anything. They're the ones who cut you off. The ball is in *their* court. Fuck that."

He nodded. "If one of my brothers made the slightest effort to contact me, I'd be open to it. But they've been horrible about the whole thing. They didn't even fucking contact me after Maren died. And I know they knew about it through friends."

I shook my head. "God, that's sick."

He attempted to shred more napkin. "Anyway, I'm totally ruining the mood."

"I'm the one who asked you about it."

"You know," he said, "your family is small—just you and your dad. But you're lucky. Chuck is an amazing man. He was so kind to Rafe when he came to visit us while you were away."

"I know I'm lucky. He's my everything."

"I'm sure he hopes you'll end up with someone worthy of you, so he doesn't have to worry."

"He just wants me to end up with a good person." I raised my shoulders. "Who knows—maybe I'll end up with no one. And you know what? I wouldn't be the only one navigating this life solo. I can handle it if that's my fate."

"Trust me. You won't end up alone."

"That's right." I winked. "I'll have Rafe. Thanks to you."

"That's very true." He smiled.

"But as for Dylan, because I know you want to ask me more about him, we're seeing where things go."

Dax's ears turned red again. "So you're gonna keep seeing him..."

"Any reason I shouldn't?" *Why do I keep pushing the envelope? Blame it on the alcohol.*

"No," he muttered before taking another long swig of beer.

I tossed my napkin on the table. As tense as this meal had been, I didn't want to leave. Because leaving this restaurant would mean going back to our "new normal." I much preferred to stay in this beer-infused bubble where it was just Dax and me, talking about life.

We ended up ordering one more flight of beer each and stayed talking for at least another hour before I finally suggested we leave.

"This day turned out to be a pleasant surprise," he said.

"We do drunk well."

"That we do." He laughed. "I would normally drive you back to your car, but I don't think either of us is in a position to drive. I know you don't take Ubers alone, so why don't we share a car? I'll have them drop you off first."

"Sounds like the only option. Thank you."

Dax lifted my coat off the hook attached to our booth. He held it open for me. I lifted my hair briefly as he placed my coat around my shoulders. I froze when I felt his hand on the back of my neck.

"What is this?" he asked. "You got a tattoo?"

Shit. Shit. Shit. The alcohol had lessened my focus, and I hadn't been thinking straight when I lifted my hair.

He rubbed his thumb over my skin. As embarrassed as I was to have to explain it to him, I closed my eyes in pleasure at his warm touch.

"I was having a particularly rough few days in France..." I explained. "Some friends and I went to Paris at night, and I got this..."

"Is that supposed to be...me?" he asked.

I nodded as my worst fear was confirmed. He *did* remember the time I'd referred to him as a deer. The tattoo depicted the V-shaped head of a little deer with antlers. It was small, but apparently not small enough for him to not notice.

"Wow." He slowly closed his fingers around my neck, putting me in a gentle chokehold before suddenly removing his hand, as if he'd caught himself teetering on the edge.

He cleared his throat. "I'm...flattered, I guess?"

"And I'm embarrassed," I said, my body still on fire.

"Embarrassed. Why?"

"Oh, I don't know. Because it makes me seem a little crazy, maybe?"

"You *are* a little crazy." He winked. "But I love that about you."

You loved me once, too. I shrugged. "It's the only permanent thing I have of us. I figured no one would ever know the meaning besides me. I never planned to let you see it, that's for sure. I wasn't even sure you'd remember I compared you to a deer."

"Was this by any chance the same night as...alabaster?"

My heart nearly stopped. *Ugh.* The drunken alabaster text—another thing I'd hoped he'd forgotten. "No, it wasn't," I informed him. "And I thought you said you'd never mention that again."

He grinned mischievously. "I still have it. I looked at it several times while you were away."

"Great."

Another night, while a bit inebriated in Paris, I'd sent Dax a now-infamous text. I'd followed it the next morning with an apology.

Dax pulled it up on his phone. He didn't have to scroll very far.

He faced the phone toward me, and I cringed as I read it.

Wren: I never realized how strange the word alabaster is. I've heard it all my life but never knew what the hell it meant. It's a color, apparently. A warm white. It's exactly the color of the seashell in your office that I shattered. That reminds me of how you shattered my heart. You're an alabastard, Moody.

The text immediately below it read:

Wren: OMG! Please disregard that! I had way too much to drink last night. I don't even remember writing this to you. You're not a bastard. I'm the bastard for sending this. Very embarrassing. Sorry!

He'd texted back a couple of hours after.

Dax: No worries. Consider it forgotten.

At the time, I'd overanalyzed the brevity of his response. Was he mad? Was he trying to cut me a break and not make an issue out of it? Did he not care about me anymore? I'd carried those words *consider it forgotten* on my shoulders for over a year, because those were the last words I had from him for a long while. *Consider it forgotten.* Consider *us* forgotten.

"You said 'consider it forgotten,' but clearly you haven't," I told him.

"There's not one second I've forgotten, Wren. About anything."

Our eyes locked, and I felt my cheeks burn. "You must've thought I was the biggest idiot when that text came in."

"Actually, I was asleep with my ringer off when you sent the first one. So I saw the apology message first."

"Well, thank God for that. I figured the delay was because you didn't know how to respond to that craziness."

He shook his head. "I remember feeling sad—sad that you were hurt when you were supposed to be out having fun. Even if it was fleeting and alcohol-induced, it made me realize you were holding on to a lot of pain when it came to me—the same pain I was holding on to, even though more than a year had passed by then. But you know, alcohol has a way of bringing our deepest feelings to the surface."

We stood in the middle of the restaurant, both of us in a daze. Feeling my emotions consume me, I cleared my throat and attempted to cut the tension. "Well, I'd like to forget about alabaster, if you don't mind. And now that you've seen my tattoo, at least I can wear my hair in a ponytail." I buttoned my jacket, ready to flee the desire pummeling me. "Anyway, we'd better get going."

His eyes lingered on mine. "Yeah. We'd better."

During the Uber ride back to my house, I kept noticing Dax stealing glances at me, looking like he wanted to say something. But he remained quiet. I looked down at his beautiful hands from time to time, wishing I could reach over and loop my fingers with his or bring his hand to my mouth to kiss it.

When the car stopped in front of my house, I said, "Thank you for a fun time."

He did air quotes. "Fun in quotation marks?"

"Fun like a root canal."

He bent his head back in laughter. "Oh...that was harsh."

I giggled.

"I'm gonna stay in the car and not walk you to the door because I don't want Chuck to see me and get the wrong idea."

"He's working. But it's better if you don't anyway." *Because I would give anything if you could come inside and fuck my brains out right now.*

"Right." He nodded. "Goodnight, Wren."

"Goodnight, Moody."

He smiled.

Even if we couldn't be together, he would always be my Moody.

CHAPTER 22

Dax

A week after my impromptu dinner with Wren in Kenmore Square, I sat at the dinner table across from Morgan. My phone chimed with a text.

> **Wren: Wanted to give you a heads up that Dylan asked me to attend the law firm's anniversary party with him this Friday. I didn't want you to be caught off guard. Not that you need a warning of my presence, but I felt weird not telling you ahead of time.**

Morgan tilted her head. "Who's that?"

Feeling guilty, I stuffed the phone in my pocket. "Wren, actually. She wanted to let me know Dylan invited her to the law firm party."

"Oh, yes. He mentioned that." She chewed. "Things seem to be going well between them."

I stuffed my mouth with pasta and muttered, "Yeah."

I was relieved that she didn't ask why Wren felt the need to text me that news. Morgan trusted me and would never in a million years have guessed that I had a history with Rafe's sister. The rest of our dinner was uneventful, though I was itching to respond to Wren. I didn't want her to assume I was upset.

Morgan did eventually head back to her apartment, and sooner than she usually did since she had to be up for an early meeting.

After she left, I finally responded to Wren's text.

Dax: Thanks for the heads up. I appreciate it. How are you?

Wren: I'm doing okay.

I debated leaving our text exchange at that. But I couldn't.

Dax: You played "The Swan" in the last video.

Wren: I did.

Dax: You haven't played it in a while. That's my favorite.

Wren: I know. That's why I played it.

My heart raced. *What the fuck am I doing?* Guilt consumed me. I'd been struggling lately. I hadn't stopped watching Wren's channel since relapsing. And I knew this was about more than liking her music. This was about staying connected with her in the only way I'd deemed appropriate. I'd convinced myself it was innocent. But it wasn't, was it?

As I was pondering whether or not to text back, Rafe popped his head into my room. Rattled, I shoved the phone under my sheets. "What's up?" I swallowed.

"Do you think I could skip school tomorrow?"

My eyes narrowed. "Why?"

"I was up all night studying yesterday. I'm still not prepared for my exam. If I can't stay home tomorrow, I'll be up all night again."

A certain smell registered. I knew what it was, but I couldn't understand why Rafe smelled like it.

"Are you wearing perfume?" I asked.

He blinked. "No. But I sprayed it in my room. It's... Mom's."

"I know," I whispered. "Where did you get it?"

"I was out with Wren once. I told her the woman in line in front of us smelled exactly how I remembered Mom smelling. She asked the woman what she was wearing, and the woman told her the name of the perfume."

"Quelques Fleurs," I whispered.

"Yeah, that's it."

"You bought it?"

"Wren bought it for me. It was part of the present she brought to the party. She gave me money and a bottle of that perfume."

Wow. That hit me in the feels. What a sweet gesture. "Well, that was very thoughtful of her."

Seeming a bit embarrassed, he fidgeted and promptly changed the subject. "You never answered my question about staying home."

"You're pushing yourself too hard with the running. It's catching up to you, Rafe."

"I really want to get a scholarship. If I fall behind on either running or my grades, that's not gonna happen."

"You do know that we're good financially to send you to college, right? You don't need to worry about a scholarship."

"You've always handed everything to me. It's important to me to accomplish this myself."

I pondered that for a moment, and then cracked a smile. "You're more like me than I thought."

"What do you mean?"

"You know how I'm estranged from my family? That's because I was determined to be successful on my own rather than take a job that was handed to me. So I can relate to how you feel. It's okay to work hard, as long as you know it's okay if the scholarship doesn't happen. Your mental health is more important."

"So, can I stay home tomorrow? Because that's for my mental health."

I had to give him credit for using my advice to his benefit. "I'm gonna say it's okay because you haven't done it before. But it can't be a regular occurrence."

He held his hand up in salute. "Got it."

I expected him to run out of the room as he typically did when he got what he wanted. Instead, he lingered in the doorway. "My sister told me she's going to Morgan's law firm party with that guy, Dylan."

I cleared my throat and nodded. "Yep."

"I asked her if she wanted to hang out on Friday, but she told me she couldn't go to the movies with Kelsey and me because Dylan had invited her..." He paused. "I don't know if I like that guy. He seems too...perfect or something."

I raised my brow. "Perfection is a bad thing?"

"I don't trust people who seem too perfect. They're usually hiding something." He hesitated. "I think that was why I didn't like you at first. I thought you seemed too perfect when my mother introduced me to you. Then when I got to know you, I realized you had a lot of flaws."

I chuckled. "Thank you...I think?"

"Morgan sort of comes across as perfect, too. Almost like, too good to be true. So I'm not sure I trust her, either."

That was the first time he'd ever mentioned Morgan like that. I wanted to hear more. I narrowed my eyes. "I thought you liked Morgan."

"There's some stuff I like about her, but some stuff I don't."

I sat up straighter. "You want to be more specific?"

"I don't like how she acts like she runs the house when she's here. She doesn't even live here."

"Is that the only thing?"

"And I heard her telling you once to take Mom's photo down."

Shit. "Ahhh." I nodded. "You do know I would never do that, right?"

"Well, I just think it says a lot about her that she would even ask you to do that."

"How come you've never expressed this concern to me before?"

"Because I don't think it's any of my business, and I didn't think it would matter."

I looked him straight in the eye. "Your opinion absolutely matters to me."

We stared at each other for a few seconds before he turned toward the hallway.

"Anyway, I gotta go study," he said.

"You should try to get some sleep tonight and study in the morning, since you're staying home tomorrow."

"Yeah." He shrugged. "Maybe."

He'd walked away when I called out, "Rafe?"

He turned back. "What?"

This conversation was yet another reminder of where my priorities needed to lie—with Rafe.

"I like this talking thing. We should do it more often."

He rolled his eyes before disappearing down the hall again.

At the end of the week, the night I'd been dreading finally arrived.

Seifert and Goldstein's twenty-fifth anniversary party was a black-tie affair held in the Four Seasons' grand ballroom. I'd worn my tux this evening, and Morgan was dressed in a long, sequined black gown. She looked gorgeous, which was no surprise because Morgan was a beautiful woman who always dressed to impress—long legs, silky golden hair, perfect skin, white teeth. My eyes should have been glued to her and her alone. Instead, I was looking all over the place for Wren, even while knowing it was going to be difficult to see her on Dylan's arm.

Maybe this was exactly what I needed, though—a wake-up call, motivation to stop going down this path of emotional destruction I seemed to be on. I was at the shit-or-get-off-the-pot point with Morgan. And I needed to leave Wren alone and let her move on with her life. And if the current situation caused me so much distress, maybe I also needed to consider whether being alone was a better option for me.

It wasn't fair to plan a future with Morgan if my heart was with someone else. Even if I couldn't be with Wren, my inability to stop thinking about her was telling. In addition, this situation gave me déjà vu. I really *wanted* things to work with Morgan—just like I'd *wanted* them to work with Maren. Both women had my respect and admiration. But neither had made me *feel* the things Wren had.

On the outside, Morgan was a good match for me. She was equally as successful, and I didn't have to worry about her wanting me for the wrong reasons. She did make me happy when we were together, and I was able to see a future with her. But after Wren came back, I'd started questioning everything. And Rafe's comments about Morgan the other night had left me unsettled. It had bothered me when she'd suggested I take Maren's photo down, but I'd put it out of my mind until he brought it up. At the time, I'd chalked her request up to insecurity. The more I thought about it, though, the more I felt it was inappropriate. It would have been one thing if Maren and I were divorced. But that photo was one of the only physical reminders Rafe had of her.

I needed to get my ruminations in check. The night was too young to start down that path. Morgan and I were seated at our table, and a live jazz band played in the corner. Deciding to release some of my nervous energy, I stood up. Squeezing Morgan's shoulder, I asked, "What can I get you to drink?"

"I'm in the mood for a vodka with seltzer and lime," she said with a smile.

"Coming right up."

I went to the bar and waited in the line, which was basically one long row of tuxedos and sparkly gowns. The cologne and perfume in the air was almost noxious. So was the smell of money.

At one point, I looked to my right, and there she was. Wren stood at the entrance to the ballroom. She was dressed in a red gown and wore her copper hair up. She looked even more stunning than I'd imagined she would. And Dylan stood beside her. A rush of adrenaline ran through me as I noticed his hand on the small of her back. Trying not to stare, I turned my attention back toward the bar and refused to look over at them until I was forced to deal with it.

I finally got our drinks and headed back toward Morgan at our table. But my pace slowed when I realized Dylan and Wren had joined her there.

"Hey, Dax," Dylan said. "How's it going?"

"Good." I feigned a smile as I set the drinks down. "You both look amazing."

"Thank you. So do you," Wren said as our eyes met for a moment.

I sat down and took a long drink of the vodka I'd ordered.

Morgan placed her hand on my arm. "I'll take any opportunity to see my handsome man in a tux." She turned to Wren. "That dress is absolutely stunning."

"So is yours."

"This old thing?" Morgan laughed. "Thank you. But seriously, yours is breathtaking. Red is definitely your color."

"Why, thank you," Dylan answered. "I picked it out."

I sucked in a breath. *He's choosing her clothes?* That explained why her tits were hanging out.

"I could never have afforded this dress," Wren said. "But I guess Dylan didn't want me showing up in a romper or ripped jeans, so he took matters into his own hands."

I'd like to take *him* into my hands right now and crush him.

Incidentally, she would've been just as beautiful in her ripped jeans and off-the-shoulder shirt. I loved Wren's casual style.

Sensing myself getting lost in my head again, I forced a conversation with Dylan. "Morgan told me about that new client you helped the firm snag," I said. "Abbott is a huge company. Congratulations."

"Thanks, man. I appreciate it."

"You didn't mention that," Wren said to him. "That's amazing."

"Thank you, beautiful. I was gonna tell you tonight."

Swallowing the bitter taste in my mouth, I moved my eyes away from them and turned my gaze to the jazz band.

The rest of the night was more of the same. I'd look over at them, notice Dylan touching Wren's leg or rubbing her back, and then force my eyes away. At one point during dinner, I struggled to keep my food down when Dylan ate something off of Wren's plate.

After the meal, Morgan and I got up to dance. Dylan and Wren followed a minute later. A time or two, Wren's eyes found mine as the four of us moved around the dance floor. I'd force myself to look away, only to get caught soon thereafter looking at her again. But she was also looking at me. When Dylan began rubbing his fingers over the deer tattoo on the back of her neck, I started to sweat. *If he only knew.*

As I wondered what story she'd told him about that ink, a possessive feeling came over me. This night felt like a turning point. I was kidding myself if I thought I could handle this dynamic. I hadn't gotten over Wren. Not even close.

She's fucking mine. She's been mine this entire time.

So where did that leave me? I couldn't do to Morgan what I'd done to Maren. I couldn't marry someone I wasn't completely in love with. I knew I was only headed toward repeating my history of hurting women I cared about. You can't fall in love with someone when you're already in love with someone else. *Damn* that was a hard thing to realize when the person you loved was currently in the arms of another man—and when you'd sworn you could never be with her anyway.

When the dance ended, I needed a breather. I excused myself to the bathroom. Long after I took a piss, I stayed at the sink, staring at the man in the mirror and hating myself for what I now knew was coming. I had to figure out how to end things with Morgan. I was about to hurt yet another woman I cared about because I couldn't control my feelings. With Maren, my sin had been not loving her passionately enough. With Morgan, my sin was secretly loving someone else.

I loosened the bowtie around my neck and prepared to head back out there. As I exited the bathroom, Wren was waiting outside in the small hallway. Her face was as red as her dress.

"Are you okay?" I asked.

She shook her head. "I'm having a hard time."

"I thought you were happy."

"Well, I'm not. I'm just a better actor than you are."

My heart sped up. "Things aren't going well with him? It's all an act?"

"They're going as well as they could be. But you know this isn't about him." Wren took a deep breath. "Did you really think I could just come home and switch you off that easily?"

"I *wished* you could," I said.

"Well, I can't. I can't switch you off like it seems you can with me."

"Is that what you think?" I looked into her eyes. "You're wrong, Wren. So very wrong. Have you not seen it in my face tonight? I haven't been able to take my eyes off you." I looked out toward the ballroom to make sure no one was coming. "All I fucking do is hurt people," I whispered.

"You don't owe anyone anything, Dax. Not Morgan. Not me. Not even Rafe. You owe it to *yourself* to be honest about how you want to live the rest of your life. Because life is short." She started to cry.

Fuck. My mind raced. Maybe I needed to tell Rafe. Maybe that was the only solution. Then almost as soon as I had the thought, I began doubting it was right. But I couldn't live like this anymore, and I needed to do something. No matter which decision I made, someone was going to get hurt.

I nodded. "I'm gonna figure this out, Wren. I—"

"What's going on?"

Morgan's voice was jarring.

She looked over at Wren. "Why is she crying?"

I'd been looking out toward the ballroom for Morgan, but she'd appeared from a different direction altogether.

Wren nor I said anything. I hoped my face didn't look as guilty as hers.

Wren wiped her eyes. "I'm sorry," she said as she rushed past us to return to the ballroom.

Left alone with Morgan, I knew this was it.

I'm not gonna lie to her.

I won't lie.

I'm done fucking living a lie.

The look of suspicion in Morgan's eyes grew with every second I remained silent. We stood facing each other.

"Are you going to say anything?" she finally asked. "What the hell is going on?"

"We need to speak in private."

She raised her voice. "No. You'll tell me right here. Right now."

"Outside on the veranda," I insisted. "Please."

She reluctantly followed as I headed for the French doors. When we got outside, I didn't waste time as I came out with it—the truth.

"Before she went to Europe, Wren and I...were lovers."

Morgan's mouth slowly opened. "What?"

"I know you're shocked."

She looked ready to explode. "Does Rafe know about this?"

The mention of his name made my chest hurt. "No."

Morgan grimaced. "How could you get involved with his sister?"

The air was chilly, but I wiped sweat off my forehead. "It's more complicated than a simple answer. She and I connected before Rafe knew she was his sister. It wasn't something I planned. Wren and I are both adults, and it just happened. We ended things before she left because we felt it was the right thing to do."

She crossed her arms protectively. "And you never thought to tell me this little factoid?"

"I didn't want to hurt you. That's all there was to it."

"Finding out like *this* was better? Catching you in a lovers' quarrel?" She huffed. "So...what—why was she crying? She still wants you?"

When I didn't say anything, she drew her own conclusion. And it was the right one.

"You still want *her*."

I took a deep breath as I tried to gather my thoughts. "Things between us weren't resolved when she left for Europe. And even though a lot of time has passed, I'm afraid things between us are *still* not resolved."

"Why the fuck did you get involved with me if you had feelings for someone else?"

I ran my hands through my hair. "I thought I'd moved past them. I have genuine feelings and nothing but the utmost respect for you."

As expected, she became angrier by the second. "This is bullshit, Dax. I can't be with you if you have feelings for someone else." She yelled up at the sky. "Nearly a year of my life down the drain."

"It wasn't my intention to waste your time, Morgan."

The evening breeze blew her hair around as she shook her head. "Well, enjoy. Now you're free to be with your little slut."

Whoa. "You can be mad at me all you want, but leave her out of it. She didn't do anything wrong, and she's most certainly not a slut."

"Only a slut would fuck her brother's stepfather." She pointed at me. "And you—who the hell fucks his stepson's sister?" She rubbed her temples. "God, it makes my head spin just saying it out loud."

I was almost relieved she was being so harsh because it lessened the blow of hurting her. Maybe I deserved it, but I still tried to defend myself.

"It wasn't cut and dried, as much as you want to paint it that way. We hadn't known each other for long before we developed a connection. And Rafe and I weren't as close then as we are now."

"That's your excuse? If you don't think it's something shameful, then why not tell him?" When I didn't answer, her face changed. "I wonder what he'd think if *I* told him." She laughed angrily.

That rattled me. I didn't know if she was serious, but if Rafe were ever to find out, it was going to be from me— not from anyone else. Over my dead body. "Why would you even joke about that? You think it's funny to hurt a kid?" I closed my eyes a moment. "Look, I understand you're shocked and upset. I don't blame you one bit. But your attitude right now is surprising. I didn't cheat on you, nor would I. You walked in on a conversation, and I'm sorry about that. I—"

"You know what?" She began walking back inside. "I'm getting an Uber, and I'm leaving. We don't have anything more to say to each other." She shook her head. "I can't believe this."

"We need to talk about this when you're less drunk and less angry," I called after her, though I knew there wasn't much more to say.

It's over.

The following morning, paranoia consumed me. I hadn't wanted to make an even bigger scene, so I'd left the party right after my blowout with Morgan. Would she do something rash to get back at me? Would she see to it that Rafe found out about me and Wren?

More to the point, how was I supposed to deal with the fact that I couldn't seem to live without Wren? I wavered between telling Rafe the truth and vowing that he would never find out. Would he understand? Would he forgive me? He was older, more mature now. Then again, he and I were *closer* now—did that make what I did even more wrong?

I'd survived a lot of things—estrangement from my family, the death of my wife, losing Wren. But I didn't think I could survive hurting that boy when I'd been the only constant in his life—when he'd been the only constant in mine.

I leaned my forearms against the kitchen table and held my head in my hands. Rafe had left earlier this morning for a track meet, so thankfully he wouldn't have to witness me in this state. I needed to use this time to figure out my next step.

"Hey," I heard.

I looked up to find Rafe standing at the entrance to the kitchen.

"What are you doing here?" I asked, my heart pounding. "I thought you were at your track meet."

"I'm not feeling well, so I told the coach I needed to sit this one out. I got a ride home from someone."

"You never skip meets. Even when you're sick."

He ignored my comment. "Why did you have your head in your hands?"

"I'm just...going through some stuff."

He continued to stand at the doorway. "Is this about my sister?"

I froze. All I could manage was, "What?"

"Are you upset because you're in love with my sister?"

What? Panic squeezed my chest. *Morgan.* She fucking told him. "Did Morgan say something to you?"

"No." He shook his head. "I did...a bad thing."

He did a bad thing? "What are you talking about?"

"I read your journal."

My throat felt like it was closing. "You...what?"

His voice shook. "I read your journal. A few months ago, I went into your drawer to look for condoms, and I found that cigar box. I didn't expect to find a notebook in there, and I wasn't planning to read it, but the page I opened to had my sister's name. So I kept reading."

Oh no. "So you've known about this for months?"

"Yeah. It was right after Thanksgiving, a couple of months before she came back. I was never gonna tell you. I didn't want you to be upset with me. But this morning before I left, I saw the pain in your eyes, and I knew I had to do something."

I scrubbed my hand over my face. The surprises kept coming.

"After I found the journal, I confronted Wren."

I looked up at him. *Wren knows about this?*

"But I swore her to secrecy because I was scared to tell you what I'd done."

I buried my face in my hands again, feeling ashamed. I couldn't even remember what I'd written. It was a total brain dump, especially that night Wren left for Europe. But I knew I'd written about having sex with her. I also remembered writing about falling in love with her.

"I can only imagine what you think of me right now," I said. "I'm so sorry you had to find out that way."

"Well, you were never gonna tell me. So I guess I would've never known at all."

"You're right. I didn't want to hurt you. For a long while, I never planned to tell you. Our relationship was so damn fragile at first. The last thing I wanted to do was hurt you, Rafe. Please know that."

"I know. I read it all. You said that in the journal. You also said you fell in love with her."

There was no denying anything anymore. "I did."

"Do you still love her?"

Without hesitation, I answered, "I do."

He nodded, blowing out a breath. "I'm not mad. I mean, it was definitely weird when I first found out. Took some getting used to. But I can see how it happened. It's not like she grew up with me. And she's closer to your age than mine. You get along. I used to think she was your girlfriend when I'd see her at the house, before I knew who she really was."

"Really? You never said that."

"I never said *anything* back then, remember?"

"I sure do."

"Anyway, Wren told me some stuff went down at the law firm party last night. I don't want her to be sad. Or you. I saw your face this morning at breakfast. I could see how upset you were. I knew you weren't gonna tell me, and I was never gonna admit what I did, either. But I don't want to see my sister sad anymore. So if you hate me for reading your—"

"Whoa. *Hate* you?" I interrupted. "Are you freaking kidding me? I'm the one who should be worried that you hate *me*. The fact that you read my journal makes me uncomfortable, sure. But I don't blame you. You did what anyone would do in that situation."

"I didn't have to read the whole thing, though."

"No, you didn't. But I can understand why you did. I'm not mad at you. *I'm* the one who should be apologizing. I don't want you to hate me for what *I* did."

"I...want you to be happy," he said. "If it's with my sister, then it's with my sister. Whatever you thought the truth might do to me, you were wrong. I don't hate you. I've never hated you." For the first time since he'd appeared in the kitchen, my blood pressure felt lower.

"When my mom died, you could've left," Rafe added after a moment. "You weren't my dad. You weren't even my friend back then. But you didn't leave. You stayed. You did everything for me when you didn't have to. You lost sleep over me. You worried about my grades. You met with my teachers and therapist. And when I got into running, you made as many of the meets as you could and cheered me on from the stands. Since the day Mom died, you've put my happiness first—before your own. You...

saved me." He paused. "I'm happy now, Dax. Truly happy." He approached me and put his hand on my shoulder. "You deserve to be happy, too." When I looked up at him, he said, "I love you."

My chest tightened with a full heart it could no longer contain. I never thought I'd hear those words come out of Rafe's mouth. I never imagined he could feel that way, but I'd known for a while that I loved him.

I'd never forget the moment I realized it. He'd collapsed on the track about a year ago at a meet. It turned out he was just dehydrated, but before I knew it wasn't serious, I'd felt like my life was ending. I realized in that moment that Rafe was my reason for being. He was the reason I'd met Maren. My purpose in life was to help raise him. I didn't need any other purpose to feel fulfilled.

I placed my hand over his. "I love you, too, Rafe. Thank you for your forgiveness."

"There's nothing to forgive. Go live your life before you're too damn old to enjoy it."

"Thanks a lot." I laughed. "You've given me a gift."

His eyes met mine, this time with a different expression—a look of warning from a protective brother. "Don't waste it."

CHAPTER 23

Dax

After the weekend, I took some rare personal time off from work to clear my head and think about my next steps. I knew I needed to close things out with Morgan more appropriately, as uncomfortable as that was going to be. But when I showed up at her house a few days after my conversation with Rafe, she refused to talk to me. I'd apparently hurt her far more than I realized. However, after her reaction at the law firm party, I'd become more certain that even if Wren didn't exist, Morgan was not the right person for me.

She was understandably angry, but there was no excuse for threatening to tell Rafe. No one should find joy in the idea of traumatizing someone. It was like a switch had flipped inside her that night that showed her true colors—a side of her that perhaps I'd intentionally turned a blind eye to, the same side that wanted to take down the picture of Maren with no regard for the impact on Rafe. Aside from all that, I wasn't in love with her. I never had been. That was clear to me now.

Morgan placed a bag of stuff I'd had at her apartment in front of her door and told me to leave. She said she never wanted to see me again. And maybe that was for the best. It was easier to be on the receiving end of her anger than her sadness.

So now that I wasn't having a conversation with Morgan, I knew my next stop. I hadn't spoken to Wren since the night of the party, but there was someone else I needed to speak to first. My gut told me I needed to start with him.

Wren worked most mornings until sometime later in the day. On Wednesday afternoon, I drove by her house to make sure her car wasn't there. Her father, on the other hand, worked nights and was home.

I knocked on the door.

When Chuck answered, he didn't look all that surprised to see me. "Hello, Dax. Wren is at work."

"I know. I came to speak to you."

"Oh?" He stepped aside. "Well, come in."

I wiped my feet before entering the house. "I know you know about Wren and me. I know she tells you everything."

He turned away. "Do you mind waiting here while I get my shotgun?"

My jaw dropped for a second, even though he had to be fucking with me. Wren must have also told him we'd joked about him wanting to shoot me.

Chuck looked back and pointed at me. "The look on your face..."

I shook my head. "I wouldn't blame you if you did get a gun."

"I don't wish you ill, son." He pointed to the couch. "You want a seat?"

I had way too much nervous energy to sit my ass down right now. "No, I prefer to stand."

"Okay."

I looked down at the ground before facing him again. "Look, I need to apologize for the way I've treated your daughter. I've toyed with her emotions because I couldn't control my feelings for her, despite the fact that I believed we couldn't be together. I made poor decisions and hurt her as a result. I would never want someone treating my daughter the way I treated her."

He nodded. "You had your reasons. This wasn't exactly a clear-cut situation. I get that."

"Well, I'm still sorry for the way I handled it. But I'm not sorry for falling in love with her. I've tried to stop...but I can't. That was never something I could control. I came here to assure you I won't be hurting her anymore."

He raised a brow. "How do you plan to prevent that?"

"I plan to just...love her. If she'll let me."

"She told me Rafe told you he knows, and he gave you his blessing." Chuck cracked a slight smile. "I'm sure that was a gamechanger."

"I guess I underestimated his level of maturity."

"He's a remarkable kid, in part because of *you*, you know. You should try to take some credit for that. You've raised him. He's been with you longer than he was with his mother."

My eyes widened. I'd never thought of it that way, but it was true. Maren had only had Rafe for three years. He'd been with me more than five.

"That's pretty unbelievable to realize," I said.

"We have a lot in common, you and I," Chuck said. "We both lost our wives prematurely. We both were left to raise a child. We've both made mistakes, even though we tried our best."

I nodded.

"We don't always understand why life happens the way it does," he continued. "But I'd venture to say that having Rafe in your life has made you a better person, just as he was lucky to have you when his mother died. Life works in funny ways."

I let out a long breath. "My marriage...it wasn't the best. A lot of that was my fault. So after Maren died, I felt like I owed it to her to look after Rafe. But as time goes on, I've realized I wouldn't have had a meaningful life without him. He gives me purpose." I paused. "You know I'm estranged from my family, right?"

"Wren mentioned that, yes."

"I now understand that true family is the one you choose, not the one you're born into."

He nodded. "I can't even explain in words how much I love my daughter. When Eileen died, I devoted my life to making sure Wren was cared for. She definitely gave me a run for my money during her teen years, but I wouldn't trade a second of it. She's a strong woman. She doesn't need a man. But all I've always wanted was for her to find someone who'd love her as much as I do, whether that be man, woman, or child. It didn't matter. Just someone so if something ever happened to me, I would know she wasn't alone." He smiled. "Because of you, she now has two people. Am I right?"

I smiled. "Yeah."

"So, no need to apologize for anything. Okay?"

This guy had given me a huge pass. I still wasn't sure I deserved it. But I nodded. "You're a good man, Chuck. I wish my father was more like you."

"If he were, you might not be who you are—powerful and independent. Our parents shape us. Sometimes their negative aspects make us stronger people, motivate us. We can learn from our parents in good ways, but we can also learn from their mistakes. Your dad led by example and showed you what *not* to do."

"I think you're right. Thank you for the insight." I chuckled. "And for not pointing a gun at me."

"There's still plenty of time for that, if you ever hurt my daughter." He winked and looked over at the clock. "I need to get to work. My shift at the factory starts at three. You're welcome to wait here for Wren. She's usually home by four. We just miss each other on the days I have to work."

"You know, if you wouldn't mind, that would be great. We have a lot to discuss."

"Make yourself at home. It's not as fancy as your place, but there's beer in the fridge and some leftover donuts on the counter."

"Thank you, Chuck. For everything."

After he left, I sat alone in the kitchen, enjoying a beer and a stale cruller donut. I looked out the window and watched the birds converge on his feeder. I felt freer than I had in years. As the sun streamed into the kitchen, it felt like the first time in forever that I could just be myself with a clear conscience—free to make mistakes and rebound from them, free to love whomever I wanted, free to let go of the guilt I'd carried since Maren died. It was euphoric to be truly excited about the future.

Of course, one more very important thing needed to happen. I had to explain all this to Wren. That's why I'd be limiting myself to one beer. I needed to be fully coherent.

Ninety minutes had passed. It was now 4 PM, and Wren still hadn't come home. I could've texted, but I wanted to surprise her. I just hoped she'd see me being here as a good thing. We hadn't spoken since that night at the Four Seasons, so I didn't know where her head was, nor did I know what had happened with Dylan after Morgan undoubtedly told him what was going on.

With nothing better to do, I ventured upstairs into Wren's bedroom. Memories of the time we'd made love here came flooding back. I lay on her mattress, relishing her scent. On one wall, I noticed something peculiar—a sketched picture of *me*. I recognized the artist's style. Rafe had drawn that. When had he drawn me and given it to Wren?

Then I heard the door close downstairs and hopped up from the bed.

I made my way down the stairs, and Wren jumped at the sight of me.

"Dax?" She held her hand over her chest. "What are you doing here? You scared the shit out of me."

"I'm sorry. Didn't mean to scare you."

"Is my dad okay?"

"Oh my God. Of course. Everything is fine. He's at work. I came to apologize to Chuck, and he told me I could hang out here until you came home."

Her eyes nearly bugged out of her head. "You came to speak to my dad?"

"Yeah. I talked to him before he left for work."

"You've been here a long time, then."

"Yes. I would've waited forever, though."

"Dax, I—"

"Before you say anything, hear me out, okay? I need to say this."

Her chest rose and fell. "Alright..."

"You deserve so much better than what I've given you, Wren." I let out a shaky breath. "You deserve to be cherished, not hidden. Loved openly, not in secret. I'm so fucking sorry if it's ever felt like I've strung you along."

She shook her head. "You couldn't help it. It was an impossible situation."

"Doesn't make it right." I took a step closer. "I haven't been in touch since the other night because there was no way I was gonna face you until I got my shit together." I paused. "Morgan and I aren't together anymore, as you might've figured. Because I couldn't stay with her...when I'm in love with you." I paused to look at her. "I'm so in love with you, Wren McCallister."

She placed her hand on her chest. "God...to hear you finally say it." She exhaled. "Rafe told me he came clean about reading your journal. It was hard keeping that from you, but he was so scared to tell you."

"I want you to know something." I cradled her cheek. "Rafe walked in on me Saturday morning with my head down in despair after the law firm party. I was debating telling him everything even before he said a word to me. He saved me from having to do that. But I already knew I couldn't live without you, and I had to do something. I just hadn't figured out what. I know now that there's only one way for this story to end, Wren. And that's with us together."

Her eyes glistened. "Does this mean I have to tell Dylan I won't marry him?"

My body tensed.

She reached up and pinched my cheek. "I'm kidding, Moody."

I fisted her hair and pulled her close. "You nearly gave me a fucking heart attack, woman."

"I went back to the table that night after Morgan ran into us talking," she said. "I waited there with Dylan, suspecting that a bomb was about to drop. Morgan came into the ballroom after leaving you and told Dylan everything right in front of me. Then she stormed off. Believe it or not, he wasn't quick to walk away or cast blame. He just wanted to understand. So we left the party and talked it over at a bar down the street. He still wanted to work things out. He really is a great guy. But ultimately, I ended things. Because I love you." She smiled. "You know that."

"Yeah. I do." I slid my arm down her back. "There's still so much I want to say, but I don't think I can keep my hands off you much longer."

"You sure you don't want to have tea?" she teased. "Maybe we should chat a little more."

"I think we've done our fair share of talking over the years. Talking can fucking wait because I need to be inside of you." I brought her lips to mine, swallowing the familiar taste I'd longed for. This kiss felt like the oxygen I'd been missing for nearly three fucking years.

"Let's go upstairs," she murmured.

"We're not leaving your bedroom tonight," I muttered over her lips. "At least not until right before Chuck gets back."

When she wrapped her arms around my neck, her fingers found the bandage there.

"What is this?" she asked. "Did you hurt yourself?"

I turned to show her it wasn't an injury. It was a clear bandage over a tattoo I'd just gotten.

She gasped. "Oh my God. You're crazy, Dax."

"*I'm* the crazy one? Do you not have a deer tattoo on the back of your neck as a symbol of me?"

"Well, yeah. But this…"

"Wren means little bird, does it not?"

She covered her mouth. "I know. I just…"

She stared at the tiny bird I'd had tattooed on the back of my neck. It wasn't just any bird. It was Tweety. It was the size of a quarter.

"You're crazy, Dax Moody! What made you choose Tweety?"

"He's a little bird, isn't he?"

"How are you going to explain Tweety to your clients?"

"I'll proudly tell them it's a symbol of the woman I love. Fuck them if they think it's weird. I love you so much, and I'd do just about anything to prove it."

"This definitely proves it." She laughed. "When did you get it?"

"Yesterday." I swooped her up. "How about a break from talking now?"

She squealed as I carried her up the stairs.

"I love it when you carry me. It's such a gentlemanly gesture."

"Nothing I'm about to do to you will be gentlemanly, Wren. *Nothing.*"

Excitement filled her eyes as I laid her down on the bed. I hovered over her and kissed her hard as she fumbled to remove my belt. She finally whipped it away and tossed it aside before lowering my pants. I kicked them off. She slid out of her own pants, and when I reached down to remove her panties, I might've ripped them. We lifted our shirts off at the same time, and they went flying. My dick ached to be inside of her—something I thought I'd never have again.

I was reaching for my pants to find a condom when she wrapped her hands around my face to look me in the eyes. "No condom," she said. "I want to feel you without anything."

My dick throbbed. "Are you sure?"

"It's okay. I was having painful periods, so my doctor put me on the pill. I'm good...but only if you want to."

My eyes went wide. "What kind of a question is that? Do you know how many times I've fantasized about coming inside you?"

"Now you get to do it for the rest of your life." She smiled up at me. "I can't wait to feel it."

"You're about to." I spread her legs wide and thrust inside in one movement. I closed my eyes briefly at the sheer pleasure of her warm pussy swallowing my throbbing cock whole. I wanted to explode right then and there. If there were such a thing as sex feeling too good, this was it.

I pulled out slowly and thrust into her again. "Fuck, Wren, this is better than I dreamed."

Slow and steady soon gave way to fast and hard, and the bed began to shake. It felt like the whole damn room was shaking, actually, as I pounded into her. I closed my eyes, trying to stave off the orgasm ready to shoot through me. If she so much as moved her hips a certain way, it would've been all over. I knew it was going to be the best damn orgasm of my life.

"Come inside me," she breathed. "Please... I can't wait anymore."

I hadn't been expecting her to climax so soon, but she didn't have to ask twice. I happily let myself go, groaning as I emptied inside of her. She continued to move her hips until neither of us had anything left. There was no better feeling than this. I knew wholeheartedly that she was mine.

We lay limp and sated for a moment. "Let me grab a towel for you," I said.

She shook her head. "Don't. I love your cum inside me."

Feeling like a goddamn caveman, I fell back into bed and nuzzled her neck. "And now I'm getting hard again."

"Good." She brushed her fingers along my abs. "Should I ride you this time?"

"Hang on." I pinched my arm. "Sorry, I needed to make sure I wasn't dreaming."

We had sex multiple times that evening, and it was 9 PM before we realized we hadn't eaten anything. So we ordered food and ate it in her room. It felt like almost everything I needed for the rest of my life was here.

After we ate, I again noticed the sketch on her wall. "What's the story behind that drawing?"

She rolled her eyes. "You weren't supposed to see that, you know. But considering you're a trespasser..."

"Rafe did it. But when?"

"I found it in his room before I moved to Europe. I asked him if I could keep it."

"He didn't think it was weird that you wanted a drawing of me?"

"Oh, he thought it was weird. He didn't suspect anything, though. He gave me a drawing of me, too. He just thought I admired his talent. That was the only image I had of you. So I cherished it."

"Wow. That's true. We've never taken a photo together." I reached for my phone. "Fuck, we need to change that."

"You're gonna take our first official photo while we're both buck naked under the sheets?"

"If that's okay with you." I held the phone out in front of us, putting it in selfie mode.

Wren laughed. "Considering our relationship started with you half-naked under a towel, I'd say that's pretty fitting."

CHAPTER 24

Wren

D ax and I had been together for six months now. Well,
we'd been in love for a lot longer than that, but we'd
been openly loving each other for half of a year.

My brother had gotten used to seeing me around the
house. We waited three months before I spent the night,
though. But since then I'd spent almost every night here.
While Rafe seemed okay with Dax and me being together,
we were always careful to curb the PDA around him as a
courtesy.

Things were going so well that I found myself paranoid that the other shoe would drop. I'd even managed
to find a music teacher position at an elementary school
in the city. My life had never been more fulfilling, both
professionally and personally. I had to constantly remind
myself to enjoy each day, rather than fear losing what I
had. When I was younger, I used to obsess about what I
would do if something happened to my dad. Now, I had
three people in my life I obsessed over losing. It was a
good problem to have, I suppose.

I'd continued filming performances for my RenCello account, but not as frequently. One time I'd introduced Dax as a special guest and filmed with him sitting next to me while I played. That video got the most hits ever, probably because of the curiosity factor generated by the title, "Meet My Boyfriend," not to mention Dax's beautiful face in the thumbnail photo. It felt like we were coming full circle, with the man who'd inspired my music for so long finally there while I played.

One Friday night in September, Dax and I were alone in the house as Rafe was out with his girlfriend, Kelsey. He was a senior now, so who knew if that relationship would last once they went away to college. But I was glad she made him happy for now.

It was about 10 PM, and Dax sat in his chair reading while I'd curled up in my spot by his feet. Even Winston had gotten used to me being around, and he lay calmly nearby, not a growl to be heard. The more I stared at my boyfriend, the more overwhelmed I became. My eyes welled up.

Dax looked up from his book. "Are you crying?"

"A little."

His forehead crinkled. "Did I miss something?"

"Nothing bad."

"Is it the old-man glasses?" He took them off. "Seriously, what's this about?"

"I got choked up for a moment, thinking about how when I was away, I never imagined I'd be back here, sitting by your feet while you read. I thought we were done. I feel so lucky that I didn't have to live the rest of my life without you."

He set his book aside. "I still feel like I have so much to make up to you."

I shook my head. "You don't owe me anything. I just need *you*, Dax. I don't need anything else but you."

"There's nothing you want that I haven't given you?"

I got up and straddled him. There was one other thing I wanted. I just wasn't sure if he wanted it, too.

"I want to have your babies," I told him.

His eyes went wide. "Not exactly what I was expecting you to say."

"I know that was a bit much. But it is something I want someday, something I dream about. But only with you, and only if you want that, too. I don't know how you feel about having kids of your own. We've never discussed it."

I'd always been afraid to bring this up, fearing his answer would not be what I wanted to hear. He used to refer to himself as not being the fatherly type when Rafe was younger. He'd never felt good enough for the job. But he'd certainly proven himself.

"I never imagined having kids of my own..." He hesitated. "Until you." His mouth curved into a smile. "Now? I can't imagine going through life without seeing a part of me inside of you, growing into a little human. Getting to raise a child with you? Getting to see what an amazing mother I know you'll be? Everything I thought I wanted when you first met me went out the window once I fell in love with you, Wren."

"Really?" I whispered, feeling so damn relieved.

He gripped my ass and squeezed. "Really, baby."

"You know, I learned a pretty big lesson in France." I looked into the fireplace. "It was so beautiful there, you know? I'd sit out on my balcony and listen to the sounds of my cute little neighborhood in Versailles. I finally had what I'd thought I wanted for so long—I'd traveled far away and experienced a new land, free to do whatever I wanted away from home. But from almost the moment I got there, I realized I had nothing without the people I love. You, my dad, Rafe. The people you love are what life is about, not a place. Places are just backdrops, like the moving scenery of a Broadway show. It's the cast of characters that matters." I smiled. "I'd be in Paris at a café, staring across at the Eiffel Tower but longing to be back in this living room—simply because you were here. All I wanted was to sit by your feet or on top of you in the very spot I am now. The most beautiful sights in the world can't beat being with the one you love."

Dax cradled my face and brought me in for a kiss. "I want to show you something," he said before lifting me off of him.

He went upstairs, leaving me alone by the fire.

When he came down, he had his black journal with the fleur-de-lis on the front—the journal Rafe had read.

I'd curled up in his chair, so he sat across from me on the sofa.

He looked down at it for a while before he spoke. "For a long time, I was too scared to look back at what I'd written—knowing Rafe had read it. But recently, I decided to open this again. I had to know what he'd seen. What you just said about how you felt looking at the Eiffel Tower reminded me of something I wrote." He opened the journal and turned the pages. "I'm gonna read you the entry from the night you left."

On the edge of my seat, I nodded.

"I just let the woman I love get on a plane and leave me. I feel completely empty. Even though I know Wren and I made the right decision to end things this way, with her moving to Europe, it doesn't make it any easier. If Rafe ever found out about us, it would devastate him. So I'm choosing to hurt myself instead. Because make no mistake about it, this is the biggest hurt I've ever felt." Dax turned the page.

"I never intended to have sex with her tonight. But the need for her body overtook me. That need had been slowly wearing me down, and I had no resilience left. I selfishly wanted to experience it, just one time before I never had the chance again. When she said she needed me the same way, utter desire trumped any inhibitions I had left." He glanced up at me. "Being inside of Wren was bar none the best thing I've ever felt. Knowing it was also goodbye made it bittersweet. And not being able to tell her I loved her? That had to be the worst feeling of all."

I placed my hand on my chest. "Wow."

Dax cleared his throat. "As painful as letting her go is, I'll always be grateful for what my time with her taught me about myself. I now know that I have the capacity to love someone in a way I didn't think possible. I now understand that love is pure, organic, and not something you can control. It has nothing to do with a place, or life circumstances, compatibility, or whether you *think* someone is right for you. Love just *is*. And there is nothing more powerful. It doesn't matter where you are or what you're doing, as long as you're with that person. I'm feeling the emptiness of her being gone so strongly right now. The pain is almost unbearable. But I have to be strong for Rafe. I have to get over her. And I have to stop writing in this journal for a while. Because when I open these pages, the only thing I want to write about is her. She was the one. And now she's gone. The rest is unwritten."

His eyes lifted to meet mine.

Wiping my tears, I whispered, "And to think I didn't think you loved me."

He closed the book. "I wasn't planning on doing this tonight. I had a plan... I was going to do it in a couple of months at Christmas. You once told me you hated Christmas because of that old boyfriend who dumped you. But this feels like the right time now. If being with you has taught me anything, it's that you can't plan what feels right. Nothing has ever felt more right in my life than you. I love you more than life itself."

My heart pounded. He wasn't talking about reading me his journal anymore.

He opened the journal again and took something out. When he lifted it, I realized it was a sparkling diamond ring.

With my heart thundering against my chest, I sat up straight as he came over and got down on one knee.

His hand trembled as he held out the ring. "It would make me the happiest man on the face of the Earth if you would be my wife, Wren."

Covering my mouth, I stared down at the shimmering diamond. "Did you just ask me to marry you, or am I dreaming?" Tears clouded my eyes.

"It's not a dream." He smiled.

"You already own my heart." I shook my head. "But yes, I will most certainly marry you, Moody."

Dax pulled me into a tight embrace. "I've always loved when you call me Moody. There's only one name I think I like better."

"What's that?"

He kissed me again and smiled. "Mrs. Moody."

EPILOGUE

Wren

I knocked on the door.

When he opened, I couldn't help but ogle him. He looked absolutely gorgeous. His hair was just wet from the shower, and he wore a white tank top that showed off his muscles.

"Hi, I'm Wren." I cleared my throat and held out my hand.

He gave me a once-over but withheld his hand. *What a tease.*

"Nice to meet you," he said as he leaned against the door.

"Are you going to let me in?" I laughed.

"Yeah. Let me get that." He reached out and grabbed my table, leaning it up against the wall.

"Thank you," I said as I entered, my heels clicking against the floor of the foyer.

He shook his head. "I'm Dax. Sorry. I should've said that." He exhaled. "I guess I got a little distracted."

"Have you ever had a massage, sir?"

"I've never taken my clothes off for a massage before, no."

"Well, I guess we're both in the same boat then."

"You're taking your clothes off, too?" he joked.

My eyes went wide. "No." I laughed. "I'm nervous because this is my first night on the job. I've had training, of course, just haven't gone into any houses yet. And I certainly haven't massaged anyone as..." I stopped short. "Never mind."

"No." He took a few steps toward me. "Say what you were gonna say."

"I've never massaged anyone as..." I looked down, then up. "...Good-looking as you."

"Well..." He inched closer. "I'm flattered." I could feel his breath on my face. "Can I be honest, too?"

My breath quivered. "Sure."

"I wasn't expecting you to be so beautiful. I'm a bit flustered right now."

I tucked a piece of my hair behind my ear. "As a professional, it's really inappropriate for me to have admitted that I find you attractive."

"I won't tell." His seductive tone practically penetrated my skin. "I love your honesty."

I looked around. "Where do you want me?"

"That's a bit of a loaded question, isn't it?" His eyes burned into mine. "Sorry. See? I'm the inappropriate one." He lifted the table and began leading me into his office.

"Is this room okay?" he asked as we entered.

Looking around, I nodded. "Yes. This is fantastic."

He walked over to the window. "I'll draw the shades."

"Probably a good idea," I agreed.

Dax turned to me and slid his hand down the length of his chest. "Do you...want me to take all my clothes off?"

"That's up to you."

"I asked you if you *wanted* me to."

Stalling, I licked my lips. "Yes. I mean, that would make it easier."

I had barely gotten the sentence out before he slipped his shirt over his head, tossing it aside. He then undid his pants, letting them slide down his legs. His huge cock practically burst through his boxer briefs, and there was a wet spot at his crotch. I salivated with an intense desire to kneel and take him into my mouth.

His brow lifted. "Like what you see?"

"Um...yeah, actually. You have an amazing body." I swallowed. "There's no denying that."

He slipped his finger into the band of his underwear. "Mind if I take these off, too?"

I gulped, feeling my body heat. "Not at all."

He lowered his boxer briefs. A bead of precum glistened on the tip of his cock. My panties were already wet as I imagined what his impressive girth would feel like between my legs. I had to tighten my muscles to contain my own arousal.

He walked over to the massage table and lay down, his cock fully hard.

"Do you start on the back or the front?" he asked.

"I'm going to start on you from the front, if you don't mind. I'm supposed to put a towel over your lower body, but I don't think it would...contain you."

"I don't mind leaving it off, if that's okay with you."

Desire pooled between my legs. "It is definitely okay."

He placed his hands behind his head as he settled in. "Good."

As I started to massage his chest, his eyes burned into mine.

"You look like you want to say something," I whispered.

"I'm not normally this forward, Wren. But I'm having a hard time keeping my feelings inside today."

"What do you want to say?" I asked.

"It's a question, actually. I'm hoping you won't take it the wrong way."

My hands glided down his hard chest. "Try me."

"I joked about this earlier...but I'm serious this time. How much more would it cost to get you to take *your* clothes off, too...while you massage me? Or is that totally out of the question?" The corner of his mouth quirked. "Feel free to tell me to go fuck myself if I'm out of line. I'll understand."

I pretended to have to think about it. "No one's ever asked me to do that before, so I don't really have a price. It would be against company rules."

He wrapped his hand around mine to stop me for a moment, then leaned up and looked me in the eye. "I want to see you naked. What do I have to pay?"

I bit my bottom lip. "If you jerk off and let me watch, I'll take off my clothes."

"That's a bargain." His eyes glimmered. "And if you're serious, I think we have a deal."

I stepped back. My chest rose and fell as he wrapped his hand around his cock and started pumping.

I unbuttoned the front of my blouse and slipped it off my shoulders. I then undid my denim skirt, letting it fall to the floor.

"Fuck." He jerked himself harder. "I knew you weren't wearing a bra. You have the best tits. I want to come all over them." He pumped faster.

My body buzzed with arousal as I slipped my panties off. Completely naked now, I slid my hand between my legs as I watched him pleasuring himself.

"I'm gonna come so good looking at that bare pussy," he groaned.

I began to massage my clit. After a minute of watching each other, it was as if we were in a competition to see who could come first.

"You know what?" I said.

"What?" he rasped.

"I changed my mind. I don't want to watch you. I want to ride you."

His eyes turned glassy as he tugged on his cock. "Get your ass over here, then."

I crawled up onto the table, straddling him before placing his cock at my entrance. I lowered myself onto him, sinking all the way down. Swaying my hips, I rode him harder and harder. I watched as his eyes rolled back in pleasure.

Dax wrapped his hands around my ass as he pushed himself deeper into me. "I need to come, but I shouldn't do it inside you," he muttered under his breath. "As much as I want to."

I thrust my hips. "It's okay. I'll take the chance if you will."

Clenching around him, I started to orgasm. His body shook as his warm cum filled me. I continued riding him slowly until our climaxes wound down. It was fast and furious, which was what we needed, because we didn't have all the time in the world. In fact, the clock was ticking fast.

Collapsing over him, I lay on his chest and listened to his ragged breaths.

Dax slapped my ass. "You're a naughty little massage therapist. I should report you."

A door slammed in the distance.

"Shit!" He groaned.

I hopped up off of him and ran to my clothes. "So much for two whole hours to roleplay."

He threw his pants on. "At least I was smart enough to lock the door after we came in here."

I buttoned my blouse. "Why are they back so soon?"

"Daddy! Mommy! Where are you?" a little voice called from behind the door.

The dog was barking like crazy now, too. Commence the circus. *Back to reality.*

"They weren't due back until three," Dax said as he threw his shirt over his head.

She was at the door now. "Daddy, are you in there?"

Dax buckled his belt. "Just a second, honeypie!"

I could hear Shannon's voice. "Fawn, leave Daddy for a bit. I think he might be busy."

She was totally on to us.

After we were both dressed, Dax caught his breath as he unlocked the door and opened it. He ran his hand through his messed-up hair. "Hey! You guys are back early!"

Shannon surveyed the space, noticing the table. "Just like old times in here."

The dog scurried in behind them.

"I was giving him a massage." I cleared my throat. "Needed to brush up on my skills... You know, in case I ever go back to it."

"Sure." Shannon smiled knowingly. "Anyway, we're back early because Miss Fawn decided she wanted mac and cheese at home instead of going out to lunch after the show. I texted you a heads up, Wren, but it doesn't look like you got it."

My phone was upstairs, so a lot of good that did.

I bent to lift my daughter. "Did you have fun at the theater?"

She nodded.

They'd gone to a matinee performance of *The Lion King*. Our little girl loved going to see musicals and movies.

Some days, I still couldn't believe I had a daughter. Dax and I had gotten married six months after our engagement. We had a small ceremony with just Rafe and my dad in attendance in Bermuda. Our now four-year-old daughter, Fawn Rafaela Moody, was born less than a year after our wedding. I'd always thought Fawn was a pretty name. It had a similar ring to it as Wren. But when I realized a baby deer was called a fawn, I knew that was the name for our daughter. And she was the spitting image of her dad, our new purpose in life, and the apple of her uncle Rafe's eye. Rafe had recently graduated from MIT and was about to start a job as a computer software engineer. He had his own apartment now in Cambridge.

"What did you like most about the musical?" I asked her.

"I cried when Simba's dad died, but it was a happy ending."

"I think Daddy had a happy ending, too." Shannon snorted.

I laughed, even though Dax looked annoyed. I loved Shannon. We were so lucky to still have her in our lives. She'd warned us that in the next couple of years she'd be retiring to New Orleans—for real this time. But we'd deal with that when the time came.

After Shannon left the room, our daughter seemed transfixed by something on the shelf in Dax's office. She pointed. "Mommy, what are those seashells?"

Dax and I froze. She'd spotted the shell where Dax kept Maren's ashes and the smaller shell next to it, which now held Winston's. It was the first time Fawn had ever pointed them out.

Our beloved dog had passed away right before Fawn was born, so she never met our big Fluffernutter, who incidentally loved *me* the most by the time he died. After Winston crossed the rainbow bridge, we hadn't planned to get another dog. But when Fawn turned one, we'd adopted a beautiful white Pomeranian. We'd visited the shelter "just to look," and I'd begged Dax to let me take her home. He'd told me we could on one condition, that he be the one to name her. Of course, I agreed, and that's how we ended up with our little Alabaster.

"You never noticed those shells before, sweetie?" I asked.

She shook her head.

"Can I touch the big one?" she asked.

Dax looked reflective as he stared up at the shell.

"It's a seashell..." I told her. "But it has something inside that's very important to Daddy. So it's not a toy."

She looked at me earnestly.

"Make sure you just look at it from afar. Never touch either of those shells, okay? Because they can break."

"Mommy learned that the hard way," Dax chimed in.

I rolled my eyes, but boy, was that ever true.

He lifted the large shell off the shelf. I don't think I'd ever seen him touch it, aside from the time he'd had to clean shattered pieces of the old one off the ground. Dax seemed lost in his head as he looked down at it, understandably reminded of Maren and all the regret and sadness I knew he would always hold in his heart.

He knelt down. "Come here, Fawn."

She walked over and leaned against him.

"It's so pretty, isn't it?" he asked.

"Yes, Daddy."

Dax carefully placed it next to her ear. "Did you know if you put a seashell up to your ear and listen, you can hear the ocean?"

OTHER BOOKS BY
Penelope Ward

The Assignment

The Aristocrat

RoomHate

The Crush

The Anti-Boyfriend

The Day He Came Back

Just One Year

When August Ends

Love Online

Gentleman Nine

Drunk Dial

Mack Daddy

Stepbrother Dearest

Neighbor Dearest

Jaded and Tyed (A novelette)

Sins of Sevin

Jake Undone (Jake #1)

Jake Understood (Jake #2)

My Skylar

Gemini

Well Played (Co-written with Vi Keeland)

Not Pretending Anymore (Co-written with Vi Keeland)

Cocky Bastard (Co-written with Vi Keeland)

Playboy Pilot (Co-written with Vi Keeland)

Mister Moneybags (Co-written with Vi Keeland)
British Bedmate (Co-written with Vi Keeland)
Park Avenue Player (Co-written with Vi Keeland)
Stuck-Up Suit (Co-written with Vi Keeland)
Rebel Heir (Co-written with Vi Keeland)
Rebel Heart (Co-written with Vi Keeland)
Hate Notes (Co-written with Vi Keeland)
Dirty Letters (Co-written with Vi Keeland)
My Favorite Souvenir (Co-written with Vi Keeland)
Happily Letter After (Co-written with Vi Keeland)

ACKNOWLEDGEMENTS

The acknowledgements are always the hardest part of the book to write. There are simply too many people that contribute to the success of a book, and it's impossible to properly thank each and every one.

First and foremost, I need to thank the readers all over the world who continue to support and promote my books. Your support and encouragement are my reasons for continuing this journey. And to all of the book bloggers/bookstagrammers/TikTokers who work tirelessly to support me book after book, please know how much I appreciate you.

To Vi – The best friend and partner in crime that I could ask for. I love creating worlds with you. It was so amazing to actually get to see you in person this year.

To Julie – A true warrior and an amazing friend. This year, more than any, you've inspired me.

To Luna – Thank you for your love, support, and friendship. I look forward to our annual visit all year, but in the meantime, we'll always have our daily messages. Waking up wouldn't be the same without you.

To Erika – It's an E thing! Thank you for your love, support, and friendship and for always holding pieces of my characters in your heart.

To Cheri – An amazing friend and supporter. Thanks for always looking out for me and for never forgetting a Wednesday.

To Darlene – The best baker and friend on the planet. Thank you for always supporting me.

To my Facebook reader group, Penelope's Peeps – I adore you all. You are my home and favorite place to be.

To my agent extraordinaire, Kimberly Brower – Thank you for everything you do and for getting my books out into the world.

To my editor Jessica Royer Ocken – It's always a pleasure working with you. I look forward to many more experiences to come.

To Elaine of Allusion Publishing – Thank you for being the best proofreader, formatter, and friend a girl could ask for.

To Julia Griffis of The Romance Bibliophile – Your eagle eye is amazing. Thank you for being so wonderful to work with.

To my assistant Brooke – Thank you for hard work in handling all of the things Vi and I can't seem to ever get to. We appreciate you so much!

To Kylie and Jo at Give Me Books – You guys are truly the best out there! Thank you for your tireless promotional work. I would be lost without you.

To Letitia Hasser of RBA Designs – My awesome cover designer. Thank you for always working with me until the finished product exactly perfect.

To my husband – Thank you for always taking on so much more than you should have to so that I am able to write. I love you so much.

To the best parents in the world – I'm so lucky to have you! Thank you for everything you have ever done for me and for always being there.

Last but not least, to my daughter and son – Mommy loves you. You are my motivation and inspiration!

ABOUT THE AUTHOR

Penelope Ward is a *New York Times, USA Today* and *#1 Wall Street Journal* bestselling author.

She grew up in Boston with five older brothers and spent most of her twenties as a television news anchor. Penelope resides in Rhode Island with her husband, son and beautiful daughter with autism.

With over two million books sold, she is a 21-time *New York Times* bestseller and the author of over twenty novels.

Penelope's books have been translated into over a dozen languages and can be found in bookstores around the world.

Subscribe to Penelope's newsletter here:
http://bit.ly/1X725rj

Made in the USA
Coppell, TX
04 February 2023

12120746R00194